JAGGED
no more

Lorelie Rozzano

D1526264

 FriesenPress

Suite 300 - 990 Fort St
Victoria, BC, V8V 3K2
Canada

www.friesenpress.com

Copyright © 2016 by Lorelie Rozzano
First Edition — 2016

We all know or love someone who struggles with the disease of addiction. Although this story is fiction the characters behaviour throughout this series is not. While addiction is a progressive illness, it is also highly predictable. Know the signs. Like any other chronic illness the sooner you seek help the more successful your chances at a full recovery will be.

All rights reserved.

No part of this publication may be reproduced in any form, or by any means, electronic or mechanical, including photocopying, recording, or any information browsing, storage, or retrieval system, without permission in writing from FriesenPress.

ISBN
978-1-4602-8792-7 (Hardcover)
978-1-4602-8793-4 (Paperback)
978-1-4602-8794-1 (eBook)

1. FICTION, MEDICAL

Distributed to the trade by The Ingram Book Company

Acknowledgement

ADDICTION IS A DIFFICULT AND CONTROVERSIAL TOPIC. Millions of people around the world struggle with it. Most will not receive *help*. If you or a loved one suffers from this disease, I hope reading the Jagged series will encourage you to reach out and ask for help. Because this illness is predictable, it is also highly treatable. There's no shame in getting well. Admitting you need help is not an act of weakness, but one of great courage.

As a recovering addict I've been helped by many. My journey started at the Edgewood treatment center in 1997. Edgewood taught me how to move beyond the chains of addiction and live with integrity. I remain forever grateful for their loving guidance.

Thank you to Rebel Ink Press, Edgewood Press and Friesen Press for believing in me and facilitating the publishing process of Gracie's Secret, Jagged Little Edges, Jagged Little Lies and Jagged No More.

Thank you to Brent Clements for including me in his team of skilled professionals over at Addiction Campuses. I contribute a weekly blog post and I'm proud to be a little part of the great work they do.

I'd like to thank my friends and co-workers for their support and encouragement over the years. I love you all very much.

I'd especially like to thank Michael Wood for his great suggestions and endless hours of grueling edits. You are an amazing friend and one talented guy!

I'd like to thank my children, nieces, nephew, siblings and parents. Like any family we have our struggles, but the upside to it is that we are learning how to fit together in peace, love, and harmony. We have come a million miles and I am so proud of each and every one of you!

I'd like to thank my biggest fan, my husband Dave. We've come a long way, Baby! There's something very beautiful about our simple, clean and sober lifestyle. I don't miss the old drama at all. Thank you for walking away from me. If you hadn't quit me that day, none of this would be possible.

Most of all, I'd like to thank you, my readers. I've had people tell me they feel like they know me, although we've never met. If you can relate to my story, we *have* met. We are kindred spirits. We need no introductions as we walk together in matters of the heart.

Lastly, it's important to acknowledge you have purpose. You were not brought here to suffer, but to do incredible things. You are needed. No matter how far down you are, you can still get up. Where there's breath, there is hope. Where there's hope, there is possibility. Never stop believing and know this: I believe in you.

Dedication

This book is dedicated to all those who lost their life to addiction. Therefore the grace of God, go I.

Metamorphosis

Her cocoon was dark and cramped. The caterpillar had outgrown it. Fearfully, she made the decision to leave its small, dark confinement. Her passage out was rough. Many times she fought the urge to return to her miserable abode. Determined to make it through, she prayed for strength. Inch by inch, she drew closer to her goal, as she crawled, guided by a light she could see far off in the distance. Many times she stumbled. Just when she thought she could go no further, she did. Exhausted, she gave a massive push and shed the last of her decaying cocoon. The little caterpillar grinned. Miraculously, she'd made it out alive! A droplet of water shimmered next to her. Thirsty, she lowered her head to sip from the liquid but halted upon seeing her reflection. She gasped in wonder at the beautiful creature staring back at her.

Her mind reeled in confusion. How was this possible?

The wind rustled the leaf she clung to and whispered. 'Fly, for you are free.'

Her wings unfurled as she leapt from the branch, doing the very thing she'd been born to do

Lorelie Rozzano.

Prologue

HIS DEAD, BUG-EYED STARE WAS CREEPY. HIS SKIN looked waxen and grayish white. Rooster's mouth gaped open. *His long, yellowed teeth would look more fitting on a rat than a man,* John thought. He shivered and looked away.

Huh. Guess Declan got his wish after all.

Naked, Rooster was diminished—and dead. Rigor mortis had set in, leaving him stiff. His flesh was marbled and cold to the touch. John checked the tag on his toe a final time before rapping on the steel door.

Outside of the morgue, Frank *was* waiting for him. "You sure took your sweet time," he said, clicking the lighter that was never far from his hand.

"Yeah, well…" John trailed off. The click from Frank's lighter annoyed him.

"Well?" Click. Frank huffed impatiently. Click, click.

Fast as a rattler, John grabbed the lighter away from Frank and tossed it into the nearby garbage can. "Hey!" Frank protested.

"Consider it a favor. You were trying to quit anyways." John scowled at Frank and pulled a pen and small notebook from his shirt pocket. Flipping open the notebook he said, "Run it by me again."

"Jeez," Frank muttered, stooping to pluck the lighter from the trash can. He stared intently at it before puckering his lips and blowing on it. Satisfied no germs remained, he smiled, plunging the lighter deep into his trouser pocket before answering. "Like I said before, the guard found him like that." Frank waved, indicating the morgue and the stiff body lying on the table inside.

"That's it? That's all you got?" John's eyebrow shot up, his cheek quivered, and for a split second, he resembled Twitch, the meth head Declan met in jail.

"Not much else to tell," Frank mumbled, rubbing longingly at the lighter in his pocket. At least John hoped it was the lighter he was rubbing. "No one knows time of death. Coulda been anywhere between lights out and this morning."

"Any blowback?"

"Nah, no one's talking." Frank shook his head. "The old guy probably just had a heart attack. As far as I can tell, there's not a mark on him."

John scribbled two words before flipping his notepad closed.

Frank rocked back and forth on the balls of his feet and pulled his lighter free. Click, click. "Are we done here?"

"Yeah," John nodded. "I guess, for now."

Without another word, Frank turned and raced off down the hallway.

John eyed Frank's receding back, glad he was no longer a slave to nicotine. She was one bitch of a mistress. Forgetting all about Frank, he opened the notebook and stared at the two words he'd written down.

Heart attack?

John scratched his head and thought back to his time in jail with Declan. His eyes narrowed and a sneer crossed his face. He flipped the notebook closed and stuffed it back into his shirt pocket.

He trod down the hallway mumbling to no one in particular. "Heart attack, my ass."

Chapter 1

DECLAN EYED THE INTERIOR. AS FAR AS HE COULD tell there was no way out. The mesh divider kept the front seat off limits and prevented him from accessing the door handles. Besides, the two officers up front would be a problem.

Fuck. Being escorted to rehab by two cops. Could it get any worse?

He sighed and looked at his 'luggage.' A big black garbage bag sat next to him on the seat holding all his worldly possessions. It was only one third full. A toothbrush, a comb, his shaving gear, a couple of magazines, and a change of clothes were all he had.

A hot, thick lump in his throat choked him. Neither his mom nor Miranda were answering his calls. For the first time in his life, he was alone. Except for the two officers riding in the front seat, but they didn't count.

A tear rolled down his cheek. He swatted it away. That's all he needed, to be known as a cry baby. Declan stared out the window not seeing the scenery. He couldn't get over Twitch turning out to be a narc. He was still trying to digest the whole thing, but one look at his surroundings brought it all back.

Twitch and the guards dragging him off to the little office, interrogating him for hours. Convinced he was part of a rival gang that were killing other gang members and bringing in drugs. Yeah, right. Declan the gangster. Declan the homicidal maniac. Except... wasn't that exactly what he was turning into?

He still couldn't figure out how Jesus got the big guard with the prison tattoos in to see him. He'd been sure he was going to die. The big guard had simply reached down and taken the phone from his trembling fingers. Declan sat waiting for it, but it never happened. At least not the way he thought it would. Instead, the guard smiled and said to him, "Jesus told me to come."

"Huh?" he squeaked, hoping he wouldn't piss himself.

"I'm one of his disciples."

"Um, okay?"

"Is there anything you need, my son?" the guard asked, his eyes blazing.

Declan tried not to stare at him as an idea began to take shape.

"Hurry," the guard whispered.

The little bag of drugs clung slickly to his belly. At any moment the door would open and he'd be escorted back to his cell. Rooster would kill him. He was sure of it. Or would they put him into protective custody? Maybe the Jesus disciple could hold onto his bag, just for safe keeping?

Declan fingered the baggy loose, the table hiding his movements. "Can I give you something to hold onto for me?"

"Anything, my son," the man agreed reverently. His pupils looked like big black balls of madness.

Something was seriously wrong with this dude's sanity, but Declan wasn't about to argue it. Instead he said, "I need you to hold onto my pills."

The blazing eyes filled with sorrow and Declan's gut twisted. "Why do you need pills, my son? Are you sick?"

"Nah." Declan attempted a smile, but it slid from his lips.

"I do not condone drugs," he warned, his eyes ablaze with righteousness.

Declan shivered. This guy was beyond crazy. His mind raced trying to come up with something. He thought back to his days in Sunday school, but all he remembered was a drawing of a shepherd's hook and a little lamb. He rubbed his eye and winced. An idea occurred to him. An eye for an eye—it just might work.

Screwing up his eyes, he tried to match the Jesus disciple's insane look. He lowered his voice, adding a throaty growl. "An eye for an eye, a tooth for a tooth," he sneered for good measure, before continuing, "Vengeance is mine!"

The disciple's eyes lit from within. He straightened his shoulders and murmured, "Praise be, my son." He looked at Declan adoringly before caressing his cheek. "Who did this to you?" he whispered.

"Rooster," Declan said, his eyes flat. "That's who the pills were for. He needs to pay for what he's done. I was going to inject him with this heavenly concoction."

"I see," the disciple replied. "An eye for an eye, tooth for tooth, hand for hand, foot for foot, burn for burn, wound for wound." His brows rose, leaving his face a twisted mess. He nodded, "Oh God of vengeance, ye shall shine forth."

"Yeah," Declan gulped, "something like that."

The disciple stared at him intently, as if trying to reach a decision. He crouched low and Declan flinched, expecting to be hit. But he was spared the beating. Instead a warm, calloused palm met his under the table. "Give them to me," he ordered.

Declan fought to unclench his hand. Everything he needed was right there. If he let go, he'd be going cold turkey. If he didn't, he'd be dead.

"Hurry," the man warned again. "They'll be coming any minute."

His fingers refused to open. His fingernails were embedded firmly in his fleshy palm. Declan reached below the table with his other hand and pried his fingers loose. They came apart with a wet sucking sound.

The guard removed the saran satchel, leaving a strangely intimate caress on his open palm. Declan squeezed his fist closed, trying to rid himself of the hideous touch, before wiping it away on the leg of his jumpsuit. His empty hand yearned to snatch the little satchel back. Instead, he plunged his hands beneath him and sat on them.

With a twisted smirk, the guard stood, stretching, and pocketed Declan's pride and joy. "God will vindicate the righteous," he said, his tone deep and solemn.

A sharp bark of laughter from the front seat brought him back to the present. Declan glanced down at his jean-clad legs. It felt weird wearing them after all the time he'd spent in a prison jumpsuit. He was showered, shaved, and dressed in 'normie' clothing. Not that he was normal. He wasn't. He didn't know what he was any more. He sure as hell wasn't the scared little kid that first entered through the prison gates. The time spent in protective custody hadn't helped him either. All it did was give him more time to think.

The bickering from the front seat distracted him from his thoughts.

"No way, it's your turn to pay. I got lunch two days in a row," Officer Wilkes, the fat cop, complained.

Officer Fernandez, the skinny cop, snorted, "Yeah right! Ya call donuts lunch?"

"Hey, you weren't complaining."

Jesus. Get a life, would you? He might be on his way to rehab, but it was better than being in these poor slobs' shoes.

How long before they arrived? He eyed the cops up front. Three big rolls of fat bulged over the back of the big guy's collar. The dark brown hair sticking out from below his hat was greasy. The thin one's shirt was flecked with dandruff. Declan shook his head. These guys wouldn't last two minutes where he'd come from.

"Hey," he shouted, trying to get their attention.

The thin one turned, showing Declan his hawkish profile. He poked a long, skinny finger into his partner's arm. Half his finger disappeared. "Nope, it's your turn to buy, end of story. And I get to pick."

"Hey!" Declan tried again. But it was pointless.

The two cops bickered back and forth up front, like he wasn't even there.

Chapter **2**

LOOSE CHANGE JANGLED IN THE POCKET OF HER skinny jeans, weighing them down. The stilettos she wore were scuffed and old. A dirty toe poked through the shoe's opening, the red nail polish chipped and flaking off. All she needed was another forty bucks. Her hips jutting out, she cocked an eyebrow at the elderly senior who passed by. "Lookin' for a little company, honey?" she rasped, trying to smile.

The man stopped, bent over his cane, and raised his head with a questioning look. "Eh?" he replied loudly, pointing at his ear.

Dee narrowed her red, blood shot eyes and peered at the old guy. Large, knobby, flesh-toned hearing aids protruded from both ears. Oh God, he must be deaf. Great, isn't that just what she needed? A deaf old bugger. Would he even be able to get it up?

Staring at him, she contemplated repeating herself. The old fellow stood by patiently, waiting. Dee swallowed, trying to work up her nerve. How she hated this. She wasn't even sure she could go through with it. "I um...." she trailed off.

Intense blue eyes met hers. His eyes were young and startling, not at all like the rest of him. "Yes?" he said, twisting the knob on his right ear.

A shaky little laugh escaped her lips. She hoped it was sexy. Her short, blunt fingers picked at an old scab on her forearm. She noticed the old man staring at it and stopped. For a moment she thought about robbing him. Right there, in broad daylight, on the street. She glanced down at his pants, wondering how easy it would be to grab his wallet and run.

A frown wrinkled the old guy's brow and he backed up a step.

Nah, she couldn't do it. There were too many people around. Maybe if it was later, but she'd never make it to later. She needed something now. Not able to fleece his wallet, she went with her original question. Tugging her shirt down to display her cleavage, she covered his hand with her own and tried again. "Are you lookin' for a little company, honey?"

One gray shaggy brow bent, nearly covering his eye. The other looked at her with suspicion. "What kind of company?"

What kind do you think? Jesus, did she have to spell it out for him?

He sucked on his teeth before giving her a shrewd look. "I guess," he said gently removing her hand from the top of his, "I wouldn't mind a cup of coffee."

Exhausted and dope sick, her mind turned over the possibilities. She eyed the street again. It was mostly families, especially mothers with their children around at this time of day. One mother stood out from the rest. She was holding her little boy's hand. The little boy looked like an older version of Billy. The child smiled up at his Mom and hugged his red Elmo doll.

Something ugly crawled in her heart. Dee grimaced and made up her mind. It was slim pickings out here anyways. "Yeah, a cup of coffee sounds good. You buyin'?" she asked, hoping he'd get the double meaning.

With his gray brows furrowed in concentration, the senior resembled a pug. He eyed her sternly, "I guess..." He trailed off, obviously not sure.

Dee switched tactics. She needed something. "Do you have a smoke I could borrow?"

The old man's hand patted his loose, dark suit jacket. He smiled for a split second and withdrew his hand. "Sometimes, I forget." he said, by way of explanation. Seeing her confused look, he added, "I had to give them up."

"Well then, could ya lend me a couple of bucks for a pack?" Dee smiled, licking her lips, and stroked the suit material covering his forearm.

Long wisps of gray hair waggled back and forth as he shook his head. "Are we going for coffee or not?" He turned away from her and headed in the direction of the café next door.

Dee watched him, torn. She didn't want a coffee, she wanted a fix. Still, not much was happening out here. She turned, following the old guy's back. Her mind was busy working on a plan to get money out of him.

Two waitresses looked up as they came through the door. The elderly gentleman knew his way around. He waved Dee towards the front of the dinette and the vacant stool. One of the waitresses smiled. "Hi Charlie, long time no see. Where you been hiding?"

The cafe was warm and smelled like bacon and eggs. The oily warmth made her gag. It was too late for breakfast and too early for lunch.

Charlie flipped over two coffee cups before replying, "Oh you know, here and there."

Aware of the curious looks she was getting, she turned her back on the two nosy waitresses and sat down on the little bar stool. Charlie placed his cane next to her and teetered over to the coffee pot.

She stared at his departing back. His pants were loose, but nothing bulged. Maybe he carried his wallet in his suit jacket pocket? Either way, it wasn't going to be easy trying to get it from him.

"Cream?" Charlie asked, interrupting her thoughts.

Dee nodded and picked up the sugar bowl. Four teaspoons later, she sipped from her cup while eyeing Charlie.

He drank his coffee black. His long knobby fingers enfolded his cup in a shaky grip. A gray shaggy brow shot up as he studied her. "What's your story?" he asked.

Still wondering how she could get the forty bucks she needed, she decided to play nice. "My story?" she asked, playing along.

"Yeah, you know." Charlie took a sip from his coffee and set it back down in the saucer. "What brought you to the streets?"

She was perplexed. Charlie should have been an easy target. Just another lonely old man wanting a quick hand job in the back alley. These old guys didn't usually ask so many questions. But this one was different. His eyes were strangely intimate. As if he knew things about her she didn't want him to know.

A tremor ran through her fingers and jerked her arm. Her coffee sloshed in its cup, spilling over to the saucer. Dee took her hand off the coffee cup and curled it in her lap. Play time was over. She was just too sick for this. With narrowed eyes, her tone turned flat. "Look Charlie, are ya interested or not?"

Seconds ticked by before he answered. "I might be. How much will it cost me for an hour of your time?"

A cold bead of sweat dampened her upper lip, tickling it. Dee eyed Charlie wondering what in the hell he needed an hour for. "One hour? Nah, I ahh, I don't think it will take you that long," she said, not wanting to offend the man.

Charlie shook his head, his eyes solemn. "No, I'll need at least an hour for what I have in mind."

All she really wanted to do was get the old bugger in a back alleyway somewhere close by, with his pants down around his ankles. She could easily steal his wallet then. By the time he had zipped up his pants, she'd be out of there.

With no intention of spending one second longer than necessary with him, Dee placed a hand on his chest. Her fingers stroked an intimate invitation.

Once again, Charlie's eye grew serious. The intense blue turned dark cobalt. As if she were no more than a child, he stopped her hand cupping it in his own gnarled mitt. He eyed her fingers, taking in the bitten nails and squared off edges.

A strange fluttering sensation erupted in her chest and she panicked, pulling her hand free of his. What exactly did Charlie have in mind? Was he some kind of twisted freak, or just a lonely old man who needed someone to talk too?

With a last gulp of his coffee, Charlie stood up and grabbed his cane. As if an afterthought, he glanced at her. "I can give you one hundred, not a penny more."

She tapped her fingers on the linoleum countertop. If he had a hundred, he probably had more. "Okay Charlie, you've got yourself a deal." The idea of easy money, and the dope she could buy with it, brought a sincere smile to her face. "And I know just the place," she said, thinking of the alleyway across the street.

"No." Charlie shook his head and buttoned up his suit jacket. "I've got somewhere in mind already."

Rule number one: never let the John name the place. Dee blinked, drawing a blank. She was becoming too dope sick to think clearly. Oh well, what was the worst thing that could happen? The old guy wasn't a threat. Not wanting him to know how sick she was, Dee set the ground rules. "Okay, but only an hour, or it will cost you double."

Besides, she thought, *the sooner we're alone, the sooner I'll get at his wallet.*

Charlie appeared to be considering her words. He stuck out his hand. "Deal," he agreed.

She shook his hand awkwardly as the waitresses picked up their pace getting ready for the noon hour rush.

Following Charlie, she exited the café, visions of black tar heroin dancing in her head.

Charlie, however, had a completely different vision in his.

Chapter 3

THE BELL ENDING THE PLAY THERAPY SESSION CHIMED softly above Billy's head. The floor around him was littered with paper, cast off toys, and broken crayons. Lyndsey eyed the floor skeptically, wondering how Kristen, the play therapist, was able to decipher meaning from all of this mess. Billy, oblivious to anything but the doll he was trying to dress, sat in the middle of the floor, intent on his task.

Lyndsey felt inadequate gawking at Billy and the mess he was making. She resisted the urge to get up from her chair and start picking up after him. She was used to sitting in a circle doing group therapy with people who were learning to communicate their feelings. But watching Billy play—she just didn't get it. How was the mess in front of her therapeutic?

Looking at the broken crayons, she shuddered. Billy had a mean streak and liked breaking things. He had chosen three colors to draw his artwork. Red, black, and yellow. First he'd scribbled a shaky circle in black on the fresh sheet of paper Kristen had given him. Then he'd used the red and yellow crayons to color it all in. After he'd finished coloring, he looked at his paper and frowned before tearing it into pieces. Clearly he wasn't impressed with his work. But why? With his artwork in pieces, Billy turned to the crayons and began breaking them. Lyndsey was sure he'd have broken every last one if Kristen hadn't intervened.

Lyndsey took her eyes off Billy and stared out the window. Her thoughts turned to the little boy's mother, Dee. They'd only heard from her once since Billy had come to live with them. Just one call, but it was enough to create even more chaos and drama. Dee was still way out there in la-la land. Her friend was operating under delusions and false promises. But she had left her with one piece of important information: Billy's birth date.

"Nyn," Billy attempted, breaking her train of thought.

"Nyn," was the best Billy could do. His speech was as underdeveloped as the rest of him, hence the play therapy sessions. Her lips lifted in a big smile. "Yes, Billy?"

Looking serious, with his face all scrunched up, he got up from the floor. Billy was beginning to fill out. His hand held tightly to the Ken doll that he'd been trying to dress. With a defiant look at Kristen, he marched over to Lyndsey and said, "Mine." Billy waved the doll excitedly in the air.

"No, honey." Lyndsey shook her head.

His bottom lip bowed, forming a big pout. Tears pooled in his eyes. Billy eyed the Ken doll and tried again. "Mine."

Lyndsey's heart broke. If only it were that easy. Just give Billy everything he wanted, regardless if it were his or not, then maybe his past would magically disappear. Yeah, right. She knew only too well that it never worked that way. She'd seen far too many parents ruin their kid's life by giving them everything they wanted. Entitlement only worked for spoiled brats and addicts. It sure as hell didn't make for healthy, well adapted children. All children needed to learn the word no. She just wished it wasn't her who had to teach it to Billy.

It was hard doing nothing. Watching Billy struggle broke her heart. As a child she'd been sure she could feel other people's emotions. Now she knew it wasn't other people's emotions she was feeling, but her own.

But she could emphasize with how Billy felt. It was awful to be the child of an addict and feel helpless and unloved.

Lyndsey steeled herself to stay in her chair as she watched Billy's face.

One tear, and then two, ran down his cheek. His lower lip trembled as he clutched the doll tightly to his chest. Billy buried his face into the doll and whispered, "Mine."

Fighting the urge to take the little boy into her arms, Lyndsey turned to Kristen for guidance.

Kristen smiled at her and then turned to Billy. "Billy, can you please put the doll back?"

The Ken doll's T-shirt hung crookedly on its plastic frame. Billy yanked on it with one hand. In his own little world he focused solely on Ken, not responding to Kristen's request.

Lyndsey turned away from Billy and looked at Kristen questioningly.

Kristen's blonde head bobbed, her brows furrowed in concentration as she observed Billy. "Hmm…" She trailed off into an awkward silence.

Oh, oh. Lyndsey recognized the tone. It spoke volumes. She should know. She'd used it many times herself. The unspoken words hung between them. To her eyes, it looked like Kristen wasn't sure what to do either. What did one do with a small child who had seen far more than he ever should have? Would it increase the trauma to Billy if they took the doll away from him? By the look on Billy's face, she was pretty certain this was one of those times when trusting your gut was the right answer.

A grunt came from Billy as he tugged on Ken's T-shirt. His face grew pink from his efforts. His motor co-ordination was off and he was clearly frustrated. Lyndsey rose from her chair, intending to help Billy clothe Ken, but before she could get there, the shirt gave out with a loud rip.

The torn T-shirt hung in Billy's hand before he flung Ken to the ground. His eyes screwed closed. His face turned purpled and he shrieked. He crumpled into a little ball on the floor and howled.

Frozen to the carpet, Lyndsey watched shocked as Billy melted down in front of them. What should she do? Glancing at Kristen, she found her answer.

"He's okay," Kristen assured in a gentle voice. "It's best if you just leave him. He needs to learn how to self-regulate. And right now, he needs to get it out."

"Oh, okay." Lyndsey re-traced her steps back to the chair and sat down. What Kristen said was probably right, but why did it feel so wrong? With grownups it made sense. They had the where-with-all to cope with their feelings. Well, except if you were an addict, or the family member of one. Oh, scrap that. People in general wanted to avoid emotions. She wished she could right now. It was heart breaking to watch Billy as he sobbed on the floor.

Kristen watched from a distance, her face calm and serene. Lyndsey found it soothing. It was easy to feel helpless in a situation like this. She was used to being the one in Kristen's chair. It had been so long. She'd forgotten what it felt like to be on the other side.

Feeling helpless is an awful feeling. Removing her thumb from her mouth, she glanced at the shredded nail in surprise. Biting her nails was something she resorted to in times of crisis. Billy's wails were bringing up old childhood wounds for her. She knew what it was like to be small and alone. Maybe Billy really did need to learn how to self-regulate, but everything within her screamed to pick him up.

Billy hiccupped as his sobs quieted. His whimpers showed his pain even if he wasn't yet able to vocalize it. It didn't feel right letting him fight through this alone. Yes, he needed to self-soothe, but he also needed love and comfort.

Not sure if she was attempting to make Billy or herself feel better, Lyndsey scooped him up against Kristen's advice. Oh God, now she was one of them!

His little body stiffened within her embrace. Rather than sit, she paced the room and whispered affirmations into his shell-like ear.

"There, there, you're all right, sweetie." Lyndsey whispered the words, but she didn't believe them.

The clock struck ten with a soft chime, reminding her of the appointment she'd made with Susan.

Susan had done a miraculous turnabout. She was one of the success stories, or spiritual awakenings, that she was so blessed to see. It was early days, but when you've supped from the bowl of misery, you'd do anything to avoid going back to that dark dinner.

A spike of anxiety pierced her. Lyndsey wasn't sure how she would manage. There was a lot on her plate and her appointment with Susan was the least of it.

Billy shifted, lying in her arms with a faraway look on his face. Sometimes little boys had to disassociate to protect themselves. He had no way of knowing he was safe in her arms. In his brief experience, shutting down and survival were key.

Safety was simply a word he couldn't comprehend.

Hugging Billy even tighter, she wished her love was a magical elixir that could mend all his broken places.

An old familiar heat rose in her throat. Pain and rage. It was a bitter brew, and one that could turn deadly if it weren't caught in time.

Billy stirred and his eyes fluttered open. His eyes were vacant, as if no one lived behind those dark black pupils.

"Billy," she called him back from wherever he'd gone.

Her words broke the spell and he blinked. The quick up and down motion of his lids restored him to the room.

Her heart broke all over again as she looked at him. God, she hated addiction. The legacy it left on the kids. The generations of families it affected. The hopelessness and despair with which it operated. And the insidious selfishness under which one functioned when consumed by it.

Addiction was a greedy monster. It was infectious, and it didn't stop with its host—it wanted their families too. It even wanted the littlest victims. Planning its future in the blood of our children.

Well, it wouldn't get Billy. Not if she could help it.

Chapter **4**

THE SMELL WAS GROSS. THE WARM AIR INSIDE THE car was thick with the rich stink of asiago cheese. The two cops rode up front oblivious to everything but the sub sandwiches they jammed into their mouths. Declan looked for a way to roll down the window, hoping he might have missed something. But there was nothing but the smooth wall of the car where the window gadget should have been.

A fresh wave of nausea rolled in his stomach. The bagged lunch sat beside him un-opened. By now, he should have had two doses of methadone in him. Although he wasn't crazy about the shit, obviously his body was. He didn't know who marketed methadone, but they lied. It was just another money maker for big pharmaceutical companies to sell to a naïve public and all those bleeding hearts. Methadone was addicting, and coming off of it was the same as coming off all the other opiates he'd ever taken.

The wet slurping sounds coming from up front added to his misery. Officer Fernandez licked the last drops of salad dressing from his fingers and belched. Declan stared out the window, wishing he was anywhere but here.

"Aren't you gonna finish that?" Officer Wilkes waved at the leftover sandwich poking out of the skinny cop's wrapper.

He'd given up on trying to get their attention. All he wanted to do now was sleep. It was the only way he'd get any relief from what he knew was going to get a lot worse.

"Nah, I'm done." Officer Fernandez shrugged, squishing the wrapper up into a ball.

"Hey!" Officer Wilkes complained. "I woulda finished it."

Fernandez snorted. "Yeah right! It really looks like you're starving."

The first wave of cramps hit. Sweat popped out on his brow. He swiped it away the with his shirt sleeve. Fuck. When would they get there? And where in the hell was this place?

"Hey kid!" The fat cop craned his neck. Rolls bulged, reshaping, to look like a bum drooping over the back of the cop's collar.

Declan decided to give them a taste of their own medicine. Two could play at this game.

But the cop wasn't playing. "Hey kid, don't make me stop this car!" The fat cop's neck turned a dark shade of red.

Maybe if he was nice, they'd get there faster. "Yeah," he mumbled.

Officer Wilkes turned, showing one side of his profile. With bread crumbs clinging to his big pink lips, he jerked a thumb at the unopened bag sitting next to him. "You gonna eat that, or what?"

No way could he eat right now, at least not without it coming right back up. Declan shook his head. "Nah, I'm not hungry."

Fernandez shifted in his seat to get a better look at him. Eyeing Declan intently he said, "You don't look so hot, kid."

No shit, Sherlock! Really? What tipped you off? He shook his head. "I'm good."

"Quit playing his mother would you, and get me his lunch," the fat cop said to Hawk-face as he pulled roughly onto the shoulder of the road.

Gravel crunched beneath the tires as the car slammed to a stop, shooting Declan into the back of the front seat. His face kissed the cold steel mesh before gravity pulled him back again.

Regaining his balance, he sat up straighter. The back door opened and Declan scooped up his lunch bag, tossing it to the thin cop. "How much longer before we're there?"

Catching the lunch bag in one hand, Officer Fernandez closed the door. The guy was way too serious, his face set like stone.

And to boot, it looked like they were back to ignoring him.

The patrol car was silent except for the rustling of the paper bag as the fat cop tore it open. Half a ham and cheese sandwich disappeared in one bite. The big cop's cheeks popped out like a hamster. "Not bad," he stated to nobody in particular.

Should he ask again or just let it go?

With his nose twisting to one side, Fernandez eyed his partner as he jammed the other half of the sandwich into his face. "You kiss your wife with that mouth?"

"Hmm," Officer Wilkes replied.

Jesus! Just what he needed, Laurel and Hardy in the front seat. He decided to let it go. They'd get there when they got there. Deep in thought, his legs bounced up and down. Rehab wasn't prison. At least he wasn't locked up.

Seemed to him that everybody and their dog were out to get control his life these days. It really pissed him off. What he did with his life was nobody's fuckin' business but his own. He stared through the window, his mood black.

Gurgling noises erupted from his belly. His tongue felt dry and pasty. The little muscle spasms and quivers had begun. He thought about the baggie he'd passed to the Jesus disciple. What he wouldn't give to have it back right now. He wondered what the freak had done with it. The guy was just crazy enough to have flushed the whole damn package down the toilet.

Snatches of conversation drifted back to him from the front seat. "Did you catch the football game?"

Saliva made his mouth wet as he counted the pills in his mind. Blocking out all else, he concentrated, seeing their shapes and colors. Each orb was tantalizing. Like a beautiful naked woman lying just beyond his grasp.

The fat cop snickered. "Did you catch those cheerleaders?"

He focused on one pill in particular. It was flat green. Like a smarty with the shine worn off. The number 80 was etched into it. It felt chalky on his fingertips as he picked it up.

"Oh yeah," Fernandez chortled. "Did you get a load of those knockers? You wonder how she could stand carrying around a rack that size."

The pill was virtually weightless in his hand. Screwing his eyes closed even tighter, he stayed with the vision.

"And what about the red-head?" said the fat cop.

He pictured himself placing the pill into his mouth. The vile, bitter taste was like sweet nirvana to his system.

"What, you don't like red-heads?" Fernandez asked. "I wish my wife could do the splits like she did."

Fighting the urge to bite down on the round green orb, he waited, wanting to prolong the pleasure.

"She'd be doing them, if she got a load of this bad boy." The fat cop harrumphed and grabbed his crotch.

The pill faded from his tongue and he strained, trying to get it back.

"Jesus! Would you shut up about my wife? I thought we agreed. The topic is not up for discussion!"

Burying his head in his hands, he knuckled his eyeballs. The little green pill faded to black. He reached for it in his mind's eye. But it was gone.

The rolls on the back of the fat cop's neck danced with merriment as he laughed. "You're so sensitive."

Little yellow halos danced behind his lids. He waited a minute longer, hoping he could re-create the sensation. The halos turned white and then disappeared.

Fernandez wasn't playing. His tone turned hard. "What's our ETA?"

Declan's eyes snapped open.

"Okay, okay," Officer Wilkes said. "Don't get your panties in a knot, for Christ's sake. We should be there in ten."

Ten what? Ten days? Ten hours? Ten minutes? By the look of the hawk-faced cop, he thought it was probably minutes. Sitting up straight, he ran a shaky hand through his hair.

The cops continued to bicker up front.

Tuning them out, he stared straight ahead. His mind raced as he braced for what was to come next.

Chapter **5**

EYES FIXED FIRMLY ON THE GROUND IN FRONT OF HER, Dee held onto her seat. She was part of a larger circle, in which sat men and women of all ages. Charlie sat to the left of her and some strange, smiling woman she'd never met sat to her right. She stewed, wanting nothing more than to run screaming from the room. But she needed her hundred bucks and Charlie said he wouldn't give it to her until the meeting was over.

So here she sat, in this bullshit place, listening to these idiots go on and on about their dumb lives.

The lady beside her stood up. "I would like to suggest powerlessness as the topic, for the newcomers in the room."

Dee closed her eyes, hoping to snooze her way through this torturous event. The coffee made it impossible and her eyes snapped back open. A constant thrum ran through her, fueled by caffeine and need. A half-eaten donut sat on her lap. She thought about throwing it away, but decided to save it for later.

A well-manicured hand patted her forearm as the woman beside her sat back down. She glanced up to see bright red lips smiling at her. What was it with this lady? She wasn't into women, or threesomes for that matter. She stared at her donut, hoping the woman would get the hint.

A man across from her stood up. "My name is Darren and I'm an alcoholic. I'd like to talk about powerlessness," he said.

Darren was a big man, maybe thirty-five, with dark hair and a goatee. He looked dangerous and was just the kinda guy she'd go for.

"When I first heard the word powerlessness, I thought it was bullshit." Darren stopped and scratched his head before starting again. "Powerlessness was for cowards and little girls. It wasn't for me."

She didn't have a clue what he was talking about, but she liked the way he looked.

"So I decided I'd show you, by hurting me." Darren laughed and the others joined in.

She looked around the room, confused. What in the hell was so funny?

"Life was getting pretty crazy for me. You know, the regular stuff. Like a warrant out for my arrest, not paying my child support, a broken marriage, fired from another job. But hey, it wasn't my fault!" Darren smiled a big, white toothed smile and met her eyes.

The people in the room roared with laughter and she squirmed. Great, she was in a room with raving lunatics. She couldn't wait to get the hell out of there. Why had Charlie brought her here, anyways?

"By this time I wasn't just drinking, I was using other substances too."

Dee yawned. Seriously, she has absolutely nothing in common with these people. She wouldn't waste a dime on booze.

"I finally found something that did the trick. It stopped the pain, and I loved it. So I put away the booze, because this stuff was better. I actually fooled myself into thinking I didn't have a drinking problem."

A hush hung over the room the way it does at a funeral. Darren cleared his throat and the smile slid from his face. "I was in a rooming house. It was ghetto-ville. I was still waiting to catch my break. Each morning I

26

woke up, I was consumed with misery. It took me all of five minutes to break the promise I'd made the night before."

A hot stabbing pain pinched her side just underneath her rib cage. She flinched and bit her lower lip. Bolting upright in her seat, she thought about fleeing the room, but stopped. Torn, she looked at Charlie, caught.

Charlie only smiled and shook his head.

She looked at Darren. "Have you lost your bloody mind?" she shouted.

Confused, Darren's jaw dropped open as he stared blankly at her. "Excuse me?"

"Promises," she drew a shaky breath and tried again. "You should never make promises! Stop doing it!"

The woman with the bright red lips smiled, patting her arm. "Keep coming back dear," she said with kind, big brown eyes.

Jerking her arm free of the woman's grasp, she muttered, "Stupid."

Darren took his eyes off hers and looked at the other people in the room. "Sober just wasn't a place I wanted to be. It was too painful and it kept reminding me of the mess I'd made of my life. Loaded, I was free. Sober, I was miserable. It was as simple as that."

And your point is? she thought. *Charlie said an hour. We must be close to it.* Her leg slid against a hard object. A brown leather purse swung slowly beside her. The woman's tan coat hung over it, trapping the purse strap beneath.

A sharp bark of laughter drew her eyes away from the purse. "So what's a guy to do?" Darren asked, laughing again.

A new idea occurred to her. She craned her head and stared around the room. Was everyone high?

"Here I was," Darren huffed, "trapped between wanting to stop, but not being able to."

Darren's eyes glistened with unshed tears. She glanced back down, not interested in what he had to say. Shifting in her seat, she moved closer to the swinging purse. Her finger stroked the brown leather strap.

"So I did what any good alcoholic would do. I gave up." Darren drew in a deep breath. "I figured, screw it. Then I got down to the business of using. Only this time, I didn't stop."

Her fingers slid down the smooth strap landing on the zipper. She grasped the tab and tugged gently.

"A kid found me in an alley way. A kid...." Darren's voice broke and trailed off.

The zipper slid smoothly along the tracks. She could see a black wallet inside the purse.

"A fuckin' kid. Can you believe that? I mean, what kind of low life scum do you have to be to do that to a kid?"

She looked up, not able to stop herself. Darren's eyes locked on hers. But he stared through her, not at her. A shiver ran down her back and her arms broke out in goose bumps.

"The kid had more sense than I did. That's for sure." Darren blinked and dropped his head.

It was like she'd been frozen for just a second. She jerked in her seat, and the purse swung wildly below.

"Without the kid's quick thinking, I wouldn't be here. The EMP said I didn't have a pulse when they found me. They shot me full of Narcon, but they weren't very hopeful."

Her shoulder made a popping sound as she reached for the purse.

"When I woke up, something had changed. I was me and yet..." Darren hesitated.

With her eyes fixed on Darren, she slid her hand down the strap expecting to find the purse open as she had just left it.

"I wasn't." Darren inhaled sharply. "I was different. I could feel it."

Instead of cold leather, her hand curled around warm, living flesh.

"You can't get any more powerless than that, in my mind. My best thinking killed me." Darren laughed, and then sobered. "If that kid hadn't called for help, I wouldn't be sitting here today."

Her heart lurched in her throat as she stared at what she grasped.

The red-lipped woman smiled, raising her hand with Dee's in a sign of victory. Instead of shouting 'thief', the woman simply kissed Dee's hand and said, "Sister, it's gonna be okay."

She stared mesmerized at the bright red lips on the back of her hand. The strange woman patted her on the arm once again, and returned her hand to her lap.

Charlie reached over and hugged her from the other side.

Sandwiched between the two, she wondered if she was hallucinating or having an out of body experience. Something was seriously wrong here. For the first time in a long time, she was stunned.

Out of options, she clung to her seat.

Chapter **6**

THE DRIVE HOME WAS A BLUR. LYNDSEY KEPT ONE eye on the rear-view mirror and one eye on the road. Billy had finally fallen asleep in his car seat. Sitting in the garage with the car idling, she didn't want to wake him up.

Could she just leave him in the car to sleep?

What did healthy parents do in situations like these? She sure as shit didn't know.

Weary, she rested her head against the car's headrest. The car was warm and she relaxed. The warm air blowing from the heater was nice.

An image of the dirty laundry sitting by the washing machine drew a sigh. She stole a glance in the rear-view mirror. Billy's cheeks were flushed rosy pink. He had one fist curled around his yellow stuffed duck.

It didn't seem right to wake him. She turned off the ignition and waited to see if he'd wake up.

Billy didn't move.

Rolling her head from side to side, she worked out the kinks. She didn't want Drake to know it, but she was beat. Taking Billy on had been her idea, but she was finding out he was a full time job, on top of her full time job.

Closing her eyes, she decided to make the best of it. Pings sounded from under the hood as the engine cooled. Her eyes grew heavy and she drifted off.

A little boy laughed as he ran through a field of green. The kite he held onto sailed high above his head. Lyndsey squinted, barely able to read the writing on the kite. 'Git wel son' rode high above her. The child raced around the field running faster and faster. He looked frantic. She stepped forward, wanting to help him, but when she got closer, she saw it was Billy. Except it wasn't.

"Linds?"

The child disappeared. Her eyes snapped opened. Drake was standing beside the car.

Billy stirred in the back seat and she held a finger to her lips.

"Were you sleeping?" Drake cocked an eyebrow, not talking quiet at all.

Glancing into the rear view mirror, she hoped Billy was still sleeping. With one eye on Billy and the other on Drake, she inched the car door open. The squeak of the hinge woke Billy up.

He didn't wake up happy. Instead, he began to cry.

"I got him, honey," Drake said, disappearing from her vision.

Feeling strangely unnerved from her dream, she gathered up her purse and car keys.

Billy's cries grew louder as Drake unbuckled him from the car seat.

She sighed. When it came to caring for Billy, she felt overwhelmed and helpless. Following Drake into the house, she ran to get Billy some toys.

Drake plopped the child on the living room carpet next to his toys. Billy looked at them with puffy eyes. Lyndsey watched, tense. He turned and reached for his truck with a scowl on his face. "Do you think he's hungry?" Her eyes met Drake's.

He shook his head. "Relax, Linds. He's okay."

"Yes, but—" she broke off as Drake kissed her.

His lips were warm on hers. For a moment she forgot about Billy. Drake drew her closer and cupped the back of her head with his hand. She nestled there against him for a moment, before growing awkward in his embrace.

Embarrassed, she pushed him away.

"Linds?"

"Should we be doing this?"

Drake scratched his head and looked confused. "Doing what?"

"Kissing." Lyndsey rolled her eyes at Billy.

"What's wrong with kissing?"

"I don't know. That's the problem. I don't seem to know anything when it comes to caring for Billy." She chewed her bottom lip. "I don't want to do anything that might re-damage him."

"Lighten up, Linds! You're taking this whole parenting thing too far."

She bristled. "That's not fair!"

"Honey, Rome wasn't built in a day, and Billy isn't one of your patients. For now, he's our little boy. I think it's okay if he sees me kissing you."

Billy made growling noises as he crashed one truck into another. She watched him wondering if his destructive behavior was a sign of oppositional defiant disorder.

Aware she had just tuned Drake out, she turned back to him. "It's easy for you to say 'relax,' but you aren't carrying around a head full of probabilities when it comes to Billy."

"Lyndsey, I'm just trying to point out that you're becoming hypervigilant. Can't you loosen up a little? Let the play therapist figure out what's wrong with Billy. You don't have to."

A loud crash put an end to their conversation. One of Billy's trucks lay broken at the foot of the fireplace. She stepped away from Drake, intent on retrieving the truck. He squeezed her hand and tugged her back. The three of them looked at one another, and Billy started to wail.

"Just let him cry, he's okay," said Drake.

Billy's cries turned to howls. His face grew red as he pointed at his truck.

"I think he wants his truck back."

"Then let him get it, Linds. He's the one that threw it over there."

Billy grasped the remaining truck and smashed it up and down on the ground. Drake shook his head and said firmly, "No Billy," then took the truck from him.

Billy stopped howling for an instant as he looked at his empty hand. Drake placed the truck on the carpet next to Billy. Billy snatched up the truck, seeming to hug it before tossing it at the fireplace. The truck hit with a loud crash and landed beside the first one.

She stood there helplessly wringing her hands, not sure what to do.

Drake frowned. "No Billy, you do not throw your trucks," he said, scooping the mangled trucks up from the fireplace and putting them on top of the mantle. Billy pointed at them and grunted. His face became bright red and his eyes screwed shut.

She tensed, waiting for it. Billy screamed long and loud. It was earpiercing. He dropped to the carpet and curled into the fetal position.

Her shoulders sagged and worry creased her brow. Biting a nail, she wished she knew what to do. She'd seen so many young people damaged by their environment.

Drake winked at her and crossed the room to pick up Billy, who had shut down and seemed unaware of Drake's presence.

Had she made a mistake? Maybe she wasn't the right one for this little boy after all.

"Don't worry, Linds," Drake said, shifting Billy on his hip. He pulled her finger from her mouth.

She stared at the bitten nail before swiping it on her leg. "Oh Drake," she whispered. "What if I made a mistake?"

The grin slid from his face. "What if you did? Would it be the end of the world?"

"I don't know..."

"Well I do." Drake tightened his grip on Billy. "No pain, no gain, hey Billy boy?"

Billy's eyes remained glued shut as Drake tousled his hair.

"Besides," he smiled at Lyndsey, "this boy is gonna make one hell of a pitcher. Aren't you, Billy?"

Leaning over, he gave her a quick kiss. "Stop fretting," he ordered.

As Drake strode from the room with Billy in his arms, she wished she had some of his confidence. But at the moment, she was anything but. In fact, she was worried sick.

With nothing better to do, she picked at a cuticle and waited for Drake to return.

Chapter 7

THE BUILDING WAS LARGE, ITS EXTERIOR A DIRTY white stucco, with black bars running vertically across all the windows. Declan's new home looked like a great big shoe box. The area around the building was landscaped in gravel. A big rusted ashtray and a couple of scraggly looking plants decorated the front entrance. The whole scene shouted ghetto.

The door beside him jerked open. "Let's go, kid. We don't have all day." Officer Wilkes stomped his foot and crooked a finger at him.

He stared at the building, feeling tense. "Are ya sure we got the right place?" he asked, not wanting to get out.

Officer Fernandez craned his neck and sneered. "What's a matter, princess? Did you think you're going to a four star hotel?"

"No..." he trailed off. Glancing around the inside of the cop car, he grabbed his bag. It couldn't get any worse than this. Could it?

Officer Wilkes walked him to the front door. "You know, you're lucky kid. If it were up to me, I'da left you to rot in your cage. Someone's pulling for you, that's for sure."

Declan eyed the seedy building, thinking he was anything but.

A small black button, circled in rust, was embedded to the left of the wooden door. Officer Wilkes pushed the button and sighed. "Hot out here," he mumbled to Fernandez.

It was hot. The plastic bag he clung to slipped from his sweaty grasp. He bent to retrieve it just as the door opened.

A large, dark-skinned man stood in the entrance way.

The fat cop flipped open his notebook and, sounding all official, announced, "I'm Officer Wilkes. I'm here to deliver inmate 22457 into your custody. Should he leave, you need to contact us immediately. A warrant will be issued for his arrest."

The man smiled at Declan and reached for his hand. "I'm Tom. Welcome."

Officer Wilkes cleared his throat, obviously not pleased with the intrusion. "If he is argumentative or acts out in any way, you're to call us and we'll come and get him right away."

Declan craned his neck, trying to see beyond Tom into the interior of the building. A large finger tapped his shoulder and he turned.

"Is that understood?" The cop asked the question, but Tom stared at him too.

"Yeah," he mumbled. A piece of paper was thrust below his nose along with a pen.

"Sign this then, and we'll be on our way."

He scratched his signature along the line reading 'sign here' without bothering to read the rest of it.

Tom and Officer Wilkes shook hands. The fat cop stared at Declan for a second before turning to Tom. "Good luck!" he chortled, indicating Tom would need it. He spun on his heel and headed back to his patrol car.

Glad to see the last of him, Declan waited obediently next to Tom. Tom gave him a long hard stare before saying, "I'll introduce you to the rest of the gang, but first we need to cover some ground rules. Follow me."

Tom flung the wooden door open, giving him his first look at the place. It wasn't pretty; as a matter of fact, it was a dive. An overstuffed couch with some of its stuffing coming loose sat next to the door. Two plastic chairs that used to be white were across from the sofa. Beside them was a pay phone.

It didn't smell good either. There was a lingering odor of rancid grease and fried onions. He stared at Tom's back, not sure what to make of it all.

After a short walk down a dark corridor, Tom turned and nodded at an open door. "In here," he pointed.

Tom took a seat behind the beat up old desk. He shot a glance at Declan and waved his hand at the vacant chair.

He sat down across from Tom and waited.

A crease wrinkled Tom's forehead. He studied his desk, eyes darting between two piles of paper. He reached out and withdrew two sheets from the pile on the left. "Okay," he muttered. "Here," Tom shoved a pen at him, "you're gonna need this."

He reached across the desk and took the pen.

"Consider this your orientation." Tom waved at the pile of papers in his hand and cleared his throat.

He nodded, not sure what else he should do.

"First thing, we're not a prison."

Declan thought about the bars on the window and wondered if he should ask.

Tom beat him to it. "The bars on the windows are simply to keep people out, not to keep them in. This isn't, um, the best neighborhood."

He tapped on his shoe with the pen, hoping to appear cool. Would they give him methadone? Or maybe they'd give him something better?

"You following me?"

He looked up from his shoe. "Yeah."

"Like I was saying, this isn't prison. It's up to you if you want to stay here or go back to jail." Tom squared the pile of papers into a neat pile and picked up the first sheet.

His legs began to bounce. The little office was claustrophobic and he was already tired of being here.

"All right, I need to read this to you." Tom grabbed the glasses out of his pocket and continued. "Stop me if you have any questions."

He nodded, not really listening.

"If you do any of the following, we will ask you to leave. If we ask you to leave, you know where you'll be going?" Tom stared at him.

He nodded.

A frown crossed Tom's face. "Say it."

"Say what?" he questioned, with a frown of his own.

"Say where you'll be going."

Jesus, the guy was into power trips. Great! "Prison," he mumbled, not wanting to give him anything else.

"That's right, prison, so you better pay attention," Tom said, having established the upper hand.

He might as well play along. What had his mother always said? You can catch more flies with honey than you can with vinegar. Something like that, anyways. If he was nice, it might work to his benefit. And maybe if he was friendly, Tom would get him something for his aches and pains. He grinned, hoping he could pull it off.

Tom seemed to buy it. He relaxed against the back of his chair and his frown smoothed out. "So, if you don't want to go back to prison, then don't do any of these things." He thrust the paper in front of Declan's eyes and snatched it back. "You following me?"

He nodded, not sure that he was.

"Number one, no drinking, drugging, gambling, or sex." Tom looked up from the paper, making eye contact.

"What about my girl?" He thought about Miranda, wherever the hell she was. "Can she come for a visit?"

Tom shrugged. "Maybe. You'll have to run it by your counselor."

He decided not to push it. He'd get his way when the time came.

Tom droned on, reading from the paper. Declan tuned him out and closed his eyes, thinking about Miranda.

"Sign here then." Tom pushed the paper across the table at him.

Before signing, he eyed the paper and came to a stop. "No drugging?" His legs bounces faster and he scratched his head. "What about detox meds?'

"Detox meds?"

"Yeah, I'm already two doses behind schedule."

"What?" Tom's eyes grew wide. "We aren't a detox center, kid. We're a treatment center. There's a difference. By the time you get here, you're supposed to be detoxed already."

"Nobody told me that." A trickle of cold sweat rolled down his temple.

"Well I'm telling you!" Tom's nostrils flared. He pointed a finger at Declan's chest. "You use anything in here and you're done. Nothing, zip, zilch, nada. Capiche?"

His legs banged the underneath of Tom's big old desk. His mind raced. What the hell? Was this some kind of sick joke? Was he being played?

"Well?" Tom nudged the paper closer to him.

The thought of prison and what was waiting for him back there brought an end to his debate. He picked up the pen, ready to sign.

Looking at him suspiciously, Tom said. "We don't have all day. Look kid, believe it or not, being here is a privilege. I'm just not sure you're ready for it."

He quickly scribbled his signature at the bottom of the page before Tom could change his mind. The telephone sitting next to him gave him an idea. "Can I call my mom? I need to tell her where I am. She still thinks I'm in jail."

Not bothering to answer him, Tom grunted and pushed the phone in his direction. He dialed quickly before Tom could change his mind. The phone only rang twice before his mom picked it up.

Under Tom's watchful eyes, he said, "Hi Mom, it's me. Ah, I'm in rehab at the Phoenix House and I was wondering if you would come and visit me. Visiting hours are…" he stopped, drawing a blank.

Tom hid a smirk and replied, "Tomorrow between 3 and 5 p.m."

Declan repeated the times and listened for a minute. "No mom, it's okay." He insisted, eyeing Tom he continued. "The guy that runs the place is sitting next to me, if you'd like to ask him yourself."

He put one hand over the phone and looked at Tom. "She's worried I'm not supposed to have visitors yet."

Tom shrugged. "Do you want me to speak to her?"

Declan shook his head and met Tom's eyes. "It's okay. I got this." Then he spoke into the receiver. "That's right mom. Good. I'll see you at 3 then?"

As he hung up the phone he wondered why his mother hadn't jumped at the chance to see him.

He didn't worry about it long, though.

His head felt like it was in a vise-grip and his stomach was woozy. For a minute, he thought he'd be sick right there.

Tom scowled at him. He jerked a thumb at the door. "We'll finish the rest of your orientation out there."

As they crossed the threshold, Declan tapped Tom on the shoulder. The big man stopped halfway out of the room. "What?"

"Um, I'm not feeling very good. Is there something you can give me?"

Tom's eyes turned a darker shade of brown. His jaw dropped open and he snorted. An eerie half grin flickered across his face. "Yeah, there's something we can give you." Tom moved beyond the doorway and walked down the hall.

Trying to match Tom's long strides and not wanting to sound too eager, he asked, "What is it?"

Tom stopped dead in his tracks and turned to face him. Gone was any hint of the anger he'd just seen. Instead, his face wore a solemn expression. Meeting his eyes he answered, "Something that just might save your life."

He licked his lips, wondering if that something might be OxyContin. He really hoped it would be.

But Tom's next words shattered the idea.

"What you need, kid, is a real good dose of reality," he said before grabbing him by his arm and steering him down the hallway.

Chapter **8**

SHE STOOD IN A CIRCLE, JOINED TO THE OTHERS BY
their hands. Hand-holding had never been her thing, and it sure as hell
wasn't now! The people in the room were saying a prayer, something
about serenity. They all seemed to know the words. Some had their
eyes closed, while others stared up at the ceiling. Dee stared at the
floor, sensing this thing was coming to an end.

"Keep coming back!" Charlie smiled at her as he tugged on her hand.

"It works if you work it!" The red-lipped woman grinned.

The circle broke apart and she yanked her hand from Charlie's. Her
eyes narrowed shrewdly. "I want my money."

Charlie acted as if he didn't hear her and turned to the red-lipped lady.
"Darlene, will you give Dee your number?"

"Of course," Darlene replied, reaching into the purse in which Dee had
just had her hand.

Darren joined them and looked at Dee. "Wanna go for coffee?"

Dee ignored him and tugged on Charlie's jacket. She was beyond
caring what people thought. Her jaw thrust forward as she spit out her
words. "Charlie, I want my fuckin' money now!"

Darren's eyes bugged open and he took a step backwards, sizing her up.
He turned to Charlie. "She needs detox."

Charlie just shrugged and shook his head. "That wasn't our deal."

Darlene thrust a piece of paper into her hand. It was all she could do not to throw it back in her face. Instead, she plunged it into her pocket and stared at Charlie.

Darren frowned at her and began stacking the chairs next to them.

Charlie nodded at the door. "Let's go outside, shall we?"

She grasped Charlie by the arm in case he got any strange ideas about trying to run away from her.

The room had emptied as they made their way out of the building. Lighters flickered in the gravel space next to the doorway. She eyed the people they passed, hoping for a hit of something. But it seemed nicotine was the only thing being smoked out here.

Charlie swatted at the air with his cane and grimaced. "Disgusting habit," he mumbled as they moved through the smokers.

Passing the parked cars, Charlie walked them to end of the dirt parking lot. He fumbled with his pants. "Hey!" she protested.

Charlie looked up from his pants, alarmed.

"That wasn't part of our deal!" she shrieked, pointing a shaky finger at him.

His face relaxed and he reached into his front pants pocket. "Ah, no offense, but I keep my wallet in my front pocket. You can't be too careful now, can you?"

She watched him carefully as he pulled his wallet from his pants.

It seemed to take the old guy forever to open it. Charlie frowned in concentration and pursed his lips. His gaze landed on her for second. Whatever he was thinking, he didn't say it. Instead, he pulled a crisp one hundred dollar bill from his wallet.

She reached out to grab it, but Charlie pulled his hand back before she could wrestle it from his grasp. "Just a minute," he warned.

On the verge of hitting him, she lunged, not caring if she pushed him to the ground.

Charlie was stronger than he looked. He thrust his cane in her face. "Wait," he said calmly, "I'd like to make you a proposition."

She snorted and bared her teeth. "I knew you were too good to be true."

He shook his head. "It's not what you think."

"Yeah right!" She eyed the cane, thinking she could probably take him, cane and all.

Charlie lowered it. "I'm going to give you this money and a lot more. All you have to do is show up here every night at 6:45."

The one hundred dollar bill floated before her eyes. She thought about the room full of people she had just left and what Charlie might want her to do with them. She wasn't into orgies, or old guys for that matter, but she'd do what she had to do.

"Each night you show up, I'll give you one of these," Charlie said, flicking the bill with a crooked finger. "No sex, no rough stuff. Just talking. You game?"

A hundred bucks a night just for talking? The man must be insane! But that wasn't her problem. Why, she could make a fortune! With what she could pick up from her other tricks and the money from Charlie...

"Well?" he asked, putting an end to her thoughts.

Not sure if he was serious, she opened her palm. "Put your money where your mouth is, Charlie."

His hand hovered just above hers. His weird young eyes locked on hers. "I know what you're going to do with this."

She snatched the bill from his hand and thrust it deep into her bra.

Charlie put his wallet back in the front pocket of his pants. He tipped his head at her. "There's more where that came from. See you tomorrow?"

"Maybe," she mumbled before turning to race off across the street.

As she waited for a car to pass, she glanced over her shoulder. Charlie was still watching her. She lowered her pants and mooned him before dashing off, laughing hysterically as she went.

Back in familiar territory, she looked for a place to score.

Crazy Warren walked up the street, slapping his face and shouting. He usually carried meth, but she wanted down. Still, he knew the streets better than she did, and he might know where everyone was hiding.

The streets had a code all their own. There was a pecking order, and you dared not cross it. Only Warren seemed to be the exception. He was able to wander from place to place with little threat. Unfortunately, she hadn't been so lucky.

For a long time she hadn't even been able to sell her own body. When she'd first started out, she'd been an escort, belonging to an agency. Then she met Dario. Dario the asshole. Dario, the love of her life.

He reminded her of Bobby, her first love. Bobby ended up being a bastard, and Dario hadn't been any different. He'd pimp her out and take all the money she made, all the time proclaiming his love for her. When she started complaining, Dario started using his fists. So the cycle began.

One nasty pimp after another, until she'd earned enough time that they began to leave her alone.

Warren stumbled past her, mumbling.

"Where is everyone?" she asked, careful to avoid eye contact.

"It's a fuckin disaster. No, no, no." Warren flung his head back. His long dark, greasy hair swung wildly around his skeletal face.

She'd learned not to look Warren in the eyes. She'd done it once before and she wouldn't do it again. Rumour was Warren had schizophrenia. He hated eye contact. The last time she'd looked at him, accidentally, he'd shrieked at her while pulling out handfuls of his hair. It gathered a lot of unwanted attention she didn't need.

A small pebble was her sole focus as she waited docilely for his answer.

Warren lurched to a stop beside her. "Hmmn?"

Dee tried again. "I'm looking for H. Who's selling?"

A grime encrusted hand appeared before her nose. "Who is? Why? Why?" Warren squawked, sounding like an insane parakeet.

Sometimes Warren liked to play dumb or act a lot crazier than he really was. Thing was, you never knew for sure if he was acting or not.

Maybe she'd need to up the ante. She thought about showing him her cash. Maybe he could help her score something quick. But she changed her mind. He was too unpredictable. Instead she asked, "You seen Doc?"

Doc was a self-proclaimed doctor who had served in the Vietnam War. She didn't think he was really a doctor. At least she'd never seen a doctor who looked like Doc before. But he did have the best heroin on the street.

"Maybe," Warren muttered, "Whass in it for me?"

Dee shrugged. "I dunno."

Warren stilled. It felt threatening.

She thought fast. "Maybe Doc will give you a little something?"

"Something for nothing, nothing for something," Warren mumbled and walked away.

With a hundred bucks she could score two points and still have money left over. After she got a little dope into her system, she could hit the streets again. Feeling generous, she stared at Warren's departing back and said, "Wait! I'll give you some."

Warren stopped, nodded, clicked his fingers, and bounced up and down on his tip-toes. With a grin twisting his face, he resembled a scary Halloween mask. "K-k-k. Get some, gotta-gotta-get some."

Repulsed, Dee shivered, hoping it was dope Warren referred to and not her.

Warren lurched off down the street five steps in front of her. He stopped suddenly, turned to her, and said simply, "This way."

As she followed his back, she prayed it wasn't a set up.

Chapter 9

LYNDSEY SNIPPED THE BOTTOMS OF THE FLOWERS AND placed them in the vase. The table was all set. Her family would be arriving any minute now. Sunday dinners had become a tradition of sorts at their house.

Billy was down for a nap and Drake was in the shower. She smiled briefly as she imagined joining him there. But no, she better not start something she couldn't finish.

The roast beef smelled delicious. Her mouth watered as she pulled it from the oven to rest on top of the stove.

"Are you sure it's done?"

She spun around, startled by Drake. Wearing a white towel around his waist, he eyed the roast. His hair was wet and stuck straight up. Her lips curled upwards and she laughed. "Relax Drake, you're being hyper-vigilant," she teased, wanting to pay him back for his earlier comment.

Drake whipped off his towel, spinning it into a weapon. He flicked it at her. "Careful woman, this is a deadly weapon!" He grinned, jutting out his hips and snapping the wet towel at her.

Lyndsey eyed his deadly weapon, which grew before her. Reaching up, she mussed his wet hair. Drake grabbed her and pulled her tight up against him. He was still wet from the shower. She pushed him away. "You're getting me all wet!"

He leered at her.

"I didn't mean it like that!" She smiled and grabbed the towel from his hand, holding it open. "Come on, put it back on. They'll be here any minute. Are you going to answer the door naked?"

"Maybe," he smiled, grabbing her again.

Drake was warm and he smelled good. She relaxed in his arms, enjoying his embrace. His tongue found hers and made love to her mouth. Heat exploded in her pelvic region. She groaned. "Stop."

"Hmm?" he whispered, nipping at her ear.

"Drake!" Lyndsey squealed, pushing him away again.

"Okay," he grinned, circling his waist with the damp towel, "but you owe me one."

"Later," she whispered, giving him a quick kiss before turning back to the roast.

With a long thin knife, she poked the middle of the roast. A small bubble of red formed when she removed the knife. Perfect! The salad was made and the potatoes were ready to be mashed. Pouring a little of the potato water into the roasting pan, she stirred the thickening gravy. It smelled delicious and bubbled tantalizingly in the pan.

A knock on the door interrupted her fussing. She opened the door, greeting her family with a smile.

"It's about time you opened the door," her father complained, shivering. "We could have frozen to death!"

"Hi Dad, it's nice to see you too," she replied, not taking the bait.

Her mother stood behind her father. She was carrying a big casserole dish. "I brought your favorite," she said with a grin.

"Is it broccoli and cauliflower with cheese sauce?"

Her mother nodded and asked, "Can I help you with anything?"

"No, I think we're almost ready." She gave the gravy a final stir and turned it down low. "Is Jean coming?"

"Not this time. Your sister got called into work."

They joined her father and Drake in the living room. A heated discussion involving politics was already taking place. Most people would ease into such a volatile topic, but not her dad. He didn't mess with such niceties as hello, or, what are your thoughts on the subject? No, he'd come right out and ask who you vote for and if it's not the candidate of his choice, he'd give you bloody hell for it. Her father still believed he knew more than everyone, and would argue tirelessly to get his point across.

Strange how much had changed. Back in the day, a conversation like this would have driven her nuts. She'd have written her dad off as an asshole, never looking behind the surface. On the surface, he appeared opinionated, gruff, and sometimes downright rude. But that was just a façade. She knew all about those—she'd worn many.

Façades are masks. Masks were for hiding. Hiding was for people who don't have the courage, or honesty, to be real. It was easier to grow scar tissue than to risk being real.

Besides, hurt people hurt other people. It really was as simple as that. As long as she didn't try to get her needs met in this relationship and she practiced acceptance and powerlessness and watched her expectations, she actually enjoyed her father's company.

She'd worked through so many issues in her recovery. Childhood trauma had been the most difficult of all. For years she'd waited patiently for "I'm sorry." But it never came. Now, it didn't matter as much. She'd stopped hurting the precious little girl she once was. She'd learned instead to parent her inner child the way she'd always deserved to be loved. She recognized that negative self-talk only hurt the child within, the child who to this day could pout and feel overwhelmed.

It was strange. Today her father was one of her biggest gifts. She wasn't victimized by his behavior anymore. Actually, she learned from it. Our gifts don't always come wrapped in pretty packages. Sometimes they came wrapped in everything we don't want. Regardless, if we pay attention, we're taught what we need to know. Although he might not say it, she knew what she meant to him. If you could read behind the lines, his grousing was as close to saying "I love you" as he could get.

Her father was stunted in so many ways. The volume in the room increased, interrupting her musings. Drake's face had gone from flushed pink to red. She stuck her tongue out at him. His pointed finger halted in mid-air. A tense silence filled the room.

Lyndsey jumped in, "Drake, can you seat everyone? I'll go get Billy."

Not wanting to startle Billy, Lyndsey opened the door softly. The door creaked and she froze. Too late! He sat up in his captain's bed, his eyes wide and clutching his blanket.

Her heart sunk as she realized the loud voices from the living room had probably scared him. "Oh Billy," she crossed the room and sat down beside him.

His eyes were glazed. His thumb was planted firmly in his mouth. She thought about removing it, but didn't. What the hell. For the moment she chose comfort over the orthodontist.

"Come on, love." She picked him up and plopped him on her hip.

He was gaining weight. Lyndsey re-adjusted him. He clung to the back of her arm pinching her skin. She shifted him again, this time holding him in front of her and gave him a cuddle.

Billy relaxed against her, snuggling into the hollow of her shoulder. Lyndsey stroked his soft hair, loving the way it felt.

Drake entered the room and snapped, "Are you coming?" Billy stiffened in her arms.

"In a minute," she nodded. "I was just trying to comfort Billy. I think he heard you yelling."

One dark eyebrow rose. "My yelling?"

"You both were. But regardless, I think Billy heard it."

"Jeez Linds," Drake puffed. "How do you put up with it?" He meant his recent conversation with her Dad.

"Honey, sometimes winning is letting go."

He scratched his head. "I don't know…"

Lyndsey plopped Billy in Drake's arms and grinned. "Well it sounds good. Don't you think? Come on, shrug it off. Let's go eat."

But it wasn't that easy. Dinner was a struggle. Billy didn't want to go into his booster seat. He stiffened into a plank, leaving her unable to bend him into the seat. Rather than fight him on it, she put him down. With Billy it was going to be baby steps, and she needed to pick her battles carefully.

Drake retreated into silence, leaving her and her mom to fill the gap.

They passed the food around the table, saying please and thank you. It was awkward and yet her father seemed unaffected by it. The mood lightened somewhat when Billy climbed up on her dad's lap.

Lyndsey tensed, expecting him to push Billy away, but instead he carefully cut a piece of roast beef and fed it to him. Billy chewed noisily and said, "Hmm."

There were these little moments in which she wished she could take a snapshot. This was one of them. A lump lodged in her throat and her eyes filled. She couldn't say why she was so moved to see her father feeding Billy. To most people it wouldn't be a big deal.

However, the moment didn't last long. Her father opened his mouth and ruined it. "What? You got something in your eye?" he said gruffly, and put Billy down.

Deciding to take a risk, she answered honestly. "No, I don't have anything in my eye."

Her mother interrupted, trying to be helpful and spoke to her father. "Maybe Lyndsey was worried that the piece of meat you cut for Billy was too big."

She shook her head. "No Mom, that wasn't it," she said. For a moment she was eight years old again and fumbled before finding the right words. "I ahh... It was just nice seeing Dad feeding Billy, is all."

Billy toddled over to her and yanked on her pants. She bent down and scooped him up, feeling safer with him in her arms.

"Oh? Well then..." Her mom trailed off, clearly not getting it. "Would anyone like seconds?" she asked, looking around the table.

Billy lunged for Lyndsey's plate and knocked it over. Food flew in all directions. She jumped up from her chair, wearing most of her dinner.

"Mine!" Billy squealed, as he picked up a piece of roast beef that landed on the carpet.

"Jesus Christ!" her dad complained.

Looking over her father's shoulder, Drake grinned at her and stuck out his tongue.

Chapter **10**

DECLAN EYED THE GLOVED HAND SUSPICIOUSLY. "What is it?"

"Tylenol. Take it or leave it," a thin, wrinkled man, who'd introduced himself as Pete, rasped.

"As in Tylenol three?" he asked, reaching for the pill.

A violent cough erupted from Pete. Declan stared at the man in alarm. The guy's skin was tinged blue and yellow. Pete gasped, fighting to catch his breath.

Not sure what else to do, Declan stood back expecting the guy to keel over.

Turning a darker shade of blue, Pete's eyes bugged out. He beat one wrinkled hand on his chest, trying to stop the cough, and pulled a soiled hanky from his shirt pocket. Putting it to his face, he gasped into it.

"Jesus man," Declan mumbled. "Do you need help?"

Pete's rooster neck craned sideways and back and forth, indicating no. He held up one long, slender finger. Wait.

He stared at Pete, grossed out but not able to look away.

Dabbing his lips with the hanky, Pete's coughing fit subsided. He eyed the soiled linen before folding it into a little square and pushed it back into his front shirt pocket. A small smile crossed his face and he muttered, "Serves me right. Lucky I can breathe at all after the shit I put into these babies." Pete pounded his chest. Then, remembering Declan, he thrust the Tylenol under his nose and said, "Well?"

Not wanting to appear eager, he studied the round white pill. Five hundred MG was stamped across its surface. "Hey!" He pushed Pete's hand away. "This isn't Tylenol three; it's just a regular one!"

"Listen kid," Pete rasped, "I'm gonna cut you a little slack on account of it being your first day and all. But if you ever touch me again, you're outta here!" He stared hard at Declan. "Got it?"

Their altercation had drawn a little crowd. Two men that he didn't know and Tom sidled in next to him.

"I don't need a babysitter!" The younger of the two men pointed at the older one.

Declan got halfway up from his chair before a big hand shoved him back down. "Stay." Tom gave him a quick glance before returning his attention to the other two.

The older one snorted. "Yeah right, Don! They say delusion is a key symptom of this illness," he said smugly.

Declan's head pounded. He eyed the Tylenol in Pete's hand, wondering if the guy was serious. But Pete was oblivious to Declan. He was caught up in the drama enfolding before their eyes.

"You're not my dad, Stewart!" Don yelled.

"Lucky for me!" Stewart snorted and rolled his eyes.

"Jesus," Declan mumbled, shaking his head. What the hell, was he back in high school?

Tom walked over to Declan and Pete and growled, "Problems?"

Pete shook his head. "Nah, just a little misunderstanding, right Declan?"

Declan eyed the three ring circus in front of him. He bit his lower lip and winced, tasting blood. Testosterone thickened the air. He thought about getting the hell out of there.

Tom pointed at Declan and turned to Pete. "If he gives you any trouble, just call the sheriff. He couldn't have gotten far. I'm sure he'll be more than happy to come and pick him up."

Declan slumped back in his chair, playing it safe for the moment.

Pete smiled. "No worries, Declan was just, ah, being careful about the kind of medication he was putting in his mouth. He wants to protect his sobriety. He asked for a regular Tylenol and not one with codeine in it, isn't that right, Declan?" Pete winked at him.

Declan blanched and stayed silent.

Tom stared at him, waiting to see if he would disagree, but loud voices coming from behind them interrupted his scrutiny.

"Stop it!" Tom barked as the two arguing men froze.

"It was his fault!" Don squealed.

"It was not!" Stewart replied. "You were the one who snuck out of dinner!" He pointed a finger at Don. "I'm just doing my duty."

"Oh yeah?" the kid shot back. "I didn't see rat on the duty roster!"

Pete grinned at Declan and rasped, "Boys will be boys."

Tom, not seeing the humor in the situation, scowled a silent message at Pete. *Smarten up.* Returning his attention to the two men standing beside him, he barked, "Get to dinner."

The two men stared at Tom for a minute, as if debating.

Tom's face went red and his eyes bulged.

Don and Stewart turned and ran off down the hall.

Declan got up wondering if he should join them, but then thought better of it. He needed something to take away these aches and pains. Tom scowled even more. He cupped his hands to his mouth and yelled, "Don't run!"

Pete smiled wickedly, obviously finding the entire situation entertaining. "Ah Tom, no yelling."

Tom's big shoulders squared, leaving him a no-neck. Looking as if he was about to argue the point, he caught sight of Declan. "Right," he mumbled, staring hard at Pete.

"As I was sayin..." Pete trailed off, pouring a glass of water from a plastic carafe sitting next to him, "Declan's just protecting his sobriety. Isn't that right, kid?"

Tom looked ready for a fight. His face was shiny and mean looking.

Declan shrugged, opting for silence until he had a better handle on this insane asylum they called a rehab.

"Here you go." Pete pushed the Dixie cup at him.

Tom thrust out his jaw, and narrowed his eyes. He watched as Declan palmed the Tylenol, like it might be a hidden hand grenade or something.

The water inside the paper cup was warm as he swallowed it and the pill down his dry throat.

Hoping to get away from these two clowns, Declan stood up. Tom placed a hand on his shoulder, stopping him.

"Sit back down, we're not finished yet." Tom thrust a finger under his nose, forcing him to meet his eyes. "You move when we tell you to, got it?"

A sudden urge to strangle Tom, or bite his finger off, left Declan puffing hard.

"Ah, Tom?" Pete asked.

Tom pulled his finger away from Declan's nose and turned to Pete. "Show him to his room." He took two steps backwards and stopped. "I need a break."

Pete's head bobbed up and down. "That's a great idea, don't ya think?" Pete winked at Declan behind Tom's back.

Tom smiled and retraced his steps. "Oh, I almost forgot!" He slapped Declan on the back. "Welcome to treatment, kid. Now get up!"

Chapter 11

The dark alleyway reeked of urine and wasted lives. Graffiti and lewd drawings colored the brick walls. The artists' tags stood out in bold, neon colors. Dee stayed close to Warren, nearly hugging his back.

Warren said Doc's place was just up ahead.

It was best to walk softly around Doc. He suffered from PTSD. Word on the street was, if you startled him, he might shoot first and ask questions later.

Warren whistled a shrill blast of air.

"What was that for?" she whispered from behind him.

"Shush," Warren whispered in response and stood still. Dee ran smack into his backside. Up close, he stank.

"Why—" she broke off when Warren spun around and covered her mouth with his grubby hand.

His crazy-eyed stare met hers. He took a big breath and his cheeks puffed out. Her eyes closed instinctively, but he didn't hit her. Instead, Warren whistled shrilly again. Both of them tensed, ready to run.

It was dark and sinister. The hairs on the back of her neck stood up. Someone was watching them. She wondered if she should tell Warren. After what seemed like a long time, a shrill whistle similar to the one

Warren had made broke the silence. Warren slumped back into his usual posture and mumbled, "K, we're good to go."

He lurched off down the dark alleyway with Dee following closely behind him. She stayed close, but not too close. One good whiff of Warren was enough for her. They walked another half block up the alleyway, stepping over trash and avoiding the garbage cans that were tossed about.

A shadow emerged from behind a large dumpster and Warren stopped. Dee patted the money inside her bra, making sure it was still there.

A low voice growled. "Whatcha lookin' for?"

Dee squinted into the dark, just able to make him out. Doc was dressed in camouflage. He wore an old baseball cap pulled down low on his forehead. Long gray hair poked out from under it.

Deciding it was time to take matters into her own hands, Dee spoke up. "I'd like to purchase two points of H, Doc. The good stuff, not the stepped on crap you sell to the tourists."

Warren mumbled something under his breath that she didn't catch, but Doc seemed to understand him.

Doc grabbed her roughly by her forearm and steered her behind the large dumpster. "We'll talk in my office."

Hoping she wasn't about to be mugged or raped or both, she allowed Doc to lead her. The need for dope outweighed any safety concerns she had. She was on the verge of puking, and didn't see any other options.

As they rounded the corner, the back side of the dumpster was even darker than the front. Doc released her arm. "Now just a sec." He fumbled for his lighter and lit a candle nearby.

Doc's office was a cleaned out spot behind the dumpster. An off-white plastic chair with one missing arm and a card board box sitting next to it were the main furniture. A rolled up sleeping mat and over-stuffed shopping cart were behind the chair.

Remembering his manners. Doc waved at the ground and said, "Please, have a seat."

Dee eyed the alleyway wondering where she should sit when Doc solved the problem for her.

"Here," Doc unrolled his sleeping bag and claimed the chair.

Warren grunted a thanks and dropped to his knees. She joined him on the bedroll.

Doc stared solemnly, at the little crowd assembled before him. "First off," he pointed a squared off finger at Dee, "Warren's finder fee comes out of your dope, not mine."

Warren waggled his head up and down beside her.

She wondered if she should argue the point, but she didn't really care. "Okay," she agreed. "How much?"

"Well now, that's up to Warren," Doc said.

The candle's flame beckoned her. She stared at it mesmerized, waiting for Warren's response.

He took his sweet time before replying. She fidgeted next to him and tried to get comfortable. Her back felt like someone had hit it with a sledge hammer.

The candle danced seductively, turning orange, yellow, white, and blue.

Finally, Warren spoke up. "I'd take half."

"Half!" she screeched, tearing her eyes away from the candle's hypnotizing flame.

Doc raised his hand. "Quiet!" he commanded.

Dee lowered her voice and poked Warren to make her point. "Half is too much. I'll give you a quarter."

"Hmm," Warren mumbled and scratched his head.

Doc the diplomat reminded Warren, "That's still half a point for you."

The candle sputtered. The tantalizing odor of smoke wafted over to her.

Warren squirmed next to her and nodded. "I guess." he agreed, and threw out a hand.

Dee looked at his hand before shaking it. It was still as grimy as she remembered. Doc chuckled now that negotiations were over. Warren stood up chanting softly and danced in a little circle. Dee reached deep into her bra and pulled out the cash. She held it for a moment, still not sure, and then pushed it at Doc.

"Two, right?"

Doc nodded, plucking the bill from her fingers. "Right." He reached inside his shirt and extracted two bright red miniature balloons. He opened one and said, "I'll cut Warren his take."

Her eyes never leaving the balloons, she watched as Doc skillfully sliced through them to reveal the black tar heroin inside. Warren's half clung to the edge of Doc's razor. Using the back of her hand as a tissue, she wiped her lips. The ritual had begun.

Doc scraped Warren's heroin onto a piece of tinfoil. Warren reached for it and grunted "nice."

Not taking her eyes off the heroin, she reached into her purse and found her spoon and hypodermic. All set, she held out her hand.

Doc dropped her dope into it and warned, "Careful, it's potent."

"Do you have any water?" she asked, not paying him any mind.

Doc got up and shuffled over to his shopping cart. He plucked out a half-filled bottle and passed it to Dee. "Go easy, girl."

Her heart raced as she ripped into the unopened balloon, placing the opened half into her purse. She'd save that one for when she had to go back out on the streets. The world shrunk to herself, her spoon, and the little black blob inside it. She was in the zone. Warren flicked a lighter next to her and chased the dragon.

Flicking her lighter, she chased a different high. The cooking process was grueling. It was all she could do not to hurry it along. She went through the motions and grit her teeth. Finally satisfied she had it just right, she threw down the lighter. With the hands of a surgeon, she pulled the elixir into her syringe.

Warren moaned next to her, exhaling a large gray plume of smoke. Doc watched the two of them from above, still in his chair.

Studying her arms, she sighed. Her veins weren't very good. They liked to roll, playing hide and seek. Maybe this time she'd get lucky. She poked one with her finger, testing. It might do. Tentatively she pushed the needle in. The vein rolled over before she could get the syringe into it. Dee yanked the elastic free from her hair and wrapped it around her arm. Opening and closing her fist, she tried again. Again the vein rolled from under her, before she could pierce it with the syringe.

"Son of a bitch!" she screamed.

"Stop!" Doc growled from his chair.

Dee looked up at him with tears in her eyes.

"Take your stuff and go!" he ordered.

"No, please, I... can't. Please, Doc," she mewled.

"If you scream again, you're outta here," he warned, his voice lowered and his tone turned menacing. "And this time, I won't ask you so nicely."

Nothing else mattered. Dee was beyond caring about anything other than getting her fix. Biting her lips, she tried again. It was a little like having sex. In and out. In and out. But slow and steady won the race.

Her persistence paid off. She hit and pulled the plunger back, sighing blissfully when the liquid inside it turned red. As if in her lover's arms, Dee pushed and pulled on the plunger prolonging the foreplay. Warmth tingled from the top of her head down to her toes.

Doc's voice floated over to her on the velvety black night air. "Be careful," he whispered. "My black magic will kiss you dead."

Enough of the foreplay, Dee thought and went for the climax, pushing the plunger all the way down. Stars burst in her head. Her body disappeared beneath her. Her last thought was of Doc. The old bastard had been right. A smile curled her lip. The needle slipped from between her fingers. A heavy blanket of warmth enveloped her. Her head hung loosely, like a bobble doll with a broken spring.

Dee floated free. Far, far away in the land of nod.

Chapter 12

LYNDSEY LOOKED AT THE PILE OF MESSAGES IN FRONT of her and wondered who to call first. Her eyes lit up as she spied a message from Susan.

"Hi Lyndsey, sorry I had to cancel our meeting. I'd like to re-book. Please call me."

With a grin, she picked up the receiver, eager to speak with her. Listening to the phone ring, she glanced over at her appointment book. Luckily, she still had a spot available.

"Hello?" Susan said.

"Hi Susan, Lyndsey here."

"Oh Lyndsey, thank God it's you! I thought it was another debt collector!"

She laughed. "Oh the joys of cleaning up the wreckage of your past!"

"Yeah," Susan snorted. "Only I don't know think I would describe it as joyful."

"It will be. You'll see. It's a relief to deal with the mess. It's a far better solution than shoving it under the carpet."

"Maybe..." Susan trailed off, clearly not convinced.

Switching topics, Lyndsey said, "I got your message. What's up?"

"I need your help."

"Oh?"

Susan expelled a big breath. "Declan called."

"And?"

"And," Susan said, "I'm not sure what to do."

She chewed the top of her pen as she listened to Susan speak. When it came to dealing with Declan, Susan had committed to reaching out for help before acting upon his requests.

"What was it like for you to get a call from him?"

Susan hesitated for a second and then said, "Weird." She laughed. "I felt different talking to him. A part of me was analyzing my reactions as we spoke. Lyndsey, he wants me to go visit him in rehab."

"Oh? Do you feel you're ready for that?"

"I'm not sure." Susan sighed. "That's why I'm calling you. I'm scared, Linds. I don't want to jump back into being his enabler, or worse, becoming that horrid, miserable old woman again."

A small plastic bit from the pen she was chewing on broke off in her mouth. She pulled it free, wondering briefly if she had an oral fixation. She really liked to chew. Gum, pens, fingernails… On second thought, maybe she was better off not knowing.

"Do you think it's healthy for me to analyze my behavior?" Susan asked, worried.

God she hoped so! She did it all the time! "Yes, I do," Lyndsey answered, throwing the pen into the garbage can beside her desk. "It's important to take your inventory and know yourself. Recovery is a little like waking up. You notice things you never did when you didn't know any better. You begin to understand your motives and whether your expectations are realistic or not."

"Good grief!" Susan wailed. "I'm overwhelmed with everything. Just answering the phone makes me anxious. How am I supposed to figure all of that out?"

"You can't! Don't forget, you can't do this alone and you're going to mistake mistakes along the way." Lyndsey frowned. "Have you called your sponsor yet?"

"No." Susan hesitated. "I don't have a sponsor. Well, that's not quite right. I have a temporary sponsor, but she seems awfully busy."

"Have you told her that? And what about your support group?"

"Irene and I had coffee yesterday. I guess it helped…" She trailed off. "I'm not sure. The problem is, I don't really want to bother anyone with my problems." Susan laughed. "I know in my head that's not right. But my heart doesn't really believe it."

Lyndsey nodded in silent agreement. She could relate. She still felt overly responsible for almost everyone she met.

"Honestly, I think asking other people for help is the hardest thing I've ever done." Susan exhaled audibly on the phone. "It's like saying I need you, and I've never said that to anyone before."

"It is hard to be vulnerable," she agreed.

"Hard!" Susan snorted. "That's an understatement!"

"Maybe it's not so much hard as it is uncomfortable."

"Oh, it's uncomfortable alright!" Her voice grew solemn. "But what should I do?"

Lyndsey frowned, thinking. She didn't want to tell Susan what to do. It was better if she helped to guide her in the right direction. Rather than give advice, she asked, "What feels right for you?"

"I don't know."

"Sure you do," she urged. "Dig a little deeper."

"Well, I want to see him. I do. But I'm also mad and hurt and disappointed, all at the same time."

"So, tell him that."

"I can't tell him that! Can I?" Susan asked.

"Why not?"

"What if I upset him?"

"What if you do?"

"I don't –" Susan broke off.

Lyndsey stayed silent, letting Susan process her thoughts.

"I guess I still think of him as my baby."

"Susan, babies don't go to jail or rehab!"

"I know."

"No, you don't know. If you did, you wouldn't be struggling with this."

"God, I'm such a mess!" she wailed.

"No you're not. You're just confused. It happens when your head and your heart play tug-of-war."

"Lyndsey, I'm afraid to tell him how I really feel." Susan sobbed. "What if he doesn't even care?"

She bit her lip. The truth was, he might not care. When you're an addict, your family members aren't exactly at the top of your priority list. Well, not unless you need dope or money, then they're number one.

"And what if he tells me I'm a terrible mother? Or that I drove his dad away?"

"Slow down, Susan! Don't make this so big. It doesn't matter what you say, or what he says. Just tell him how you feel and ask him how he's doing. Seriously, don't over-complicate this."

"I…" Susan blew her nose. "Do you think I drove his dad away?"

"I don't know if you drove him away. I can't speak for your ex-husband, but I do know it takes two to tango. Besides, who drove who away doesn't really matter, it's just another way to avoid your emotions. It's far easier to stay stuck in your head debating the question than it is to grieve the reality of it."

"I don't think I'm ready to take that one on yet," Susan said.

"One thing at a time then." She agreed, but knew Susan was already taking it on.

"Lyndsey, can I ask you a favor?"

Lyndsey's back stiffened. Favors in the past had always come with conditions she didn't like. Caution steeled her tone. Careful to remain neutral, she replied, "You can, however I don't know how I'll respond until I hear the question."

"Do you, um, do you think you could come with me? To visit Declan, I mean?"

"I'm, well," she hesitated, thrown by Susan's question. "I'm not sure. Isn't there anyone else you could ask?"

"No, not really. Well, Irene I guess, but I don't think…" Susan trailed off.

Lyndsey read her mind. Irene and her cane wouldn't be the best scenario for a first visit.

"I don't expect you to do anything, it's just, I need your help. I don't think I can do this alone."

Lyndsey thought quickly. Maybe she could kill two birds with one stone? Susan's son Declan was the same young man John, aka Twitch, had wanted her to admit into their facility. Although they hadn't had an extra bed available then, they still might be able to accommodate him in long term housing.

"Please," Susan whispered.

Her heart rolled over. She knew how hard it must have been for Susan to ask. "Okay, I'll come with you."

"You will?" Susan said, clearly surprised.

"Sure." Lyndsey plucked a new pen from the cup holding them. Pulling her calendar close, she asked. "When were you planning on going?"

"His message said he could have visitors tomorrow, between three and five p.m." Susan paused. "Will that time work for you?"

She'd have to scramble a bit, but she thought she could pull it off. "I can make it work. I'll call you back if something changes, but I think we're good to go."

"Oh Lyndsey!" Susan squealed. "Thank you, I'm so relieved."

They talked for a few more minutes before she hung up the phone. Lyndsey stared at her desk, mortified. She'd just added more stress to her life by committing to help Susan out.

She grinned. Oh well, what was a little stress in the grand scheme of things?

Besides, she was blessed to be sober. If she couldn't help others, she didn't deserve the life she had. A rush of joy brought tears to her eyes. Sometimes she still couldn't believe it. Her life was one big miracle, and her duty was to pay it forward.

The pile of messages caught her attention, bringing her back to the present moment. She picked up the phone to answer some of her calls and stopped.

'Git wel son' hung crookedly on the wall. Determined to straighten it once and for all, she taped down all four corners. Scraping the scotch tape with her finger nail to make sure it held, she was satisfied.

Standing back, she admired the child's handy work.

Git wel son. It had become her talisman.

It was a powerful message, and one she hoped Susan would learn soon.

Chapter 13

PETE YANKED OPEN THE CUPBOARD DOOR. "YOU CAN put your stuff in here," he said, waving at the space inside.

Declan tossed his garbage bag inside and closed the door.

Pete cocked a brow at him and grinned. "Okay, I guess you can unpack later."

The room was barely big enough to accommodate the four beds in it. He grimaced, seeing one of his roommates. A gray haired man lay on the bed staring up at the ceiling with his mouth hanging open.

He turned to Pete. "Can I get a private room?"

"A private room huh?" Pete slapped his knee and laughed. "One that comes with room service, I presume?"

The old man sat up and rubbed his red eyes. The guy reeked of yesterday's booze. Twenty-four hours later, it was sour and nasty. Declan's stomach rolled.

Pete waved at the gray haired man. "Gary, meet your new roommate."

Gary ignored him and looked sheepishly at Pete. "I guess you're surprised to see me back here so soon."

"Nah," Pete shook his head. "I'd be more surprised if you weren't back here. You never had a chance in hell of staying sober. That's what we tried tellin' you."

"Yeah, well, I shoulda listened." Gary's red eyes watered. "This time it'll be different, you'll see."

Pete looked at Declan and shook his head. "You can learn a lot from Gary, kid. He knows a hell of a lot... about staying drunk!"

"Aww, come on!" Gary groaned.

"Gary, you scare me. Don't tell me it's gonna be different this time, show me. Chances are in three or four days, you're gonna feel better and think you know it all again. That's when you decide you've learned enough and you walk out of treatment. I'd say the likelihood of you ever staying sober is pretty much nil."

Declan leaned against the wall, all but forgotten.

Pete raised a finger and pointed it at Gary. "There are those too who suffer from grave emotional and mental disorders, but many of them do recover if they have the capacity to be honest."

"Aww Jesus, Pete, please don't quote the Big Book to me. You know I hate it when you do that."

Pete's eyes bulged. He strode across the room and pushed a finger into Gary's chest. "Yeah, well you better learn to love it! Cuz you ain't stayin' sober without it! You're an end stage, hopeless drunk!"

Too tired to stand anymore, Declan eyed the bed he'd been assigned. It looked clean. Parking his butt, he hoped it didn't have cooties.

"Come on, Pete!" Gary argued. "That's not fair. I'm not that bad."

Pete snorted. "Gary, you have no fuckin' idea! You're about as sick as I've ever seen. You're so fuckin' sick, you don't even know it!"

He pulled the sheets back cautiously. He couldn't see any stains or short curly hairs on them.

Gary folded his skinny arms across his large, round belly. "That's no way to talk to me, Pete. You know I've been thinking about suicide."

"Don't play that shit with me, Gary! You might be able to manipulate others with that talk, but it won't work on me."

The pillow was on the lean side. He bunched it up under his head and stretched out.

"Give me a break, Pete. I feel like shit."

"Yeah, well whose fault is that?"

Tuning them out, he settled in, hoping to grab a nap. His mind wandered. He figured his mom should be making plans to come and see him by now. Who knows? Maybe by this time tomorrow, he might even be out of here. If he could talk to her, he knew he could get her to see things his way. An idea occurred to him. Maybe his lawyer could get him out on house arrest instead of rehab. Wouldn't that be great!

He pulled the sheet up over his head. Pete and Gary's arguing was interrupting his plans.

"Pete, it's not my fault. I got a disease! Isn't that what you teach us in here?"

A terse silence filled the room. Declan peered out at Pete from between the covers. Pete's face had gone from gray to a mottled red. For a second he thought Pete might hit Gary, but he managed to restrain himself.

Pete calmed himself by drawing in a big breath. "You got a disease all right! It's called bullshit of the brain! Stop the BS and get up. There's nothing worse than a pathetic drunk lying in bed all day and feeling sorry for himself!"

"I can't," Gary mewled. "I'm sick. Real sick, I think my liver might have packed it in this time."

He tossed and turned, but they kept him awake.

"Gary," Pete snorted. "I imagine your liver packed it in a long time ago. What do you think that is hangin' there, poking out of your belly like that?"

Declan scowled and rolled over. He was either going to have to get up, or get these two bozos the hell out of his room.

"Stop it, Pete! You're scarin' the shit outta me!"

"Yeah," Pete agreed. "The truth will do that to you!"

Declan threw the covers aside and sat up.

Pete was staring at Gary with his arms folded across his skinny chest.

Gary looked like an aged wayward child as he stared off across the room, not able to meet Pete's eyes. His gaze landed on Declan for a split-second and lit with interest before skittering away. Declan felt a rush and looked at Gary with renewed interest. This old boy may be of some use to him after all.

Satisfied he'd put Gary in his place, Pete turned to Declan. "Get up!" he snapped. "We're not a flop-house, for Christ's sake."

Confused, Declan stared at Pete, trying to figure him out. One minute he seemed kind of okay and the next minute, he snapped. Maybe Pete was crazy? Or bi-polar? He seemed unpredictable. He wasn't afraid of bad asses, but crazy? Now that scared the living shit out of him!

Pete's eyes narrowed as he moved closer to Declan's bed. "Well?"

Declan decided he better go along with Pete. At least for the time being. It wasn't smart, starting out with Pete riding his ass. If he appeared willing, he'd be watched less. Hoping to look friendly, he smiled.

Pete didn't smile back. Instead, he pointed a finger at Declan. "I want you out at the front desk in five minutes. Now get unpacked!"

As Pete turned away from him, Gary saluted his back.

Declan laughed, actually amused. The old guy was growing on him.

Pete turned and glared at them. "What's so funny?"

"Nothing," Gary mumbled and looked away.

Declan got busy unpacking his belongings. Pete watched him for a minute, and then dug in his pocket. Pulling out a quarter, he flipped it high in the air. "Heads or tails?" he shouted.

"Heads," Gary replied.

Pete caught the quarter and turned to Declan with a questioning look.

"Um, tails?" Jesus, what the hell was left?

Removing his hand from the top of the quarter, Pete grinned. "Heads it is, boys!" He puckered his lips and whistled a tune from an old Clint Eastwood movie he'd watched as a kid as he walked out of the room.

Aware his mouth was hanging open, Declan closed it. He turned to Gary. "What the hell was that all about?"

Gary slumped in bed, his face green. Declan looked around the room for a garbage can. Spying one, he moved it next to Gary's bed.

Gary moaned and rubbed his stomach, "What?"

"That!" Declan jerked a thumb at the door.

"Oh that," Gary said. "Don't pay any mind to Pete. If the quarter had landed on tails, you woulda seen his nasty side. Heads, Pete's a joker. Tails, he's a mean son of a bitch."

"What? Are you telling me his moods are dependent on the flip of a coin?"

Gary scrunched up his forehead and gently poked at the large protrusion in his belly. He winced. "Yup." He nodded, glancing up at him. "That's what I'm telling you."

Eyes wide, he stared at Gary. "This place is fuckin' crazy!"

Gary nodded, still distracted by his belly, and mumbled, "Pretty much."

Closing the cupboard door, he stored his garbage bag under the bed. Wow! He couldn't believe this. Seriously, he'd landed in the nut house.

His mind raced with possibilities. As far as he could see, there were three. He could stay here, go back to jail, or go home.

Home. There must be a way.

He'd have to do some serious ass kissing with his mom, but he could do it. It wasn't anything new. He'd promise her the world, say whatever she wanted to hear, and if he was convincing enough, he just might be outta here. The way he heard it, house arrest was easy. Plus, he could always get one of the guys to swing by with a little care package. He grinned as he imagined it.

His grin faded when Gary moaned loudly and vomited all over the bed.

Chapter **14**

Loud voices buzzed in her ear. She moaned, opening her eyes. The bright light shot a bolt of pain into her head. Confused and squinting, she looked around. Oh my god! What happened? She closed her eyes as she struggled to remember.

She'd been with Weasel at Doc's place. She'd been… The night before came rushing back. Her dope! Dee sat up and took stock.

Her bed was nothing but a gurney, with the rails pulled high to prevent her from falling out. So she was in the hospital. But how did she get there?

An IV tube trailed from the inside crook of her arm. She was dressed in a sheet-like nightie with nothing on underneath it. In the harsh light of day, the track marks and bruising up and down her pale limbs really stood out. Anyone who saw them would know she was a junkie. Shame clawed at her. She shivered, wishing she was invisible. She had to get out of here fast!

A nurse walked by and she croaked, "Hey!"

The nurse stopped and turned in her direction. Her dark skin glistened with a light sheen. Her dark hair was swept up high into a bee hive. Her red lips turned down. The nurse looked at her through veiled eyes. Dee felt as though she were a specimen under a microscope.

"Yes?"

"My clothes... my purse," she stammered. "Where are they?"

The nurse's dark brown eyes met hers. "Your belongings are safe."

Dee pulled the sheet up to hide her track marks and stared just past the nurse's nose.

"How are you feeling?'

She shifted in the gurney. She felt like shit, but she wasn't about to tell the nurse that. Instead she replied, "I feel fine."

One brown eyebrow rose. "You don't look fine. You look sick."

Yeah, well, it's nothing a little black tar heroin couldn't cure. If she could ever find her clothes, that was!

"Are you hungry?"

Her stomach was queasy. The thought of food made her feel even sicker. "I'm not hungry," Dee replied, and then seeing the nurse's frown, said, "I'll eat later. I really need my belongings. Can you get them for me? Please." She tried to smile sweetly.

"Not right now, I can't." The nurse shook her head. "We're moving you downstairs in a few minutes. Dr. Peterson will be by to see you shortly. He can answer any questions you have."

Alarm slammed though her. "No! You don't understand! I'm not staying. I need to go!"

The nurse looked at her, and then at her arms. Reaching a decision, she said, "Can I be frank with you?"

Dee didn't give a shit what the nurse did, as long as she brought her stuff. Maybe if she was nice, she could get outta here faster. She nodded, giving the nurse permission to speak.

"You might think you're fine, but you're not."

Dee eyed the IV line and had an idea. "Well, now that you mention it…" she said, rubbing her back. If you wanted good pain meds, complain about your back. The doctors couldn't prove you were lying that way. "I am a little sore. Can you give me something for pain?"

Wrinkles appeared on the nurse's forehead. "You just said you were fine."

Thinking fast, Dee wondered if she should go for it or just get the hell out. Either way, she needed something pretty quick.

What the hell. She figured she'd give it a shot. Maybe she could score some free dope and then get the hell outta here. She moaned and curled into a ball. "It hurts," she whined.

Through the slits in her eyes, she watched as the nurse folded her arms across her chest.

Instead of rushing off to get her pain meds, the nurse smiled. "You remind me of my brother," she said.

Who the hell cared about this chick's brother? Maybe Dee needed to up the ante. She rocked back and forth and moaned louder. "Oh, oh."

Not fazed, the nurse continued. "He was an addict, just like you."

"Ahhhh," she wailed. "My back hurts bad!"

"Only he got clean, and you can too."

Fuck! She wasn't buying it. Dee sat up and spat out, "Get my stuff!"

"Problems?" A low voice interrupted them.

"Dr. Peterson!" The nurse smiled.

Dee curled into a little ball once more. Maybe she could still score off the doctor.

"No problems. I was just explaining to Dee here that you'd be along shortly. She wants her stuff."

"I see," the doctor responded. "Are you in pain?'

Dee moaned and nodded. "My back," she wailed. If she was loud enough, they usually gave her something.

A silent message passed between physician and nurse. Her heart sunk.

Dr. Peterson looked at her. "Do you have any allergies? Are you taking any other medications?"

Hope replaced despair and Dee shook her head. Trying to be helpful, she added, "I usually get morphine for my back when it's this sore."

Dr. Peterson nodded and turned to the nurse. "Eight hundred milligrams of Neurontin, please."

"Good call," the nurse agreed and hurried to do the doctor's bidding.

Dee tried to figure out what kind of morphine Neurontin was. Casually, she asked, "Is Neurontin very strong? I have a very high tolerance."

The doctor nodded. "It is strong. It's the best anti-inflammatory you can get."

Weird… If it was that good, why hadn't she heard of it? Still playing it on the low down, she asked, "What type of narcotic is it?"

The doctor frowned and shook his head. "It isn't a narcotic."

'What?" she sputtered.

"It's a non-narcotic pain reliever, and a much better choice for you."

Dee shook her head. The room spun and she stopped. "Non-narcotic pain meds don't work on me," she insisted.

"Why don't we give it a chance and see? You haven't even tried it yet."

"Forget it!" she cried. "I want my things. I'm leaving!"

"I don't recommend you leave," the doctor replied, remaining calm and cool.

Dee reached out and grabbed him by his arm. The doctor flinched and looked at her with surprise. Dee's face twisted. She gritted her teeth. "I said I'm going," she hissed.

Dr. Peterson removed her hand from his arm, and backed up a step. A mask of sorts had dropped over his face. He looked at her. "Well then, you'll have to sign yourself out."

Dee nodded, having been down this road before.

"But before you do, I want to talk about last night."

"Last night?" To tell the truth, she couldn't remember much about last night. There was a great big, gaping hole where it should have been.

"Do you remember how you got here?"

Dee shook her head. "No," she admitted.

"I didn't think so." He scrubbed a hand over his face. The doctor looked exhausted. He met her gaze. His eyes were serious. "Death will do that to you."

"Death! What?" Dee bolted upright on the gurney. What the hell was this quack talking about? The room grew cold. She shrank against the back of the gurney at she heard his next words.

"You died last night."

No way! She looked at the IV in her arm. "That's ridiculous!"

"No, it's not ridiculous." He shook his head. "If it wasn't for the drug Naloxone, we wouldn't even be having this conversation."

"But that's impossible," Dee whispered. Bits and pieces were coming back to her. The syringe, the flame, the black tar heroin, Doc's warning…

"When the paramedics found you, you were barely breathing. You died in the ambulance. They got to you just in the nick of time. Five minutes longer and you'd be on the slab downstairs instead of on this gurney."

It couldn't be. She shook her head. No way had she died. The doctor was just trying to scare her.

"Before you leave, I'm sending in one of our liaisons who volunteers here. Perhaps he'll have a few words of advice for you."

She was barely listening. She was still trying to wrap her head around what he'd just told her.

A sheet of white paper appeared under her nose. A pen followed and she looked up. The doctor pointed at the sheet. "This form is for voluntary withdrawal. It states you're leaving against medical advice."

Dee scratched her signature across the paper. It was a shaky mess.

"I'll send someone with your belongings." Dr. Peterson's eyes searched hers before he looked away. His shoulders sagged. "I guess that's it, then."

Was it possible? Did she really die? Tears sprang to her eyes. Maybe she would have been better off if she did. She thought about Billy and cringed. A picture of black tar heroin pushed everything else aside.

An orderly appeared at her side and placed a white plastic bag at the foot of her gurney. Shaking his head at her, he left. Not paying him any mind, she eyed her IV. She thought she might have the perfect solution to all her troubles. Dee tore open the bag and searched through her clothing and purse.

Nothing! Fuck! Nothing!

Not believing what she was seeing, she looked again. But it didn't matter how many times she looked. The heroin was gone. Weasel or Doc must have stolen it from her. Determined to find them and reclaim what was hers, she dressed as fast as she could. She'd kick their asses! She was so pissed! It was all she could do not to scream.

With her eyes on the ground in front of her, she marched down the hallway consumed by anger. Bumping into someone, she snarled, "move!"

"Going somewhere?" a familiar old voice asked.

Dee looked up, wondering if this day could possibly get any worse. Apparently, it could.

Charlie grinned at her. "I bet you're surprised to see me here," he said, and then grabbed her by the arm.

Chapter **15**

Up, down. Up, down. Lyndsey went faster and faster. Billy held onto her leg and squealed with delight, "Giddy up, horsey!" She grinned, going even faster.

Laughing, Billy waved his arms in the air. For a moment it was perfect. Billy's laughter was infectious, and she laughed too.

She could listen to him laugh forever. That is, if her leg wasn't getting so sore. "More!" Billy shouted as she slowed down.

Her leg wasn't just sore, it was tired. But she shook it anyways, switching from a horse to a truck. "Vroom," she growled and shook him up and down.

"More, more, more!" Billy demanded.

A charley horse made Lyndsey wince with pain. "Sorry Billy, no more." She pulled him off her leg and put him down.

His lower lip thrust out. His eyes watered. "More!"

Lyndsey shook her head no. She wasn't being mean, her leg really hurt! Billy scrunched up his face. He started to cry and curled up into a little ball on the carpet.

Should she pick him up? When it came to parenting Billy, she was torn. Her instinct to coddle him was strong. She wished she knew what to do. 'No' was a very important word, and a difficult one to teach.

"Hey." Drake poked his head in the doorway. "Aren't you going to be late?"

Dragging her eyes away from Billy, Lyndsey met his gaze. "I wanted to spend some quality time with Billy before I left."

Drake glanced at Billy. His face remained calm, as if it were no big deal, Billy having a tantrum on the carpet like that. Billy's meltdowns didn't seem to bother him the same way they bothered her, and that bugged her. Was Drake indifferent of Billy? Didn't he care?

Tears blurred her vision. This feeling of helplessness when it came to Billy was not enjoyable at all. "How can I leave him like that? Do you think I should go to work today? Maybe they can get someone to cover my appointments? Look at him, Drake, he's so upset!"

"Linds," Drake shook his head, "he'll be fine." He stepped over Billy and sat down beside her.

"How can you say that?" she pointed a finger at Billy. "Look at him!"

"He's doing what every toddler does when they don't get their own way. He's having a tantrum. He'll get over it." Drake cupped her chin, directing her eyes to his. "It's you I'm worried about."

"Me!" She bristled. "What do you mean? Why would you be worried about me?"

His beautiful brown eyes grew serious. "I think he's triggering something from your childhood."

"What? That's ridiculous!" She snorted. "Why would you say that?"

"Because, honey, you're a strong beautiful, intelligent woman. But when it comes to Billy, you sit there helplessly wringing your hands."

"Jesus, Drake! Just because I care doesn't mean I'm being triggered. Maybe if you cared more, I wouldn't feel quite so helpless!"

"Stop it, Linds." He gave her a hard stare. "You're not being fair. You know I care, but you're making mountains out of molehills."

Lyndsey pulled her chin free from his hand. Was she creating chaos where there was none? God she was so confused!

"Maybe you should join a parent's support group." He shrugged. "It might help."

One support group was enough. She barely had time to breathe, for God's sake. Lyndsey jumped off the couch. She really did need to go.

Billy stopped wailing long enough to take a big breath. Drake pulled a toy truck free from the cushion behind him and said, "Look Billy, I found your truck!"

Billy's wail cut off in mid-air. He sat up rubbing his eyes. Drake raced the truck up and down his jean clad leg and said, "Vrmm, vrmm."

Billy eyed the truck and stood up. Determined, he reached for it. "Mine!" He grabbed it from Drake.

"Say please," Drake insisted, not letting go of the truck.

Lyndsey sighed. Billy's mood swings were wearing her out. Or was it her response to them that was the real problem?

"Your coffee's getting cold." Drake eyed her cup sitting on the coffee table as he tug-a-warred with Billy.

Maybe Drake was right. She really was taking this whole thing too seriously. Retracing her steps, she picked up her cup.

"What have you got going for today?" Drake tugged on the truck and Billy giggled.

"I'm helping a client with a difficult visit. What about you?"

Drake let go of the truck and Billy shrieked with victory. He held the truck tightly to his chest, his face serene, and settled back onto the carpet.

"I'm doing some juggling right now. The commercial project on Heckett Street is coming to an end, and I have two residentials on the go."

Lyndsey wondered how he did it. The construction trade was notorious for men who had chronic problems with drugs and alcohol. Drake learned a long time ago not to give pay loans in the middle of the week, or your crew would be a no show the next day.

Drake bent down to scoop up Billy. "Why don't you let me drop him off at daycare today?"

"Are you sure?"

He winked at her. "You can make it up to me later."

Lyndsey grinned. "Deal." Giving Drake a great big hug, she kissed Billy on his forehead. "I should be home by six."

"Call me later. If I'm off before you, I'll swing by and pick Billy up."

"Okay, thanks." She blew them both a kiss and headed for the door.

Traffic inched along at a snail's pace. Why was it that every time she was running late, traffic was slow and she hit every red light? Lyndsey drummed her fingers on the steering wheel. The back of her neck hurt—a sure sign she was taking life far too seriously. Leaning back in her seat, she turned on the radio and decided to enjoy the ride.

Entering the building through the back entrance, she avoided the main reception area. The hallways buzzed with energy. She made it to her office with a minute to spare.

Another pile of messages had accumulated overnight. Lyndsey scanned them, stopping when she spotted one about a past client who had relapsed. Damn it!

Relapse wasn't a surprise. Some even believed it was inevitable. But Lyndsey didn't buy that. Relapse happened when you cut corners, or you were being dishonest and hanging out in dangerous places.

Making a note to call the young man, she organized her schedule.

The phone beeped. "Lyndsey, I have Calvin on three." Debbie, the new receptionist, chirped.

Speak of the devil! She picked up the phone. "Hi Calvin, I'm glad you called."

"I fucked up," Calvin said, through a nose full of cotton.

"Okay. Tell me about it."

"I wanted to hang out with a couple of my old buddies. They were going to the club. I figured if I drank pop, I'd be okay. I could be the designated driver. Kind of like service work. Right?"

As she listened to Calvin, Lyndsey remembered how he had struggled to stay away from his old using buddies. He'd always referred to them as family. The trick was to find a new family. One that was sober. That's why joining a twelve step group was so important.

Addiction was so much more than what you used. It was a lifestyle that was every bit as addictive as the substance itself.

"So there I was at the club with all my buddies, and it was weird." Calvin stopped and blew his nose loudly before continuing. "At first, my bros were like, hey man, we're so proud of you! But after my buddies had had a few drinks, that all changed."

Something wasn't sitting right with her. Lyndsey frowned. "Calvin, did you really think designated driving for your using buddies was the same thing as doing service work?"

"Well…" he trailed off.

"If you're going to be dishonest, we're wasting our time. And just so you know it, my time is too precious to waste. So what's it going to be?"

"Jeez," Calvin mumbled.

"Do you want to be clean?"

"What the hell kinda question, is that?"

"An honest one! Look, Calvin, you know what to do, you just have to do it."

"Yeah, I guess," he said, sounding defeated.

"How are you feeling?"

"Like shit!" He snorted. "I guess I'm a loser, huh?"

"No, Calvin, you're not a loser. Today is a new day. You've learned an important lesson. Go to a meeting, tell on yourself, and then get on with it. And the next time you have a good idea, make sure to run it by your sponsor first."

Lyndsey hung up the phone deep in thought. Many people thought getting clean and sober was about being abstinent. But that was the easy part. What getting clean and sober really meant was learning how to be honest, and doing that was far more difficult.

The phone beeped, interrupting her train of thought.

"Lyndsey, Susan is here to see you." Debbie paused. "Do you want me to send her down?"

Now? Susan was way too early. She scanned the office, noting the confidential paperwork and messages scattered across her desk. Her eyes stopped on 'Git wel son'. The tape was doing its job. At last, the picture hung straight.

Picking up the phone, she said. "Don't send her down, I'm coming up."

Chapter **16**

They were at the beach, playing in the surf. In his dream, Miranda looked killer in her miniscule bikini. He held her tightly in his arms. She was wet and slippery. Laughing, she wiggled away from him. "No, please don't go!"

Declan's eyes blinked open and his hard-on faded.

Pulling the covers up, he settled in, hoping to recapture the dream. But it was no use. He was wide-awake now.

Turning over, he saw that Gary was staring at him from his bed across the room. Gone was the green man from the night before. Gary looked like he was up to no good. He stared back at Gary, wondering what his deal was.

Gary's eyes darted to the door and then back. "Listen kid, I'm gonna be leaving today. Do you have a couple of bucks I could borrow?"

"Nah." Declan shook his head. "I'm busted."

Gary's eyes narrowed. "Look, I know a place where we can get some cash, but it's tricky. Can I trust you?"

What was the old bugger up to? Declan shrugged, not wanting to get involved.

"Well?" Gary insisted.

"I guess." he said, more to shut the old guy up than to agree with him.

"Good," Gary grunted. "I had a feeling about you."

Not sure what he meant, Declan stayed quiet.

"There's a petty cash tin in Tom's office. I need you to keep him busy so I can go in and get it."

Cash? Now Gary had his attention. Declan sat up straight, thinking. "Won't the door be locked?"

A sly grin crossed Gary's face as he fished in his covers. "I have the key!" he chortled, holding up a single key and waving it before Declan.

Declan thought fast. If his mom managed to get him out today, he'd need some cash for sure. He'd planned on hitting her up for it, but this could work out better. He'd use the money Gary gave him, and with his mom's money, he might be able to start up a little business. Only this time, he wouldn't be so stupid as to get caught.

The smile slid from Gary's face. "You better not screw me over, kid."

Declan shook his head. "Don't worry, I won't. When do you want to do this?"

Gary got out of bed and walked across the floor. Boxers that were once white sagged from his bottom. He opened a cupboard drawer and withdrew a small black comb. As he ran it through his thinning hair he said, "I was thinking visiting time might the best. That way, everyone will be distracted."

"Hmm, I've got a visitor coming. It might not work."

Gary frowned and then looked at him closely, "Oh yeah? Who?"

Declan didn't want to tell Gary it was his mom, but he couldn't see any other option. "My mom," he mumbled.

"Oh?" Gary's face lit up. "Does she have any money?'

He bristled. Gary was a piece of shit who wanted a piece of his action. His mom was loaded, but he wasn't going to tell Gary that. Instead, he shook his head. "Nah."

Tapping one crooked finger on his chin, Gary asked. "Is she single?"

"What?"

"Is she single?" Gary repeated. "You never know, I might just be the highlight of her day!" He chuckled, amused by the thought.

"She's divorced." Declan kept a straight face. "No offense Gary, but you're not really her type."

Gary smirked. "No offense kid, but you don't really know her type. After all, you're in here too, aren't you? Besides," he patted his crotch. "I have a secret weapon."

The idea of his mom with Gary was just ludicrous. He decided to change the subject. "Where are the showers?"

"All in good time," Gary said, not one to be redirected so easily. "I want you to introduce me to your mom when she gets here. Tell her I'm one of the counselors."

"Why?"

"Because I'm pretty sure I'm not the only one who wants to leave. I get the feeling you do too."

He nodded. "I do, but I'm court ordered to be here."

"We'll figure it out as we go, but if you're mom thinks I'm your counselor, I can encourage her to appeal to your lawyer. Maybe a nice cushy house arrest is in order, hey kid?"

Declan stared at Gary in surprise. They were thinking along the same lines. He didn't know whether to be disgusted or afraid.

"Then, when you're at home, I can drop by and say I'm following up on your case."

The idea of seeing Gary again was not at all appealing. Still, the guy had a point. If his mom was suspicious of him, she'd certainly believe his 'counselor.'

Declan eyed Gary as if seeing him for the first time. Gary had a big red, bulbous nose. He needed a shave and a shower. Cleaned up and with the right clothes, it might work.

Gary stuffed his comb back into the drawer and flung open the wardrobe. "I got this from the Salvation Army." He held up a blue pin stripped suit. "What do you think?"

Before Declan could say anything, Tom entered the room carrying towels.

"Morning, gentlemen." He glanced at Gary. "It looks like you're feeling better today. Does this mean you'll be leaving us?"

Gary put the suit on his bed. His shoulders drooped. "You don't have any faith in me at all, do you Tom?"

Tom shook his head. "Nope. Not much."

Gary put his hand over his heart. He turned to Declan. "How's that for support?"

Tom pointed a finger at Gary. "Leave him outta this. He still has a chance. You, on the other hand…" Tom trailed off, but his meaning was clear.

Gary shook his head. "You know Tom, I'm not feeling the love."

Ignoring that, Tom handed Declan a towel. "I figured you might need this. You got a busy day ahead of you."

He nodded. He did have a busy day ahead of him, but it wasn't the one Tom had planned.

All business now, Tom waved at the white binder on his desk. "Check the schedule in your handbook. You have twenty minutes to shower and make your bed. And don't forget to clean your bathroom." He jerked a thumb at the tiny space masquerading as a bathroom. It was a two piece, with only a toilet and sink.

Tom's jaw thrust out and he barked, "Twenty minutes starting now!"

Declan stared at Tom, not getting it.

Tom tapped his watch.

Shit! Tom was timing him! He launched into action, making the bed under Tom's critical eye. Gary hummed an off-beat tune as he made his.

Satisfied, Tom looked at the beds and nodded. "I'll walk you to the showers."

Declan hesitated. He was hoping to talk more with Gary. Tom stood at the door, waiting. Clearly, he wasn't going to leave without Declan. Declan looked at Gary, hoping he'd come up with something. But Gary just picked a piece of lint off his suit, as if he didn't have a care in the world.

"Don't forget your towel," Tom said, pointing at the towel on the chair.

He fussed with his binder, stalling for time. Maybe Tom would grow tired of waiting for him. But he didn't. He just stood by the door, waiting. He couldn't stall any longer. He picked up the towel and walked towards Tom.

Gary caught his eye and winked. "Don't worry, Declan. I'll show you how it's done."

Tom's lips turned downwards. Ignoring Gary, he looked at Declan. "Let me give you a piece of advice." He waggled a finger at Gary, "Whatever you do, don't get involved with any of his shenanigans."

Declan looked back and forth between Gary and Tom, then said innocently, "Jeez Tom, Gary's been nothing but nice to me."

Tom shook his head. "God help us all." He turned away and walked through the doorway. Hiding his smirk, Declan followed Tom down the hall.

Chapter 17

"YOU CAN'T LEAVE LIKE THAT!" CHARLIE HUFFED, pointing at the IV protruding from her arm.

"Fuck off, Charlie," Dee snapped.

He yanked on her arm. "You've got to get that thing out before you go."

"Would you mind your own business?" She got up in his face. "Now let go of my arm or I'll scream!"

Charlie backed up a step and shook his head. With the back of her hand, she swiped her runny nose. God she felt sick. Tears blurred her vision. The thought of going back to the streets to earn money was more than she could bear right now.

Charlie scratched his head and looked at her. "Is there anyone you can ask for help? What about your friends or family?"

Family? Now that's a laugh. Dee thought about her mother. She hadn't seen her in a long time. It was more than five years. The last time they were together, her mother had been falling down drunk and they'd gotten into an argument.

"There must be someone I could call?" Charlie fumbled in his coat pocket and pulled out his cell phone. "What about your mother?"

"Yeah, right!" She snorted. "Sorry, she's busy."

A frown creased his brow. "I'm sure she's not so busy she couldn't find the time to speak with you."

"Forget it., Charlie."

"Why? What can be more important to her than you? Is it work? What does she do?"

"She's a nun in a monastery." Dee rolled her eyes. "She's on sabbatical."

Charlie grinned. "Okay, I get it. I'm told laughter is the best medicine when something is ailing you."

Sweat broke out on her upper lip and she groaned.

A look of concern passed over Charlie's face. "Are you alright?"

Too tired to pretend, she shook her head. "No Charlie, I'm not. I'm sick and it's gonna get worse. Now would you please get out of my way so I can go out and find my medicine?"

"I know what that's like." His eyes met hers.

She eyed him shrewdly. "No, you don't. You don't have a clue and I'm too sick to try and explain it to you."

Charlie stared at her. The way he looked at her hurt. Kindness wasn't something Dee was comfortable with, so she looked away.

"Well," Charlie harrumphed, "there must be something I can do to help you."

A twisted smile flittered across her lips. "Unless you're carrying dope or give me some money, there's nothing you can do. Your words won't help me Charlie; they're merely prolonging my agony."

"Hmm." He looked up at the ceiling, as if talking to God.

The twitchy restless bounce pushed her shins up and down. Just standing was wearing her out. Turning from Charlie, she said, "I gotta go."

She'd only gone two steps when he shouted at her. "Wait!"

Sick with need, Dee walked faster.

But Charlie was quicker. Grabbing her sleeve, he said, "I have an idea."

Wow! The old boy was relentless! She couldn't figure him out.

"Why don't you stay with me for a few days?"

Her eyes narrowed. Was this what it was all about? Was Charlie trying to make her one of his girls? Disappointment washed over her. For a moment, she actually thought he cared. Still, she couldn't go back to her room. She was behind on the rent. And she needed a place to shower.

"Of course, we must talk first." Charlie jerked a thumb at her IV. "And you need to get that thing out."

One thing in her favor was she had experience when it came to negotiating with pimps. "Let's cut to the chase. What's in this for you?"

He waved at a passing nurse. As soon as she'd passed, he said, "Follow me."

She walked beside him, wondering what he had in mind.

Rounding a corner, they came upon a little alcove. Leather banquet seats lined one wall. A sign above their heads read 'X-ray.'

Charlie stopped and sat down. He patted the seat next to him.

Glad to be off her feet, Dee sank down next to him.

A round, older woman wearing glasses with short gray hair was sitting at the desk across from them. She stopped writing and watched them.

Charlie didn't seem to notice the woman across from him as he focused on Dee. "To answer your question," he said, taking a big breath. "A long time ago, someone helped me."

"And?"

"And," Charlie smiled, "they saved my life."

Slapping her thigh, she snickered. "Charlie, cut the crap! I don't need another pimp. What's your angle?"

The woman sitting at the desk gasped.

Charlie frowned. "Lower your voice, please."

"I won't lower my voice!" Dee shouted, on the verge of hysteria. "I've had enough!"

"Excuse me," the woman interjected.

Charlie smiled. "It's okay," he assured the gray haired woman. "We're just trying to work out a few details."

"Well, I.. I.." the woman stammered, pushing up her glasses and glaring at them.

Dee almost laughed. If she wasn't so sick, it would be funny. Charlie was the oldest pimp she'd ever seen.

He nudged her. "Well?"

Exhaustion weighed on her. She stared at the IV line, wishing she had something to put into it. Her head felt heavy on her neck. She sighed and ran a hand through her oily tresses.

The old woman harrumphed and slid the window closed. She got up from her chair and stomped off.

Charlie scowled at the woman's abrupt departure. His face smoothed out as his eyes found Dee's. "I have an idea. Why don't I get the medication you need to keep you from getting sick. Then we can concentrate on getting you well."

Her eyes widened in surprise. Dee hadn't expected this, but what the hell! If Charlie was willing to score her some dope, she sure as hell was willing to let him.

"It's not what you think," he warned.

Dee didn't give a rat's ass what Charlie had in mind, as long as she could get her hands on some dope. She'd deal with everything else later.

"So, we're in agreement then?"

A big smile broke out on her face. Raising her little finger," she said, "pinky swear."

Charlie reached out and touched his pinky to hers. "Okay. You wait here." He got up. "I'll be right back."

Big goose bumps broke out on her flesh. Dee shivered, cold to the bone. Her teeth chattered.

Charlie had only gone two steps when he turned back to her. "If you're still here when I get back, I'll bring you something that will help with those aches."

Rubbing her arms for warmth, she stared after him. What the hell was he was up to now?"

Chapter 18

Susan paced back and forth in the front entrance of the lobby. Her arms wrapped around her mid-section as she walked.

Lyndsey pushed through the door and waved.

Susan stopped abruptly and asked, "Are you ready?"

"Hello would be more appropriate."

Susan walked closer to her. "Hello." She paused a beat before adding, "Well, are you?"

"Yes." Lyndsey grinned and held up a set of car keys. "For insurance purposes, we need to use the company vehicle."

"Oh?" A trace of irritation passed over Susan's face. "I guess."

"Is there a problem?"

"No," Susan looked at her. "It's just, well, I'm not a very good passenger." She shrugged, then confessed, "I'm a back seat driver."

With the keys still grasped firmly in her fingers, Lyndsey joked. "I guess you'll just have to sit in the backseat then."

Susan blanched.

Her grin vanished as she noticed Susan's pallor. They didn't have a lot of time. Maybe they could talk it out in the car on their way. "We better go." Lyndsey pushed open the door and waited for Susan to go through it.

As they settled into the car, Lyndsey adjusted the mirrors. Satisfied she could see, she backed out of the parking space. Susan was silent beside her. Her fingers turned white as she gripped the arm rest.

The black Tahoe was smooth. What a pleasure to drive! On any other occasion she'd be enjoying this, but Susan's anxiety was sucking the fun out of it. Lyndsey stared out of the window. The scenery was amazing. With the vibrant colors of the tree blossoms and the different hues of grass, it was a little like driving through a painting.

The Tahoe was making good time. She dragged her eyes away from the scenery outside and glanced over at Susan. "Do you want to talk about it?"

Susan shrugged. Her shoulders slumped, and her lips turned down. She had bags under her eyes.

Worried, Lyndsey looked at her closely.

Susan turned to face her. "Wouldn't it be better if you kept your eyes on the road?"

"Right." She turned back to the road before continuing. "Well?"

Susan drummed her fingers on the armrest and blew out a breath. "I didn't sleep much last night," she admitted.

"Oh?"

"My head wouldn't shut up. The noise kept getting louder. I know most of what I was worrying about wasn't real, but at three a.m., it didn't seem to matter."

Can I ever relate, Lyndsey thought. She'd experienced those nights too, and they sucked.

"I was thinking about Declan and wondering if I should bring him a gift. But then I thought I probably shouldn't reward him for doing the right thing."

Lyndsey took her foot off the gas and pulled into the slow lane. Susan needed to get it all out before they saw Declan.

Now that she'd started, Susan spoke fast. "I mean, isn't that what I've done his whole life? I've rewarded him for doing the right thing. And worse, I've even rewarded him for doing the wrong thing!"

Lyndsey kept silent as Susan fished in her purse for a Kleenex.

Dabbing at her eyes, Susan lowered her voice. "I'm not sure if you can relate, Lyndsey, but it's really hard being a mother. You never know if you're doing the right thing. It's a heavy responsibility. If you don't do it right, your child could end up being a criminal or something. So here I am at three a.m. feeling like the biggest piece of shit, and then it occurred to me. Declan being in jail and now rehab is all my fault!"

To Lyndsey's ears, it sounded like Susan was making progress. At least she wasn't blaming her ex-husband for everything anymore.

"You know, I even thought about my own parents." Susan blew her nose. "They were such simple people. So was it their fault I ended up in rehab myself?"

"You went to rehab because you were addicted to Ativan. Which was a blessing in disguise." Lyndsey smiled. "Or you would still be enabling and playing the victim."

Susan smiled her first real smile of the day. "Yeah, well, it sure was a lot easier."

"Uh huh," Lyndsey agreed. "But do you remember how it felt?"

"I do. I'll never forget." Susan nodded. "It's like being smothered in a blanket of misery. I felt infectious. I couldn't stand people, but mostly I couldn't stand me."

Susan stopped talking, but that was okay. She'd said what she'd needed to. Lyndsey put her blinker on and resumed speed. They drove in silence, but this time it wasn't tense. A little while later, Susan waved her hand at the scenery outside the window. "It sure is pretty out there."

"It is," Lyndsey agreed, glad that Susan was able to see it again.

But their reprieve didn't last long. Tension filled the air as Lyndsey pulled into the rehab facility where Declan was staying.

"Shit," Susan said. "Is this it?"

"It is."

"But it's… awful!" Susan stared at the ugly stuccoed building. "Why are there bars on the windows? I thought this was supposed to be a rehab facility, not a prison!"

"It's not a prison. The bars are likely to keep others from getting in. With court mandated rehab facilities, they can't have their clientele climbing out of the windows any time they feel like it either."

"I don't know." Susan frowned.

A flash of anger hardened Lyndsey's tone. "Susan, this place will be good for him. From what you've told me, Declan needs a reality check. And this is it."

"I guess." Susan didn't sound convinced.

"You can still change your mind. If you go in there feeling sorry for him, he's going to sense it and use it to his advantage."

"You're right. It's just… he's not used to living in something that looks so awful!"

"Susan," Lyndsey said, "Declan was just in prison."

Susan turned to her, eyes wide. "You see! It's starting again! When it comes to Declan, I can't help it."

"Yes, you can. You just need to practice." Lyndsey pointed at the door. "And inside that door is your new practice ground."

"Okay." Susan took a big breath. "I can do this."

"Yes, you can."

Susan flipped open the visor above her head and looked in the mirror. "I look like shit," she said and opened her purse to remove a tube of lipstick.

As Susan ran the tube of lipstick over her lips, Lyndsey thought about addressing Susan's belittling self-talk. If they'd been in group therapy, she would have addressed it for sure. But given the circumstances, she chose to let it slide.

Smacking her lips, Susan shoved the tube of lipstick back in her purse and grabbed a sheet of Kleenex. "I don't know if it's better or worse." She grumbled, dabbing her lips and turned to Lyndsey. "What do you think?"

"I think," Lyndsey grinned, "you have lipstick on your teeth."

"Oh!" Susan squealed, scrubbing at her teeth with the Kleenex.

She squeezed Susan's shoulder. "Are you ready?"

Susan swiped a final dab at her teeth and tossed the Kleenex into the trash can on the floor. "I think so," she whispered.

Before she could get out of the car, Susan grabbed her.

"Wait!" she said, clinging to her arm. "What if he asks me for money?"

"What if he does?"

"You don't think I should give him any, do you?"

"Susan, this isn't about what I think. What feels right for you?"

She blinked back her tears. "I don't know…" she stammered and rubbed her temples.

"How about we just go in and see what unfolds? There's no use in playing the 'what if' game. You're trying to micromanage. Do you remember what control is really about?"

Susan nodded. "I remember. It's about fear. I'm afraid and I want to avoid this feeling, so I'm trying to control everything."

"That's right. Now that you know what you're doing, does it help?"

Susan stared at the dirty stucco building in front of them and shook her head. "Not really." She flung open her car door.

They walked in silence to the front door. The old wooden door had seen better days. There was paint peeling off it in long strips, inviting splinters to anyone who knocked.

Spying a little black button circled in rust, Lyndsey pushed it. The tinny whine of a bell shrilled inside.

Through the door they could hear, "I'll get it."

Susan stiffened beside her. "That's Declan!"

The door wrenched open with a loud squeak.

Lyndsey gasped when she saw who was standing there.

Chapter 19

DECLAN EYED THE CONTENTS OF HIS WARDROBE AND wondered if he should pack up now. It wouldn't take long. He didn't have much, but that was going to change fast. As soon as his Mom got here, he'd go to work on her. It was only a matter of time until she said yes, and when she did, he wanted to be ready.

He felt pretty good today. The hot shower had worked the kinks in his muscles loose. He still had a twinge of nausea, but his bones weren't killing him and his nose had stopped running.

Pulling on the jeans he'd worn yesterday, Declan frowned. They hung loosely on him. He wished he had his belt. They'd taken it from him in prison and he never got it back. His frown disappeared as he pictured the shopping spree he'd soon be going on. Hell, he'd buy ten belts!

You couldn't blame a guy for wanting to look good. He'd need a haircut, he thought, and his nails needed a good buffing. His hands looked rough and cracked. The prison laundry had left them chapped. Didn't matter, he'd get it all taken care of before they got back home.

Whistling one of his favorite tunes, he strode into the bathroom. The toilet lid was up. Gary had pissed all over it. Jesus! He grabbed his toothbrush and toothpaste and left the room. No way was he going to brush his teeth in there.

What was with these old guys? First Rooster and now Gary. Were all old men such pigs? Christ, if it ever got that bad, he hoped someone would take him out and shoot him.

While he brushed his teeth, he planned out the day. After him and his mom had finished shopping, he'd call Miranda. It pissed him off that he still hadn't heard from her. Come to think of it, he'd need a new phone too. One with all the bells and whistles. Yes, a phone was priority. Declan chuckled, thinking of ways he could put it to use. The first thing he'd do when he got to his mom's place was hit up her medicine cabinet. In the past, she usually kept a few goodies hidden there. Then he'd call a couple of his old buddies and...

Gary strode into the room. "Didn't anyone ever teach you to brush your teeth over the sink?"

"Didn't anyone ever teach you not to piss all over the toilet seat?" Declan shot back.

"Who says it was me?'

"Who said it wasn't?" Declan snorted and grabbed Gary by his arm. He steered him into the bathroom and pointed. "Look! That's disgusting. Clean it up."

Gary stared at the toilet. He turned to Declan, his big, bulbous nose almost touching his. "You don't know that was me."

"If you want me to help you today, you're going to do it my way." He poked Gary in the chest for emphasis.

Gary looked at the messy toilet and back at Declan. Shrugging his shoulders, he said. "Okay kid, we'll play it your way. For now."

While Gary was cleaning the toilet, Declan finished getting ready. Eyeing himself in the mirror, he liked what he saw. Any traces of the boy he'd once been were gone. The dark stubble on his cheeks made him look tough, but it was his eyes that had changed the most. He thought they were cool. They looked cold and flat, like a shark's.

From now on his mission was to get as high as he could, as soon as he could, and fuck anyone who tried to get in his way.

"Breakfast in five!" a deep male voice from the hallway bellowed.

They didn't have much time to get the kinks ironed out. As far as Declan was concerned, Gary could take all the risks and they would split the profit.

Declan poked his head into the bathroom. Gary looked ridiculous. He was bent over the toilet dabbing at the yellow spots with a piece of Kleenex. "Jesus, Gary, get a cloth. You'll be there all day!"

Gary looked up and scowled at him.

"Here," Declan tossed the hand towel at him, "use this."

The hand towel landed on Gary's head. "For Christ's sake," Gary yelled, grabbing it.

Leaning against the wall, Declan folded his arms across his chest. "Are you sure we can pull this off?"

Gary swiped the hand towel over the toilet bowl and grunted. Declan noticed the tremor in Gary's hands.

Gary leaned on the toilet bowl and stood up. He looked at Declan and then down at the toilet. "Satisfied?"

Declan nodded. He didn't give a shit about the toilet anymore. If his plans went accordingly, he'd never have to piss in it again. "I'll meet you back here after breakfast. We can figure out the details then."

Gary tossed the wet hand towel into the sink and shook his head. "There's not much to figure out. You're gonna keep 'em busy while I hit up the cash tin."

"I dunno Gary, that's a pretty vague plan. A million things could go wrong. We need to fine tune it. But first, breakfast, or Tom will be on our ass."

Gary scrubbed his wet hands on his pants. Declan winced and followed Gary from the room.

Bedroom doors along the hallway were open. Gary looked into each one, calculating. He nudged Declan in the ribs. "Rule number one, be alert and if you see something you like, take it."

Gary veered off into one of the rooms. Declan watched him from the hallway. A men's wrist watch was sitting on a bedside table. Gary picked it up, studied it, and then stuffed it into his pocket. A lighter was next to it. Gary took it too.

Not wanting to get caught in the hallway, Declan whispered. "Come on, Gary!"

Gary looked around the room a final time and not seeing anything else he could steal, slithered out.

Somewhat amazed at the old guy's brass balls, Declan stared at Gary's back. As Declan followed him down the hallway, he looked inside each room. If there was something worthwhile to steal, he wanted to get his hands on it before Gary could. The old guy really was cool as a cucumber. He'd obviously done this many times before.

They rounded a corner and Declan could suddenly smell bacon. He nudged Gary from behind as he cased out yet another room. "Hurry up, will ya? The food will be gone."

Gary shrugged and mumbled, "Not hungry." He glanced up and down the hallway and then entered the room.

Irritated, Declan ground his teeth. The old guy better not get them busted before they even get started! He figured it was too risky to be waiting out in the hallway, so he whispered loudly. "Gary, I'll see you in the dining hall."

Not waiting for a response, Declan left him to his own devices. His stomach rumbled as he picked up his pace.

The dining hall in the rehab center was much like the one in prison. Men of all ages sat at the tables shoving food into their mouths. Declan stood in the entranceway, unsure how to proceed.

Tom spied him and pointed to the lineup. He nodded, joining the line. A guy in front of him handed him a tray as he waited. The line moved forward at a snail's pace. Chewing the inside of his lip, he counted the floor tiles.

Eventually Declan made it to the front of the line. He grabbed the plate off his tray and stared at the food. The stainless steel counter held warming plates filled with bacon, eggs, and toast. He scooped up two ladles of scrambled eggs, a half dozen pieces of bacon, and four pieces of toast.

"Hey! Save some for the rest of us!" Gary winked at him to show he was kidding.

Noting two free seats, Declan joined the table and began wolfing down his breakfast. He wasn't interested in conversation and ate as fast as he could chew.

Gary pushed in next to him and picked at his food. Declan eyed Gary's plate for a second, and then remembered Gary had just had his hands in the shitter.

Forking a lump of scrambled eggs, Gary waved it at him. "You should see what I just picked up!"

Expecting a wad of cash or something like it, Declan smiled. "What?"

Gary set the fork down with the scrambled eggs still embedded in the tines. He reached in his pocket and leered. "Look!" he waved, indicating an object below the table.

Looking down, he saw what Gary held. A picture of a young woman in a bikini stared up at him.

"I took it from room 312." Gary waggled his eyebrows. "Think of this as a community service. The young man it belonged to had it hidden well. Of course, we're not allowed pictures like this one. So in a way I did him a favor by removing it before it got him busted!" Gary rubbed the picture on his crotch and closed his eyes. "Me and her are gonna get to know each other real well!"

Oh gross! Declan pushed his plate away, no longer hungry. He couldn't get out of here fast enough! Keeping his face blank, he got up. "I'll see you back in the room." *You disgusting pig*, he wanted to add, but bit his tongue.

Declan hadn't gone two steps before Tom caught up to him. "Group in five minutes," he said.

Declan didn't need group, he needed out. He looked up at Tom. "I'm not feeling well. Can I lie down?"

Tom just threw back his head and laughed. Declan stared at him in confusion. The noise in the dining hall quieted as the scene played out.

Tom slapped him on the shoulder and stopped laughing. His face grew serious. He drew close enough to Declan that he could smell Tom's bad breath.

"You're going to group!" he barked.

A droplet of spittle landed on Declan's cheek. Wiping it away, he flinched as Tom grasped him by his arm.

"I'll show you where to go," Tom said, as if he were doing him a favor.

Tom's long strides were hard to keep up with. Luckily they didn't have far to go. Tom flung open a door. "Make room for the newcomer," he shouted into the room.

Chairs scraped against the linoleum floor as the men moved to make room for him. Once Declan was settled in, Tom smiled. "I want you to focus on Step One."

A thick blue book was shoved into Declan's hands. He looked at it blankly. The guy beside him took it and flipped through the pages. "Here." He pointed to a highlighted paragraph in the book.

Satisfied all was well, Tom nodded at the group and retreated from the room.

A middle-aged man across from him began reading.

Declan yawned. The room was warm and his stomach full. He closed his eyes, lulled by the man's monotone voice.

Dozing off, Declan thought of Miranda. His head fell forward as he slept, unaware that the group had finished their big book study and left him there, alone.

A loud voice woke him. Declan sat up in his chair, blinking and disoriented, as he looked around at the empty room.

A male voice yelled from the hallway. "Has anyone seen Declan? He has a visitor."

Chapter **20**

C HARLIE PEERED THROUGH THE DOORWAY INTO THE darkened bedroom, observing his guest. A frown crossed his face as he glanced at his watch. *Better hurry*, he thought, as he walked down the hallway into the kitchen. The pill bottle was next to the sink. A big sigh escaped his lips as he opened the cupboard and reached for a water glass. He'd better be ready, for he was in for one hell of a ride!

Her legs pumped up and down, but she wasn't getting anywhere. Dee ran faster. Her lungs burned as she gasped for air. Footsteps were closing in on her. Not able to help herself, she glanced over her shoulder. The faceless men were almost on top of her. Billy weighed heavily on one hip as he clung to her tightly. She drew in a ragged breath and re-doubled her efforts. Clouds shuttered the moon, engulfing her in an eerie, glowing darkness. The loud thud of her pursuers' boot heels drew closer. Billy remained strangely silent. Her legs wobbled and shook as her steps slowed. Her heart thundered. Dee trembled, clutching tightly to Billy. "Please," she begged, "don't hurt us." The men drew close, surrounding her on all sides. Dee could smell their unwashed bodies. "Please!" she begged again. "My child is with me. Let me put him down. Please don't hurt him!" She plopped Billy on the ground and whispered into his ear. "Run, Billy, run." A large fist flashed before her face. She ducked, barely avoiding the punch. She pulled Billy up, but he wouldn't stand. Instead, he crumpled before her, slumping to the ground. A loud crack shattered the quiet. Her head rocked back as a fist connected with it. Stars exploded in front of her eyes. Her legs buckled as she landed on the ground beside Billy. Dee opened her mouth and screamed.

"Shush, you're okay," Charlie said softly and flipped on the light.

Dee bolted upright in bed and stared wildly around the room.

Charlie set a glass of water on the bedside table and lowered himself onto the side of the bed. "May I?" he asked, although he was already sitting.

Dee's heart hammered madly inside her chest. She stared at Charlie, disoriented.

"It was just a dream," Charlie assured her, patting her arm. "You're safe, Dee. It wasn't real."

The sheets tangled on her legs as she jerked away from him. The hideous image of Billy, not moving as he lay crumpled on the ground, was still fresh in her mind. She ran a shaky hand across her face as her heart rate began to slow.

"Do you want to talk about it?" Charlie asked.

Her teeth chattered, sending a wave of sharp pain to her jaw. Awake now, Dee moaned and shook her head. The room spun and she nearly vomited.

"Is it bad?"

What a stupid fuckin question, she thought. Pissed, Dee said, "What the fuck do you think, Charlie? Of course it's bad!" She gritted her teeth and rocked back and forth. The achy bones weren't the worst of it though. She was colder than a corpse. She yanked the blankets up, hoping to get warm. At times like these, she yearned for death.

Charlie plucked the pill bottle from his shirt pocket and grinned. He waved it in front of her face.

She flinched.

The smile slid from Charlie's lips. He shook his head. "Oh shit. I didn't think. Sorry."

Not interested in what Charlie had to say, Dee stared at what he held in his hand.

"Here," he said, passing the water on the bedside table to her. "This should help."

It took both of her hands to hold the glass, and it still shook. Water sloshed outside the glass and spilled onto her stomach. "Hurry," she urged.

Charlie said, "Just a sec." He unscrewed the cap on the bottle and poured one tablet into his palm.

"What is it? Oxy?"

Charlie shook his head.

"Fentanyl?"

Charlie twisted the cap back onto the bottle and palmed the pill. He pushed the bottle of pills into his trouser pocket and said, "No, it's not fentanyl or oxy. It's something better."

Intrigued and suspicious, she glared at Charlie. "It better not be Percocet or Tylenol 3! That shit doesn't work on me."

"It's not," Charlie assured her and then added. "You don't drink the water until after the tablet has dissolved. You'll need to put it under your tongue."

"That's ridiculous, Charlie! I'll chew it. It works faster that way." She looked down at the half empty glass. "Can you get me warm water? It helps the pill to dissolve in my stomach quicker. Of course the best way would be IV…" She trailed off, looking for her purse.

"You can't chew it. It won't work." he said. "How about we follow the doctor's orders? After all, I don't suppose you or I have a medical degree?"

A folded cream colored blanket sat atop the room's only chair, but her purse wasn't on it. She was never without her purse. Alarmed, she looked around the room. "Where's my purse?"

"Your purse is safe. It's on the kitchen table. I'll get it for you in a minute, but first your medication." Charlie opened his palm to reveal the tablet nestled inside.

Dee stared at the orange, stop sign-shaped pill. It was imprinted with an N and the number 8. She plucked it from Charlie's palm and pushed it under her tongue. "This shit better be good!" she warned.

"Oh, it is." He chuckled.

She waited for the pill to dissolve under her tongue. The urge to chew it was strong. If the tablet worked, she'd take the whole bottle from Charlie. But in the meantime, she thought she might have a little something stashed in her purse. Laying back against the bed, Dee stretched. You know, this might not be so bad. Maybe she'd live off the old boy for a while. It sure as hell beat living out on the streets or in dumpy hotel rooms.

An idea began to take shape. Maybe she'd landed on her feet after all! She'd take advantage of Charlie's kindness all right. She'd have him eating out of her hand in no time at all. Dee snickered. If he wasn't careful, she just might kick him to the curb and keep his house! Imagine what she could do with this place. She'd run girls of her own. No more laying down with the johns. She'd even get Billy back.

A fierce cramp in her bowel interrupted her fantasy. Hugging her stomach she asked, "Charlie, can you bring me my purse?"

Charlie leaned an elbow on his knee and peered at her dubiously.

"Please," Dee whined. "I really need it."

As Charlie left the room, Dee smiled.

Charlie didn't know it yet, but he'd just invited a viper into his nest.

Chapter **21**

AN OLDER MAN WITH A LARGE RED, BULBOUS NOSE burst through the front door. Startled, Lyndsey gasped. The blue pinstripe suit hung loosely on his thin frame. He bobbed his head up and down and grinned at her. His fingers circled her forearm, pinching. Speechless, she pried the strange man's fingers loose from her arm.

"Hi, I'm Gary, and you must be Declan's mom."

Irritated, Lyndsey shook her head and frowned. "No, I'm …" She trailed off, not sure how to identify herself.

Gary's face clouded in confusion. His eyes narrowed as he checked her out. He broke their stare and turned his eyes on Susan. Lyndsey watched with interest. Gary silently assessed Susan. His eyes ran up and down her body and landed briefly on her purse. The cloudy expression faded, to be replaced by a cold, calculating one.

Susan must have felt it too. She pulled her purse in close to her side and said, "I'm Susan, Declan's mother."

Gary's eyes lit up and he grinned. Shoving Lyndsey aside, he reached for Susan's arm. "Wellll Heellooo!" His eyes bulged as he emphasized hello.

Writing him off as just another con man who'd ended up in treatment, Lyndsey shook her head.

Susan looked upset. She pulled her hand away from Gary and asked, "Is Declan here?"

Gary, not one to be put off, nodded and reclaimed Susan's arm. He smiled an even bigger smile, exposing off-white, ill-fitting dentures.

Lyndsey decided it was time to take matters into her own hands. "Gary, please tell Declan we're here to see him."

Gary turned to her with a flicker of annoyance. "All in good time," he murmured. Ignoring her request, he turned back to Susan. "I'm Declan's counselor. Why don't we find a quiet room and get to know one another, hey? Is there anywhere you can put your, um, friend?"

Counselor! Gary was a counselor? Wow! He was the flakiest counselor she'd ever met. And he had some serious boundary issues! Lyndsey glanced at Susan, who looked shocked. She was in a bit of a bind. She didn't want to break Susan's confidentiality by admitting she was her counselor, but Lyndsey didn't want the poor woman to have to tolerate Gary's inappropriate behavior either.

Lyndsey met Susan's eyes. Susan shrugged as if asking, what now?

Gary turned to Lyndsey. "Why don't you wait in the dining hall while Susan and I talk?"

Susan frowned and shook her head. "No, I'm afraid that won't work, Gary. We are both here to see Declan."

Gary rubbed his chin. "Hmm." His shoulders sagged. He appeared to be mulling something over. "Can I take your coats?" he asked, switching topics.

"I'm fine," Lyndsey said, shaking her head.

Susan slipped out of her coat and handed it to Gary.

Gary reached for the coat and grasped Susan's hand, holding it longer than necessary. "You have lovely hands," he murmured, baring his oversized dentures.

Things were getting very strange. Lyndsey's bullshit radar was beeping. Something was wrong with this situation.

With Susan's coat folded neatly over one arm, Gary released her hand and said, "Follow me, please."

Susan shot her a questioning look before turning to follow Gary down the hallway. Lyndsey grinned behind Susan's back. Let's face it; she still got off on a little chaos.

The rehab facility was more than just a little tired. It was long overdue for a remodel. The walls, which might once have been cream-colored, were now colored dirty-gray. The carpet below her feet was badly stained. Still, you didn't need a castle to sober up in.

As if he was hosting a dinner party, Gary bowed as he entered the dining hall. "Ladies," he said, waving at the empty seats.

Pulling a chair out, Lyndsey glanced around. White fold-up tables and plastic chairs were stacked up against the wall, waiting for the next meal.

Gary cleared his throat. "Why don't I see if Declan is available?"

"Please do," Susan said, rolling her eyes.

Gary ogled Susan before he abruptly turned away.

As soon as Gary was out of hearing distance, Lyndsey turned to Susan. "I don't like this. Something's wrong."

Susan didn't hear her. She fished inside her purse and pulled out a pink compact mirror. Flipping it open, she held it with a shaky hand and looked at her image. Looking in the mirror, she asked, "Do I look okay?"

No, you look like shit. But of course she wouldn't say it. Not wanting to upset her, Lyndsey avoided the question. "How are you feeling?" she asked instead.

Susan took her eyes from the mirror and frowned. "Anxious, worried and… scared." She whispered the last word as a tear dribbled down her cheek.

Tears were good. Gary, on the other hand, was not. She needed to warn her. "Susan, I'm not sure about Gary," she said, and then bit her lip. It wasn't cool to talk bad about another therapist.

Susan dabbed her eyes and then pushed the tissue up her sleeve. She reached into her purse and pulled out a tube of lipstick. Puckering her lips, she eyed the mirror and dabbed it on. Her hand jerked and lipstick smeared on her nose. "Shit!"

Lyndsey pulled a clean tissue from her own purse. "Here," she offered.

Tears spilled down Susan's cheeks. "I feel like I'm having a heart attack!" she cried, mopping her lips, making a red streaky mess.

"You're not," Lyndsey assured her. She pointed to a red streak and said, "You missed a spot."

"Do you think he'll be happy to see me?" Susan asked, wetting the tissue and scrubbing her face with it.

"I'm not sure. Does it matter?"

Satisfied she'd gotten the lipstick off, Susan put the tube back into her purse. Snapping the compact closed, she turned to Lyndsey. "I keep forgetting that feelings aren't good or bad, they just are. I still want Declan to feel happy all the time. I know that's not realistic. But knowing it doesn't stop it from happening. I bounce between wanting to smother him with love and wanting to murder him!"

Lyndsey nodded. She could relate.

Susan smiled. "See, this is why I needed you to come with me. I feel so much better now that I've said it out loud."

"As much as I'd like to take credit for your well-being, it was you who opened up. It works every time!" Lyndsey grinned at her.

"Mom?"

Susan's face went white. Lyndsey turned to catch a glimpse of the young man who was causing his mother such grief. Lyndsey's heart stopped. The blood drained from her face. It couldn't be! It couldn't!

She rubbed her eyes and looked again. It was!

Oh my god! HIM was standing right in front of her!

Chapter 22

DECLAN SMASHED A FIST INTO HIS PALM. HE FELT like punching someone or breaking something. Instead, he eyed the picture on the night table next to his bed. His mom had brought it with her. It was taken years ago. In it, they were both tanned and smiling as he licked his ice-cream cone at the beach.

What the fuck was going on? He dragged his eyes away from the picture. Miranda wasn't returning his calls and now his mother had decided she needed time to think about his request. Time! Since when had she ever needed time when it came to him? He ground his teeth, not liking this new side to her at all.

That Lyndsey chick really pissed him off too. At first, she stared at him like she'd seen a ghost. He still couldn't figure out why his mom had brought a stranger with her to visit him. Talk about awkward!

He tossed on the bed. By now he should have been on his way home. A wave of self-pity rode him, hard. A big lump wedged in his throat. He seriously felt like strangling someone.

Not able to lie still any longer, he got up and paced around the room. Ten steps one way, eight the other. Claustrophobia set in. He needed freedom! Correction, what he really needed was to get wasted. And if that Lyndsey chick hadn't come with his mom, he was pretty sure he'd have been well on his way by now.

Maybe he should just leave? It was tempting. The thought of freedom brought a grin to his face. But it faded as reality set in. If he left, he wouldn't get far. Tom would call the sheriff's department and they would put an APB out on him.

Still, he could have one hell of a party before they caught up to him. Declan strode to the doorway and poked his head out. The hallway was clear. He could picture it. He'd grab his things and find a window to climb out of.

Nah, it wouldn't work. He needed money. He wondered where Gary was and if he'd had any luck with the cash tin. With less than five minutes until dinner, Declan went in search of Gary.

***

Gary wiggled the paper clip and slid it free of the keyhole. He thought with a few minor adjustments he might just have it. His hand trembled. The paper clip fell to the ground. He bent to retrieve it, wiping the sweat from his brow. God, he needed a drink in the worst way!

Fitting the paper clip back into the hole, he wriggled it back and forth. Okay, that was better. He was getting closer. Much closer.

***

Declan went out to the back yard, thinking Gary might be out there having a smoke. He eyed the crowd, but he didn't see him.

A tall, thin guy with spiky hair dyed orange and green on the tips smiled at him. "Hey man, can I borrow a smoke?"

Declan shrugged his shoulders. "Sorry man, I'm busted."

The guy smiled and held out his hand. "No worries, bro. They call me Lite-bright. And who might you be?"

Someone who wants to get the hell outta here! He shook Lite-bright's hand and replied, "Declan."

"Cool!" Lite-bright flashed him a big smile. "You just get in? What's your DOC?"

"DOC?"

"Yeah, you know. Like what's your drug of choice?"

Declan eyed Lite-bright, trying to figure him out. Was this dude actually happy to be here?

Lite-bright snapped his fingers. "Guess what mine is."

Was this guy comin' on to him? He backed up a few steps.

Lite-bright moved in closer. "Come on!" he urged. "Try and guess."

Declan eyed Lite-bright's yellow and white striped Tee shirt and noted the cashmere sweater he had tied around his neck. The guy wore a pair of jeans that were baby blue, and his runners were bright white. Whatever this dude's DOC was, he had the smell of money about him.

Just for shits and giggles, Declan decided to play along. His forehead wrinkled. "Hmm." He tapped a finger to his chin, as if deep in thought.

Lite-bright grinned and slapped his thigh.

"Maybe heroin?" Declan shook his head. "Nah, that wouldn't be it."

"Not heroin," Lite-bright trilled.

"Maybe speed?"

Lite-bright pointed one long, finger at him. "You're getting clossserrr!"

"Betcha five bucks I can get it on the next try," Declan said.

"Why you naughty boy. Weren't you paying attention? We're not supposed to bet." Lite-bright grinned. "But what the hell, you're on!"

Declan hid his smirk. It was like taking candy from a baby. Straight-faced, he stared at Lite-bright as if still guessing. "You started with E."

Lite-bright's eyes grew round.

"But it wasn't enough." Declan shook his head. "You wanted more."

Lite-bright nodded.

"So you gave crystal meth a try. And there was no going back after you used that greedy bitch."

Lite-bright frowned. "Who told you?"

Declan grinned and held out his palm. "Pay up!"

"No fair! You cheated!"

"I did not!"

"Come on! How else would you have known?"

Declan eyed the guy's teeth and wondered if he should tell him. Nah, it'd probably just piss him off. So he lied. Hoping to look convincing, he shrugged. "I just know stuff," he mumbled.

One pale blonde eyebrow rose high. "What do you mean, you just know stuff? Like do you mean you're a physic or something?"

Declan put a finger to his lips. "Shhh. Don't say nothing, but yeah, it's something like that."

Lite-bright didn't look convinced, but he pulled out his wallet. Declan watched him with interest.

Lite-bright flipped through a couple of twenties before plucking a fiver out. Handing it to him, he said. "K, we're square." He shoved the wallet back in his pocket. "Now it's my turn to guess."

He shook his head as he spied Tom closing in on them. "Later dude, we don't want to be late for dinner."

Lite-bright opened his mouth to protest, but Tom beat him to it.

"Colon, Declan, dinner!"

Declan shot Lite-bright a questioning look. The kid's cheeks flushed red as he stepped in front of Declan. Tom stopped him as he was about to rush by.

"Colon?" Declan asked Lite-bright.

Lite-bright turned a darker shade of red. He frowned at Tom before turning back to Declan. "Yeah, well…" he trailed off.

Tom poked one large finger at Lite-bright. "Are you using your club name again?"

Lite-bright shrugged and lowered his head. He kicked at a pebble and mumbled, "I guess."

Club name? What the hell? Declan cast a sideways glance at Lite-bright.

Tom scowled at Declan. "Have you been telling war stories out here?"

Declan shook his head, "No, I was just reminding Lite-bright, er… I mean Colon… we were going to be late for dinner if we didn't hurry."

Tom snorted. "Yeah, I bet that's what you were doing!" He shook his head and laughed.

Declan didn't know if he should try to convince Tom he wasn't doing anything wrong, or if he should just head to dinner.

Tom made the decision for him. He cleared his throat and looked serious. He looked at Lite-bright and said, "Using your club name is relapse behavior. You're either working on your relapse, or you're working on your recovery. War stories just glorify your pathetic past. Now get to dinner!" Tom cranked his head around to include Declan. "Both of you!"

"Yes sir!" Lite-bright replied cheekily and saluted.

Tom frowned. "Knock it off!"

Declan grabbed Lite-bright by his arm and yanked him through the doorway. He didn't really give a shit about Lite-bright. The money in his wallet however, now that was a different story.

Chapter 23

The soft boiled egg wasn't sitting well. Dee squirmed in her chair, trying to get comfortable. Charlie sat next to her, his eyes firmly fixed on the man speaking in front of them.

Dee eyed the motley crew. They were a strange mixture of people. Some of the men were well-dressed and clean, sporting nice haircuts and shiny gold jewelry. Others wore tattered T-shirts and jeans. The woman varied between sweat pants and business suits. She couldn't figure them out. This group didn't seem to have anything in common and yet, here they were in this room together.

The object of Charlie's interest had introduced himself as Samuel. He was a tall dark man with big round cheeks, who spoke passionately as he wagged a finger and said, "Acceptance is the answer to all my problems today."

As he spoke, heads bobbed up and down around the room.

Dee didn't have a clue what they were talking about, but she picked up on their excitement and sat up straighter in her chair.

"You're right where you're supposed to be, brother!" Samuel shouted, pointing at a man sitting in the crowd.

Next to her, Charlie whispered, "Amen."

She shot Charlie a dubious look. The poor old bugger was brainwashed and he didn't even know it!

"My best thinking was killing me." Samuel paused to clear his throat and stared up at the ceiling. The room went completely silent. Samuel took a deep breath and lowered his eyes. "And it wasn't just me that got hurt. My kids, my woman…" Samuels's voice cracked. "What I put them through is unimaginable."

Again, dead silence, only this time she felt like she was at a funeral. She shifted in her chair and rubbed her arms. Charlie blew out a breath beside her.

Closing her eyes, Dee tried to nap. The deal she'd struck with Charlie had her attending one of these meetings every day. She never said she'd stay awake for them, she'd just agreed to go.

Samuel droned on. "They said it was vehicular homicide. But that's just a nice way of saying it. I killed my lady, sure as I put my hands to her throat and strangled the life right out of her."

Not sure she'd heard him correctly, Dee opened her eyes. Samuel was weeping.

"My lady begged me not to drive and I laughed in her face. She wouldn't give me the keys, so I hit her."

Was this guy serious? You didn't tell people shit like that! Why would he share something so awful with these strangers? Dee looked around the room expecting to see angry faces. Instead, she saw compassionate ones. A lump wedged in her throat. Tears gathered in her eyes at the unexpected sight.

"I couldn't get her out of the car. I didn't want her nagging at me, but she wouldn't stop. So, I decided to show her." Samuel rocked back on his heels and keened.

The hairs on the back of her neck stood up.

Samuel blinked and swallowed, his Adams apple bobbed up and down. Gathering up his composure, he continued. "I drove as fast as I could. I don't remember much. They say a blackout is an alcoholic's best friend.

Robin Williams called it sleepwalking with activities. I don't know. Maybe Robin's right. The next thing I know, I'm waking up in the hospital and being told she didn't make it."

Charlie pulled a Kleenex from his pocket and offered it to Dee. She shook her head, embarrassed he'd seen her tears.

"I wanted to die. Right then and there." Samuel lowered his head and looked around the room. His eyes met hers, briefly.

Samuel's pain was enormous. Dee looked away, saddened by what she'd seen in his eyes.

"For a long time after that, I tried to kill myself. Oh, I wasn't brave enough to get a gun and blow my brains out. I was too much a coward for that. So instead, I drank. Every day I'd get up and get as wasted as I could. I couldn't stand the pain. If I drank enough, I could make it go away. Trouble was, it wouldn't stay gone."

His words pulled her back. She stared at Samuel. Nothing else existed. The room disappeared, as did Charlie next to her.

"I woke up one morning with nothing to drink. I was in bad shape, puking my guts out and wishing I was dead. I had just made one hell of a mess on the bathroom floor and was on my way back to bed when I passed my son's room."

Dee's heart beat madly against her rib cage. She felt panicked. She wanted to run, and yet she had the wildest urge to help this strange man. But what could she do?

"My little boy was kneeling beside his bed and praying. He asked God for all the things I couldn't." Samuel wiped the sweat from his brow.

The urge to run grew. Dee wanted to spring up from her chair and run like hell. She didn't care where, as long as it was far, far, away from here. But she couldn't move. She was frozen to her seat.

"He asked that God look after his mommy and to please tell her he missed her." Samuel broke off and closed his eyes. Dee bit her fist to keep from screaming.

Samuel drew a ragged breath and continued. "He asked God to please forgive his daddy and to help him get well. He said that without a mommy, he needed his daddy more than ever. And then…" Samuel scrubbed his eyes, and continued. "And then he cried."

Charlie thrust a Kleenex at Dee, breaking the strange trance she'd been in. He took one and mopped his face.

"I don't know what made me do it." Samuel shook his dark head. "It was like something else was steering me. I went into my little boy's room and got down on my knees beside him. He tensed up, as if expecting me to hit him, but I put my arm around him instead. He relaxed against me, and I asked him to say the prayer again, only this time, I joined in. It was something else. I couldn't get well on my own, not even for my children, but with the help of God and you folks in these rooms, I've not touched a drop since."

A collective sigh rose from within the room. The members of this strange group were blotting their eyes and shaking Samuel's hand. Dee couldn't figure them out for the life of her. If she'd told a story like that, she'd have gotten rocks thrown at her! What made this group so different? It was like you were encouraged to share your shit.

Charlie said, "Thanks for sharing, Samuel. We're almost out of time. Does anyone have a burning desire to share?"

Horrified, Dee ducked her head as Charlie looked right at her. The room grew silent. She kicked Charlie in the leg and muttered, "Asshole!"

Charlie winced. "Dee, would you like to share?"

Wishing she could disappear, she felt her cheeks grow warm. She glared at Charlie and whispered, "I don't know what to say."

"Just say the first thing that comes to mind," Charlie whispered back.

How she hated him! She disliked being put on the spot. She couldn't wait to get away from him and this room full of weirdos.

He might have the upper hand for now, but not for long. She'd had enough. Fuck these people and their sad stories. Dee sat up straight in her chair and glared angrily around the room.

Her eyes locked on Samuel's. He smiled at her. Her heart lurched.

Charlie nudged her. "Dee?"

Furious, she yelled, "Fuck you, Charlie!"

Laughter broke out around the room. She looked on with confusion.

Charlie chuckled and said, "Well on that note, will you join me in saying the serenity prayer?"

Dee jumped up from her chair, eager to get this whole thing over with when a thought stopped her dead in her tracks. She'd just gone a whole hour without using.

Chapter 24

THE RIDE BACK WAS A BLUR. LYNDSEY WAS LUCKY she didn't hit anyone. Declan's face floated before her eyes the entire way. She felt sick. Seeing Declan reminded her of HIM. And she hadn't thought of HIM in years.

In a way, the years with HIM had been the worst years of her life. And yet, they had also been the most blessed. Moisture blurred her vision and her arms felt empty. She flashed back on the hospital room in which her son had been born.

It had been a cold, sterile environment. Not at all like the cheery welcoming hospital rooms in which most mothers delivered their babies today. She'd been alone and scared, and in pain. Dear God, the pain!

Her fingers gripped the steering wheel. It was so unfair! Hot tears scalded her eyes as she remembered the precious little bundle that was laid in her arms. She'd never forget how he smelled, or how he felt cradled next to her heart. She blinked away the tears and the memories. She snuck a quick glance at Susan.

It was a good thing Susan was distracted. She hadn't noticed Lyndsey's shock at seeing her son. Now Lyndsey couldn't stop replaying that moment in her head. Had she gasped or cried out? She didn't think so. She was pretty certain she'd froze upon seeing Declan.

He looked to be about twenty. She did the math and shivered. It couldn't be. Of course it wasn't! Still… She snuck another glance at Susan.

Susan's head was bowed. She twisted a Kleenex between her fingers and stared at her lap. She was curled up into a little ball in her chair. A sure sign she was experiencing anxiety too.

Fear crawled up Lyndsey's throat, bringing with it a bitter aftertaste. Should she ask Susan what Declan's birthday was? Would Susan be suspicious if she did?

Lyndsey's son's birthday was engraved in her heart. July 16, 1991. She'd only seen him once after they'd taken him from her. At the time, she hadn't even known it was him she was seeing. She'd needed a smoke in the worst way and had been waddling down the hallway in search of an exit door when she'd passed the nursery. She'd glanced into the large window, taking in all the bassinets with their brand new swaddled babies. She hadn't looked for long. It was just too painful, but she remembered seeing the name tags on each bassinette. One held a baby boy swaddled in a blue blanket. It hid the baby, leaving only a little white hat peeking out. On the bassinette was the name, 'Baby Doe.'

Had she known it was her baby, she'd have gone into the nursery right there and then, snatched him up, and ran. Of course, she wouldn't get far. Still living at home, a teenager with no job or money, and in high school, she never had a chance.

What sad times. Her past wasn't something Lyndsey liked thinking about.

Susan let out a big sigh.

She drummed the steering wheel with her fingertips and flipped on the radio. Pharrell Williams was singing 'Happy.' She flipped it off. She loved the song, but the atmosphere in the car was anything but. Besides, she wasn't supposed to be playing music in the company vehicle.

Susan sniffed and dabbed at her cheeks. She reached over and grabbed Lyndsey's arm. The steering wheel jerked under her fingers and she cried out, "Susan! What are you doing?"

"Lyndsey, we need to turn around! Right now!"

Lyndsey put the blinker on and pulled off to the side of the road. Putting the car into park, she turned to Susan.

"I made a mistake!" Susan's nostrils flared. "I shouldn't have listened to you!"

Lyndsey frowned. "You know it's normal to feel guilty after you set a boundary."

"A boundary?" Susan shrieked. "Is that what you call it? I just left my son—MY SON, Lyndsey!—in a rehab facility that looks like it's ready to be demolished."

"Susan, he was just in prison," she reminded. "This is a step up."

"No, I don't think it is. Did you see the way he looked at me? I've never told him no before. He's already lost his Dad and—"

"Susan!" Lyndsey interrupted her. "Your son is not a victim. He made poor choices and now he's facing the consequences. Please don't get in the way of that."

"Maybe it isn't me who's getting in the way!" Susan glared at her, her cheeks sporting twin red spots.

Lyndsey let that sink in. Susan was back to where she'd started. Rather than argue, Lyndsey remained silent. Looking over her shoulder, she pulled back onto the road.

The rest of the ride was spent in tense silence. Susan withdrew even farther. She rolled up into a tight little ball and turned her back on her. Giving her space, Lyndsey focused on the road.

Back at the center, she pulled into the reserved spot and turned off the car. Pulling the keys free from the ignition, she turned to Susan and winced.

Susan's knees were up to her chest and she'd locked her arms around them. She was rocking back and forth, with her head tucked down.

"Susan." She reached over and squeezed her shoulder.

Susan stopped rocking and raised her head. She looked at her coldly.

Ignoring her cold stare, Lyndsey said, "What are you going to do to look after yourself today?"

Uncurling her legs, Susan stretched them out in front of her. She gathered up her purse and pushed her soggy Kleenex into it. Glancing at Lyndsey she said, "Maybe I'll find a new counselor. One who knows what the hell she's doing." She didn't quite meet her eyes.

"Susan, stop," Lyndsey said gently. "How are you feeling?"

"Don't ask me that! I hate it when you do that! How do you think I'm feeling?" Susan covered her face.

"Please don't hide from your emotions. I can't know how you're feeling until you tell me."

Susan lowered her hands. Their eyes met briefly before Susan looked away.

"Why don't you come in and we can talk about it?" Lyndsey asked, jerking a thumb at the main building.

Susan shook her head. "I can't." Then she corrected, "I don't want to."

"What do you think is going to happen if you don't talk about the way you're feeling?"

"I don't know. I just need some time to think."

"No you don't!" Lyndsey snorted. "That's the last thing you need. Your mind is a dangerous neighborhood. Don't go there alone. You know what's going to happen if you don't talk about this."

Susan turned her head to look out the window.

Lyndsey wasn't sure if she was trying to tune her out, or just needed some space. "If you don't talk about this, you'll act on it."

"How?" Susan turned away from the window and glanced over at her. "What do you mean?"

"I mean," Lyndsey's eyes grew serious. "The guilt will eat you up and pretty soon, you'll be back at Declan's rehab, co-signing his BS."

"How do you know it's BS?"

"Of course it's BS!" She said too loudly, then reigned in her emotions. "He's far better off at rehab than he is at your house."

Susan's shoulders sagged. She turned to Lyndsey. "I know," she whispered. "It's just, I feel so bad for him."

"What you're feeling is guilt. It has nothing to do with Declan. It has to do with you. It's the same thing the addict does. He uses substances to feel better. Guess what you use?"

Susan's brows knitted together as she stared at Lyndsey blankly.

"Come on," Lyndsey urged, wanting Susan to come to the conclusion. "You know this."

Susan shook her head.

"What would make you feel better right now?" Lyndsey prodded.

"Saying yes to Declan and bringing him home with me would make me feel better," she replied easily.

Lyndsey nodded. "That's right. When you say yes, it makes you feel better. It has nothing to do with Declan, and it's certainly not in his best interest. When you say yes, your anxiety goes away. When an addict uses, their anxiety goes away. It's a quick fix, and it's the same thing. The only difference is, you use enabling to mood-alter and Declan uses drugs."

Susan's jaw dropped open. "I never thought of it that way!"

"Of course you haven't. This is a very manipulative and dishonest disease."

"So I've been doing the same thing as Declan all these years?'

"In a way, yes." Lyndsey nodded. "But let's not go back. Analyzing the situation is just another way to avoid your feelings."

Susan shook her head. "I'd rather avoid the emotions. They're, um, messy. I don't like messy."

Lyndsey laughed. "You're not alone there. But if you avoid the feelings, you act out on unhealthy behaviors. And that's not fun either."

"No, it's not," Susan agreed. "Okay, you win. I'll phone Irene and see if she wants to go to a meeting."

Lyndsey grinned. "Actually, it's you who wins. But I'll be happy to take the credit!"

Susan reached over and gave her a brief hug. She opened the car door and stopped. "I'll check in with you tomorrow."

Lyndsey nodded. "You know where to find me."

Susan said, "Yes I do," and closed the door.

Lyndsey watched her as she climbed into her car and drove away.

Declan's face came back to her and merged with the image of HIM.

She shuddered.

No. It couldn't be.

Could it?

Chapter 25

THE SALT SHAKER CRASHED INTO HIS PLATE WITH A bang. Declan raised his head and scowled. Lite-bright jumped up from his seat smiling and high-fived the guy sitting across the table from him. "Pay up!" he crowed.

"Double or nothing!" the other man retorted.

Declan bent his head and shovelled more food into his mouth. He kept an eye on the game playing out in front of him.

Lite-bright nudged him on the shoulder. "You want in on this?"

Declan shrugged. "Maybe. Can you spot me a fiver?"

Lite-bright nodded and reached into his pocket.

Declan hid his smile. He'd pegged him right. Lite-bright was one of those guys that would do anything for you. The guy was so hungry for friends, he'd give you the shirt off his back.

"Here," Lite-bright said, slapping a five dollar bill down on the table in front of him.

"Thanks," Declan said, thrusting the bill into his pocket.

"Hey!" Lite-bright protested. "Aren't you gonna bet?"

"Nah," Declan shook his head. "We can get kicked out for that."

"But," Lite-bright paused when he saw who was standing at the door.

Tom glowered at them. "Five minutes!" he bellowed.

Declan pushed his plate away and rubbed his stomach, regretting the seconds he'd had. It was gross feeling this full, but he hadn't been able to resist the extra serving. He'd noticed his food habits were changing. He seemed to gorge more than eat these days. Oh well, maybe he was just bored.

Lite-bright reached over and scooped up Declan's plate along with his own. "Are you coming?" he asked, rolling his eyes at the doorway.

Declan nodded and stood. "I'll catch up with you later," he said, after spying Gary farther down the table.

Lite-bright frowned. He looked serious. "Dude, you don't want to be late for Step study. Tom will have your ass!"

"Yeah, if he's lucky!" Declan snorted. "Hey, can you grab my book? I'll meet you there in a sec."

Lite-bright beamed, glad to be of service. "Sure!"

Declan glanced around the cafeteria. An overly medicated old man shuffled a broom around in one corner. Other than him, he and Gary were alone.

"Psst." He knelt down beside Gary.

Gary's plate was still full as he tried navigating a trembling fork into his open mouth.

"Jesus man," Declan reached out and steadied the fork. "You're gonna take out an eye."

Gary turned and looked up at Declan. Bits of corn and meatloaf clung to the corners of his mouth. He chewed a mouthful of food and said, "Thanks."

"No problem." Declan drummed his fingers on the tabletop and wondered how to broach the subject.

Gary dropped his fork. It landed with a crash and he jumped. "Jesus," Gary whispered, running a shaky hand through his greasy, gray hair.

Deciding to be blunt, Declan blurted, "Did you get it?"

Gary picked up his fork and managed to spear a chunk of hamburger with it. The meat hung on the tine precariously as it bounced its way into his mouth.

"Well?"

Gary put his fork down and stared at Declan. The whites of his eyes were yellow, with little red veins running through them. But that wasn't the worst of it. Gary was yellow. Piss-colored yellow.

Declan backed up a step wondering if Gary was contagious.

Gary wiped his mouth with one hand and then rubbed it on his leg. He covered his mouth and let out a loud belch. Talking to no one in particular, he said, "That's better."

"Did you get into the safe?"

"I'm hungry." Gary lowered his head and picked up his fork to start the tortuous process all over again.

Declan glanced at the clock. Three minutes. What the fuck. "Here," he said, taking Gary's fork from his trembling grip. "Let me help you."

Gary opened his mouth.

Declan reined in his anger. What he really wanted to do was shove the fork down Gary's throat. Instead, Declan scooped up a lump of mashed potatoes and jammed them into Gary's mouth. He bent next to Gary's ear and whispered. "We've got about one minute until Tom is gonna come lookin' for us. If we do this right, we can get out of here tonight, but first I gotta know. Did. You. Get. In. The. Safe?"

Gary smacked his lips and pointed to his plate.

Declan reloaded the fork and let it hover near Gary's open mouth. "Well?" he insisted.

Gary rolled his eyes and huffed. "Yeah, I got in."

"Shit! Really?" Declan scooped a forkful of food into Gary's mouth and thought fast.

Gary gagged and pushed his hand away.

Declan removed the fork and patted Gary's back. "Sorry," he mumbled, thinking it served the pathetic old bugger right.

Declan wondered how much dough Gary had scored. What would his cut be? Seeing's how Declan hadn't actually watched the door, maybe Gary wasn't planning on giving him any. He glanced at Gary hoping to read his thoughts.

Big beads of sweat gathered on Gary's forehead. He moaned and clutched his stomach. "I think I'm gonna be sick."

He wrung his hands, wondering if he should punch Gary in the head, steal his wallet, and run—or help him to the infirmary.

Fast approaching footsteps solved the problem for him. "Come on," he leaned over Gary to help him stand. "Let's go and find the nurse."

"One minute!" Lite-bright shouted from the hallway waving Declan's book in the air.

"Hey!" Declan shouted at Lite-bright. "I need a hand over here."

Gary hung onto his shoulder and stood up on wobbly legs.

"Just a sec," Declan warned. Gary hung on him, knocking him off balance. Declan staggered and righted himself. Gary turned to Declan. His eyelashes were encrusted in yellow gunk. He blinked his red eyes rapidly and coughed.

A gust of rotten old alcohol fumes blasted Declan in the face. He gagged and stared at Gary. "Where'd you get the booze?"

"Sssnot," Gary mumbled.

"Huh?"

"Sssnot," Gary repeated.

Lite-bright tossed the book onto the table. "Phew!" He shook his head and backed away.

What the hell? Declan stared at Gary, looking for pocket bulges. He must have a bottle hidden on him somewhere. His suit jacket hung open. His shirt pocket lay flat against his chest. Declan patted Gary's pockets, but didn't feel anything in them.

Lite-bright pointed an accusing finger at Gary. "You better not have drunk all our hand sanitizer again!"

"Hand sanitizer?" Declan gaped at Lite-bright. "What the fuck?"

"Yeah, it's pure alcohol. The shit gets you seriously wasted."

Jesus! Declan couldn't believe these two morons. Who the hell would drink hand sanitizer? He might have his own problems, but he was nowhere near as fucked up as these two.

Gary moaned into his shoulder. Declan's skin crawled. All he wanted to do was get the fuck out of here. Fuck the consequences. Fuck tomorrow. Fuck Gary and fuck Lite-bright.

Declan didn't give a shit anymore. "Gary, give me my money."

"What money?" Lite-bright asked.

Ignoring the question, Declan said, "Help me hold him up."

"You'll get your share," Gary slurred.

Lite-bright slung one of Gary's arms over his shoulder and turned to Declan. "What money?" he insisted.

"Shut the fuck up," Declan hissed.

"Okay, okay," Lite-bright mumbled. "Lighten up."

"Not another word!"

"Okay!"

"Help me get his wallet." Declan spun Gary around. "You hold him still."

"Um, I don't know…"

"Come on!" Declan's eyes narrowed. "Are you chicken?"

Gary struggled in his grasp, trying to pull away. Declan held him tighter.

Gary bit him on the shoulder.

"Ouch!" Declan screamed, throwing Gary to the floor.

He hit with a loud smack. He moaned once and then began to bounce. His head came up off the floor and slammed back down. His back arched up and flattened. His teeth chattered and then his eyes rolled back.

Lite-bright looked around wildly before whispering, "Aww jeez! We're fucked!"

Chapter **26**

"CHARLIE, I'M GOING OUT FOR A WHILE," DEE holered down the hallway, her purse slung over one arm as she stood by the door.

"Charlie?"

She stomped her foot and swore. She didn't have time for these stupid games. Torn, she hesitated. She wanted Charlie's reassurance she'd be welcomed back. Better yet, she wanted his house keys. Reaching down, she unstrapped her shoes. The six-inch heels were killer to walk in.

The only noise in the house was the kitchen clock. It beat a steady tick, tick, tick. Maybe the old guy was having a nap? Dee thought about crawling in bed with him. She'd give him the fuck of a lifetime and then ask him for money and his keys.

Determined to find him, she walked down the hallway and stopped outside his bedroom door. Placing her ear to the door, she listened, but all was quiet. Twisting the doorknob in her hand, the door swung wide. Standing in the doorway, she blinked. The room was dark and the curtains were drawn. Charlie's bed was neatly made. On the bedside table next to it was a large gold ornate picture frame. A picture of his deceased wife stared across the room at Dee. On the opposite bedside table was the big blue book she'd seen at the meeting. Beside it was a large silver cross.

Dee's shoulders sagged and she sighed. She felt relieved Charlie wasn't napping. It was weird, incestual even, to think about fucking him.

Backing out of the room, she closed the door behind her and yelled, "Charlie?" She took a left into the kitchen and found him sitting at the table.

He was dunking a tea bag into a round blue mug. He looked old with his head bowed, and his shoulders stooped.

Dee stared at him. The only indicator Charlie was awake was the up and down motion of his hand as he dipped the tea bag in and out of his steaming cup. "Charlie?" she repeated.

Pulling the teabag free, Charlie laid it beside his mug. It made a brown puddle around his cup. He frowned, looking at the mess, and then glanced up at her. Trying to be helpful, Dee grabbed the hand towel hanging from the fridge door and swiped at the puddle.

Charlie placed a gnarled hand over hers and shook his head. He stood up and grabbed the towel away from her. "Don't use that."

"Jesus," she huffed, feeling hurt. "I was just trying to help!"

He walked over to the sink and picked up the dish cloth. Charlie mumbled, "Don't get your knickers in a knot." After cleaning up his spill, he threw the wet dish cloth into the sink and turned to face her. "You know, I haven't said that since my wife died."

"Ah…" Dee trailed off. She hoped Charlie wasn't about to start rambling.

"She'd get so mad!" He grinned, looking right through her.

Tuning him out, Dee wondered if she should take another pill before she left. She scanned the kitchen looking for the bottle, but didn't see it.

"I never knew you could miss someone so badly." Charlie shook his head. His eyes were shiny as they met Dee's. "It's like she was part of me, you know? And now she's gone. You'd think with each year it'd get easier, but it doesn't. Don't ever let anyone tell you that time heals all wounds." Charlie shrugged and sat back down. He picked up his cup of tea and slurped from it.

While Charlie was busy with his tea, Dee began opening cupboard doors.

"I wasted so many years," he said into his cup. "Back when I was drinking, it was the bottle that came first, me second, and then her somewhere far behind."

The first cupboard she looked into held nothing but drinking glasses. The pills weren't in there. She closed the door and opened the one next to it.

Charlie didn't seem to notice, he was so engrossed in his story. "Do you know," he whispered, "I picked on her just to start a fight. I wanted the drink so bad, and she'd have nothing to do with it."

Dee murmured something she hoped sounded sympathetic and stared at the contents in the cupboard. Dinner plates, soup bowls, and salad plates. But no pills.

"I called her a nagging wife and worse." Charlie sounded like he was going to cry. She glanced over at him, but all she could see was his back.

Still talking into his teacup, he said, "I wonder why she never left me." Answering his own question, he said, "Most didn't in those days, I suppose."

Dee opened the next cupboard door.

"Back then, divorce was scandalous. Why, it would have been worse than my drinking!"

Canned goods, boxes of cereal, oatmeal, pasta and sauces, and canned vegetables. But no pill bottles. She wanted to scream.

"I even cheated on her once."

Dee froze.

Charlie cleared his throat and continued. "She never found out. I thought about telling her when I sobered up. Then my sponsor reminded me, we don't make amends if it's going to injure the person you're making them to."

He lost her. Dee bent down to look in the cupboard below the sink.

"For a long time, I wasn't sure if I was doing the right thing. Sometimes when we'd lay in bed at night, she'd reach for my hand. She'd say, Charlie, I love you to the moon and back. Then I'd get a big lump in my throat and that was a good thing. It kept me from talking."

The interior of the cupboard was darker than the ones above it. It took a moment for her eyes to adjust.

"I probably would have blown it if it wasn't for that lump. I felt like such a shmuck!" Charlie sighed.

Windex, dish soap, garbage bags, Lysol disinfectant aerosol spray, drain cleaner, and a roll of paper towels, but still no pills. Fuck!

"She would have stood by me for almost anything. And she did. But she wouldn't have stood by for that!"

Dee stood on tip-toes eyeing the top of the refrigerator.

"I don't know what I was thinking. Ha!" Charlie snorted. "That's the problem, I wasn't."

A thick layer of dust coated the top of Charlie's fridge. No pills there.

"Life is strange, you know. As you're living it, you don't appreciate it. I sure took my sweet lady for granted."

Dee opened the oven door.

"I'd give everything I owned to have her back in my arms again."

It looked new, or clean. Maybe Charlie was a clean freak. Whatever he was, he wasn't hiding the pills there.

Charlie whistled off-tune. She thought it was his rendition of "I only have eyes for you." The melody was haunting and sad and it moved her. Straightening up, Dee stared at Charlie's back.

Maybe she should just ask him? With no other cupboards to look in, Dee walked around the table to face him. His eyes were closed. His cheeks puffed as he blew out air. She gripped the back of the chair, preparing to interrupt him mid-whistle, when his eyes snapped open.

A sly smile broke out over his wrinkled face. Charlie reached into his trouser pocket. She took a step back. He fished around in his pocket before holding his hand in front of her face and shaking it at her.

Dee eyed the pill bottle she'd been so desperately seeking.

"Is this what you're looking for?" Charlie asked smugly.

Chapter **27**

LYNDSEY SIDE-STEPPED THE TOYS AND BITS OF colored paper scattered over the carpet. Billy was curled up on a tiny Spiderman couch, engrossed in a movie. A little girl and boy near him were playing tug-of-war with a Barbie doll. Barbie was losing.

She knelt down beside Billy and ruffled his hair. "Hello, kiddo."

Billy scrunched up his face and frowned, but his eyes never left the TV.

Lyndsey frowned too. Her stomach sunk. It was going to be another one of those days. Billy didn't do well with change. It was helpful to give five minute warnings. "Billy, we need to go home now."

His lip thrust out farther. He shook his head no.

Eyeing Billy, she thought fast. It was crazy. When it came to a room full of drunks, she knew exactly what to do. Why then did she feel so clueless with this child? She glanced at the television. A green turtle was being chased by a dragon. She had an idea. Sitting down next to Billy, she wrapped her arm around him and pulled him close. Poking his side, she tickled him. Maybe she could distract him from the TV?

But Billy wasn't having it. He stiffened in her arms and pushed her away. "Stop!" he insisted.

She let him go of him immediately. Scooting as far from her on the tiny couch as he could get, his message was clear.

Wow! She really sucked when it came to raising kids! There must be a better way to do this, but damned if she could think of one. It crossed her mind to pick him up and drag him from daycare, kicking and screaming. But no, it would only make him distrust her even more.

A sharp scream rang in the air. The little girl who'd been playing tug-of-war with the Barbie came racing past. Her eyes wide, she held Barbie's dangling head in her hands. The little boy held what was left of the doll in his.

"He killed Barbie!" she said, pointing to the little boy and waving the doll's head in front of her.

Billy jumped up off the couch and awkwardly put his arms around the child, but she refused to be consoled and pushed him away. Landing on his butt, Billy glared up at her.

Lyndsey wondered if she should intervene, but decided against it.

Billy scrunched his forehead, pointed at the little girl and said, "Bad." Wearing a big frown and a nasty attitude, he got up and walked over to the little boy. Eyeing the doll's body, he yanked the rest of Barbie from his hands. The little boy wasn't about to give up his toy so easily. They were wrestling back and forth when Billy leaned over and bit the child on the arm.

Lyndsey jumped up from the couch and ran to Billy. "No Billy, stop!"

Billy had his teeth sunk into the little boy's arm the way a dog might with his favorite toy. The child's eyes grew huge and he screamed. His face turned purple.

Panicking, she grabbed for Billy. "Let go!" she yelled. But Billy was in another world.

As carefully as she could, Lyndsey took the little boy's arm and pried it from Billy's mouth. The child was hysterical. She scooped him up, forgetting about Billy for the moment.

Running to find the daycare worker and a first aid kit, she glanced down. The skin on the child's forearm was broken, and branded on it was a perfect impression of Billy's teeth.

"Corrie," she yelled, wondering where the hell she was.

"Coming," Corrie yelled back from the top of the stairs.

Lyndsey cooed to the little boy in her arms. He was sweaty and shaking, and crying inconsolably.

"What's all the fuss?" Corrie's eyes went wide seeing the child in Lyndsey's arms.

Lyndsey rocked the little boy and looked at Corrie. "We need Polysporin and bandages."

Corrie turned and raced back up the stairs without saying another word. Lyndsey glanced over at Billy. He was playing with Barbie pieces. The little girl was on the opposite side of the room, looking like she might cry.

First-aid kit in hand, Corrie flew back down the stairs and reached for the little boy. "Come here, Darnell."

Lyndsey gave him to Corrie and opened the kit. Corrie hunkered down and sat cross-legged on the carpet with Darnell in her arms. She picked out a bottle of peroxide and sat down next to Corrie.

"How did this happen?" Corrie asked, nodding at the bite on the child's arm.

Dousing a sterile gauze pad in the antiseptic, Lyndsey dabbed at the bite and shrugged. "Billy bit him."

Darnell pulled his arm away and screamed louder. "Shush. You're okay, honey," Lyndsey assured him. "It won't hurt, it's just cold."

Corrie's nostrils flared. "I can see that Billy bit him!" Her eyes rolled as she looked at the welt. "But why?"

"I think he wanted the Barbie. I'm not sure. He might have been trying to help. Billy has, um, issues."

"I know he has issues." Corrie's eyes wandered over to Billy.

"I'm not making excuses for him," Lyndsey said. "This type of behavior is not okay."

Corrie nodded. Her body language said duh! But she didn't say it. Instead she said, "You're right, it's not."

Screwing the lid down tight on the peroxide, Lyndsey peeled a bandage and placed it on Darnell's arm. She smiled a weak grin at him and said, "All better!"

Darnell hid his head in Corrie's blouse.

Corrie frowned. "No Lyndsey, it's not all better."

Dread squeezed Lyndsey's throat. She swallowed, fighting the feeling of shame she carried to this day. No matter how much work she did on herself, there were times when she felt small and insignificant. Bad, even.

Wishing she could just go to back to bed and pull the covers up, she stood. Glancing at Billy, she hoped to assure Corrie. "He's seeing a play therapist. He's getting help. If you knew his story, you'd understand…" She trailed off, realizing she was only making more excuses.

Corrie shook her head and touched the bandage on Darnell's arm. "What am I supposed to say to his mother?"

"I'm not sure." Lyndsey bit her lip. "Do you want me to tell her?"

Darnell poked his head out from under Corrie's arm. He looked over at Billy. "Bad boy!" he scolded.

No, he's not, Lyndsey thought. *He's troubled, not bad.* She stared over at Billy. He grunted with effort as he tried to push Barbie's head back onto her body.

Determined to put an end to this and hoping to make it up to Darnell, Lyndsey marched over and took the Barbie from Billy. He opened his mouth wide, getting ready to throw a tantrum. "Let me fix it," she said, stopping the tantrum dead in its tracks.

Billy pushed a thumb into his mouth and waited. Grasping the doll tightly, she twisted Barbie's head onto her neck. The head connected to the rest of the body with a pop. Billy's face lit up and his arms shot out.

"No." She shook her head and took his hand. Marching Billy over to Darnell, she said, "Darnell's turn."

Corrie put Darnell down. He took a small step forward, still unsure. Looking at Billy, she explained. "You have to share."

Lyndsey tensed as Corrie handed the Barbie to Darnell, but he just hugged the Barbie tightly and walked away.

Corrie smiled. "Well then, that wasn't so—" she broke off. Billy launched at Corrie and attached himself to her leg. Lyndsey stood frozen to the ground as the scene played out in slow motion.

"Ow!" Corrie yelped as Billy bit her.

Finally, her brain told her body to move. Lyndsey reached down and stuck her hand in Billy's mouth. Careful not to gouge Corrie with her nails, she applied pressure to Billy's gums. She succeeded in breaking his hold on Carrie's leg, only to have him bite her on the hand. "Billy!" she screamed. Son of a bitch, it hurt!

Billy let go of her hand. He dropped to the ground and rolled up into a tight ball.

Corrie pulled up her jeans and inspected her calf. The skin was still intact. She looked worriedly at Lyndsey and whispered, "Something's very wrong with him. He's not right. That child needs serious help."

Eyeing the teeth prints in the back of her hand, Lyndsey nodded grimly and whispered back, "You're right. He does."

Chapter 28

Tom glowered at him from across the desk. "Well?"

Declan stared at the floor. The carpet was dirty. Rusty colored coffee spills, he imagined. His mind spun. He couldn't believe this shit. A fuckin' piss test! And all because of Gary. He hoped the old bastard was happy.

Gary had still been bouncing on the floor when Tom had come in and called for Pete. They'd whisked Gary off to see the nurse and when Tom had returned, Declan had been called into this little meeting. Now Tom was accusing him of drinking hand sanitizer too. Jesus!

"I'm not playin' with you, son," Tom stated.

"I already told you." Declan glared at Tom. "I didn't drink hand sanitizer. I'm not an alcoholic, if that's what you think!"

Tom smirked and rolled his eyes. "Yeah, excuse me for not buying your story. You know how I know you're lying?"

"I'm not lying!" He met Tom's eyes, but felt weirdly guilty when he said it. Even though he was innocent of drinking hand sanitizer, Declan couldn't hold eye contact, and looked down at the floor. Curiosity got the better of him and he mumbled, "How?"

"Well," Tom chortled, and slapped his knee, "because your lips were moving!"

Declan bit his tongue. What he wanted to say would only make things worse. He fantasized about jumping up and punching Tom right between the eyes. But he didn't do it. Instead, he leaned an elbow on one knee and thought fast.

"It's either take the urine test, or go back to jail. The choice is yours. You have one minute to decide."

Declan sure as shit wasn't going back to jail. Trouble was, he didn't want to take the piss test either. He'd heard guys talking about them. How a staff member had to go into the pisser with you to watch while you did your business. The thought of one of these bozos watching him made his skin crawl.

Tom stared at his watch. Jesus! The fucker was timing him!

"Can I ask you a question?"

Tom snorted and tapped his watch. "You better talk fast!"

"How, um…" Declan trailed off, not exactly sure how to put it.

"Spit it out!"

He sat up straighter, and his face grew warm. Christ, he was blushing! "How do you do it? I mean, I've never been tested before."

"Yeah," Tom chortled, "well, nothing like a new experience, now is there?"

"I know but—"

"Listen kid," Tom interrupted. "You gonna pee or not?"

Christ, Declan wasn't even sure he could take a piss in front of this guy! Tom picked up the phone.

"Okay! Okay, relax will ya? I'll take the test."

Tom smiled. "Good choice."

"Now will you answer my question?"

Tom rolled his neck. It made popping sounds. Declan stared at him, waiting.

"Yeah, I guess." Tom nodded.

"So, as I was saying, I've never had this test before. What happens if I can't pee?"

Tom laughed. "Oh, you'll pee."

Declan scratched his head. "How? What if I don't have to?"

Tom glanced at his watch again. He got the feeling Tom was a busy guy. That might just work to his benefit. Busy guys were also easily distracted.

"Look," Tom barked, the earlier laughter fading from his face. "It's not rocket science. You drink water until you gotta go."

"Oh?" Declan stalled. Maybe he could get to Gary first. Find a way to get the cash and ditch Tom.

Tom stood and jerked a thumb at the door. "Let's get this over with."

Declan stood up. He was shorter than Tom by about six inches. He didn't like looking up at him, but did it anyways. "Where should I meet you?"

Tom frowned. "Meet me? What do you mean?"

"I need to go to my room first. Where should I meet you for this test?"

"Ha!" Tom's brow crinkled. "You're not meeting me anywhere. You're not leaving my sight until you've peed. Jesus," he mumbled. "Do you think I was born yesterday?"

"Oh, well I thought…"

"Yeah!" Tom chuckled. "That's the problem. You're thinking again!"

"But I..."

Tom cut him off. "No buts! Now follow me."

Declan's mind raced trying to come up with another tactic, but he drew a blank.

Tom marched over to the door and jerked it open with unnecessary force. He held it wide. "Comin?"

"Yeah," Declan mumbled and followed him through the door.

He followed Tom down the hallway and into the common area. Pete sat behind the front desk, flipping through a small magazine titled Grapevine. Declan craned his neck but he couldn't see Gary anywhere. Good. Hopefully they'd sent him back to bed. One way or another, he was going to find where he'd stashed the money.

"Pete!" Tom hollered.

Pete looked up and threw the magazine down on the counter before him. "Yes boss!"

"Pete," Tom pointed a finger at him. "I don't like it when you call me that!"

Declan caught Pete's smirk. This place was nuts! The staff was crazier than the clientele!

"Whatcha need?" Pete asked, suddenly cooperative.

Tom pointed to the chair and said to Declan, "Sit."

Turning back to Pete, Tom said, "We need a urinalysis on Declan here."

Jeez, why don't you let everyone know! Declan glanced around the room. The three guys who'd been concentrating on some kind of paperwork gawked at him.

Declan wagged his middle finger at them and mouthed, "Fuck off."

"Who's gonna do it?" Pete asked Tom.

"You are."

"I did the last one!" Pete complained.

Tom shook his head at Pete.

Pete scooped up the plastic pouch and mumbled, "Fine!"

Grinning, Pete leered at Declan. "It's your lucky day!" He waved the plastic pouch at him and said, "Follow me."

The staff bathroom wasn't any fancier than the rest of the building. It was small. There was barely enough room for the two of them in it. A toilet and sink took up most of the room. A paper towel dispenser hung on the wall across from it. A Dixie cup dispenser was next to it. The mirror over the sink was cracked and the room smelled like mould. Declan sneezed.

"What's the matter, are your allergies acting up?" Pete asked, making conversation as he tore open the plastic pouch.

Rather than rub up against Pete, Declan sat on the toilet. He watched Pete pull out a clear small plastic cup and a little box from inside the plastic pouch.

Then Pete pulled a cardboard dip-stick from the box, which he placed on the sink's ledge. He twisted the cap off the plastic cup and placed it beside the dip-stick. Reaching into his back pocket, he pulled out a pair of latex gloves.

Snapping on the gloves, Pete thrust the plastic cup at him.

"Whoa!" Declan stared at the plastic gloves. "What are those for?"

"Relax," Pete shook the plastic cup. "Getting urine on me isn't part of my job description, although it does happen…" Pete trailed off and waggled his hands. "That's why I wear these."

Relieved to know the gloves wouldn't be used on him, Declan grabbed for the plastic cup. "Can you step outside please?"

"Why sure, of course!" Pete grinned, opening the door and then slammed it shut. The grin slid from his face. "Are you kidding me?" He pointed a latex sheathed finger. "I'm not going anywhere. I'm going to watch you like a hawk!"

"Yeah, well, you'll get a bird's eye view in this space!" Declan retorted, pulling his zipper down. He positioned himself in front of the toilet and placed the cup under his limp dick.

He strained, hoping for a trickle. Nothing.

Pete didn't help matters by complaining. "Come on, we haven't got all day."

Declan stared at the toilet water below and focused. The pressure in his lower abdomen said he was ready. He strained again. Nothing. Fuck!

"Here." Pete tapped him on the back.

He took the Dixie cup from Pete and filled it to the brim. He chugged it down and refilled it. The water was warm. It tasted nasty. He drank the second cup and crumpled the empty container in his hand.

"Try again," Pete urged, taking the mangled Dixie cup from him.

The wall in front of him bore a tiny heart-shaped rust spot. He stared at it and tried to relax. Inserting his penis into the cup, he made his mind go blank. Pressure built up. This time his bladder let go. As instructed, he pulled out mid-stream. Pulling up his zipper, he thrust the warm cup at Pete. "Here."

With a gloved hand, Pete carefully twisted the lid on. He didn't spill a drop. He waved at the bathroom door. "Go wait at the front desk."

"No," Declan shook his head. "I want to watch you make an asshole of yourself when you see it's clean."

Pete placed the plastic cup on the back of the toilet tank and studied him. "You're not very smart, are you, kid?"

"Yeah, well at least I'm not testing piss for a living!"

"Oh yeah?" Pete snorted. "You think you're better than me? What's it like not having Mommy here to fight your battles?"

"She doesn't—" Declan broke off. It was stupid wasting time with Pete when he could be talking to Gary.

"Whatever kid." Pete shrugged and picked up the plastic cup. He swung the bathroom door wide and followed Pete, wondering what would happen next.

Chapter 29

DEE LUNGED ACROSS THE TABLE AND GRABBED Charlie by his forearm. She wrestled his arm into her side. Damn! Charlie might be thin, but he wasn't frail. "Give them to me!" she screamed in his face. With both hands she tried prying Charlie's fingers apart.

It was no easy task. Charlie's bony fingers were like steel. No way could she move them. Rage burned the back of her throat. She needed the pills, now! With one hand still trying to pry open Charlie's fist, she reached back, and with as much force as she could muster, punched him in the arm.

Charlie's eyes widened. He sprang up from his chair and shoved her hard.

Landing on the floor, tears filled Dee's eyes. The old bastard was a lot tougher than he looked!

Charlie shoved the pills into his trouser pocket and frowned. He shook his head. "If you hit me again," he wagged a long twisted finger in front of her nose, "you're gone."

Using the floor as leverage, Dee got to her feet. Her backside hurt. She hoped it wasn't bruised. Eyeing Charlie, she wondered if she wasn't better off back on the street.

"I know you're hurting," Charlie's face softened. "But your behavior is inexcusable."

Nausea kicked in and Dee grimaced. If she didn't get something in her soon, she'd be puking all over Charlie's nice, shiny floor.

"You need to learn to ask, rather than take." Charlie lectured as he pulled a glass from the cupboard and filled it with water. He sat the glass down on the kitchen table and looked at her. "You're not an animal, Dee, so stop acting like one."

A cramp twisted her bowel. Dee broke out in a sweat. Shit! She'd waited too long! A moan escaped her lips as she grabbed the back of the chair, trying to stand.

"Here," Charlie said, putting his arm around her. "Let me help you."

Gratefully, she sank into the chair Charlie held out. Icy shivers ran down her back. Her jaw locked.

"I probably should have given you these sooner."

The rattle of the pill bottle was music to Dee's ears. Her mouth watered. She thought about snorting them. They'd work faster that way. She'd much rather shoot them, but she didn't think Charlie would go for it.

"I suppose," Charlie's hand appeared before her face, "I'm somewhat responsible for the state you're in. I'm afraid I forget. It's been a long time since I've felt dope sick."

Charlie held two peach colored tablets shaped like a stop sign in the palm of his hand. Dee scooped them up before he could change his mind. "Do you have a razor blade?" she asked, ignoring the glass of water in front of her.

"A razor blade?" Charlie repeated, scratching his head. "Why do you need a razor blade? You're not thinking of doing something foolish, are you?"

"I wasn't thinking of slashing my wrists, if that's what you mean." Dee touched the tablets lovingly and then put them down. She was already feeling better. "Oh, and I'll need a straw."

"A straw?"

"Yeah," Dee met Charlie's eyes. "You know, like the kind you drink out of."

Charlie's eyes widened. "You want to snort them!"

A smile curled her lip. "Now you're catchin' on, Charlie."

"Jeez," Charlie shook his head. He pulled the pill bottle from his trousers and thrust it in her face. "Do you see anything written on this bottle that says to snort your medication?"

"Calm down," she replied, noting his bulging eyes.

"It says," he jerked a thumb at the small print on the label, "To take the tablets orally."

Dee smiled. "Now you're talkin!"

Charlie fiddled with a button on his cardigan. She caught the blush on his cheeks.

"Charlie," she wheedled, "no offense to doctors, but they don't know what they're talking about. If I chop this up and snort it, it's gonna work a lot faster."

Charlie took a deep breath. "I'm not going to give you a straw or a razor blade. If you want to take them, you'll need to follow doctor's orders."

Her bottom lip thrust out. "You're such a party pooper!"

"And you're…" He trailed off staring over her head. "Sick," he finished.

Play time was over. Dee tossed both pills into her mouth and chased them down with water. She glanced at the clock on the wall. Twenty minutes. She'd wait another twenty minutes and then she was getting the hell out of here.

With a quick trick or two, she'd find something a hell of a lot better than these pills. An image of black tar heroin came to mind. She'd shoot just enough to go back out. She figured she could probably pull off four dates. Living at Charlie's place, she didn't need to worry about food or rent money. This time, she was going to make some serious coin. This time, things would be different!

"Miriam's coming over," Charlie said. "She's going to get you started on step one."

Ignoring him, Dee did the math. Four tricks would get her two hundred bucks. That should buy enough H to last a couple of days if she was careful.

"Before you can get well, you need to understand you're sick," Charlie murmured in the background.

"Hmm," she said, not really listening. Of course, if she was lucky, she might be able to pull off five tricks. It would be easier if she had her own place. She wondered if she could bring the johns here. Maybe she could slip sleeping pills into Charlie's tea?

"Just so you know, step one isn't something you can learn overnight. It took me a good year to understand what it really meant."

What a great idea! Why hadn't she thought of it before? With Charlie conked out, she could bring as many tricks over as she wanted. It sure beat the hell out of a car or back alleyway!

"You'll probably get hung up on the alcohol thing. Step one says, "We admitted we were powerless over alcohol."" Charlie poked her in the arm. "Are you listening to me?"

"Uh huh." Dee met his gaze.

"Good." Charlie thought for a moment. "Just replace the word alcohol with heroin. It will make more sense to you that way."

"Okay," she said, playing along. She didn't have a clue what he was blabbering on about.

"Of course you shouldn't say it out loud. Heroin, I mean." Charlie pushed the skin down on a cuticle. "It's a respect thing. In AA you talk about alcohol, not drugs. Personally, I don't care, but we don't want to get anyone riled up."

"Hmm." Dee glanced up at the clock. Almost time. She'd have to hit the drugstore tonight. She'd see what she could find for old Charlie boy. She grinned. Sweet dreams, Charlie Brown!

"Oh, and there's one other thing." Charlie reached into his shirt pocket and pulled out his phone.

Maybe she could find something on the street that was stronger than sleep medication? She'd have to ask Doc. He'd know.

Charlie squinted at his phone and punched in numbers.

Seeing how Charlie was distracted with the phone, Dee decided it was time to go. "Uh, Charlie, I have an errand to run..." She never got to finish her sentence.

Charlie shook his head and held up a finger. Wait. A woman's voice answered.

The hair on the back of her neck stood up. Oh my god, it was Lyndsey!

Charlie thrust the phone at her. "Talk to your son," he growled.

Chapter **30**

Lyndsey's head felt like it would explode. Her shoulders ached from being bunched so tight. She rubbed her temple and blew out a breath she didn't know she was holding.

Fuck!

This was a day from hell! She unstrapped Billy from his car seat and pulled him from the car. Using her foot, she kicked the car door closed and headed for the house. Billy was doing his stiff, board-like imitation with his eyes scrunched closed. She wondered for the hundredth time what went on in his mind when he got like this.

A sharp bark of laughter came from her mouth. She shook her head. What the hell had she been thinking, bringing Billy home to live with them?

Should she tell Drake about Billy's biting episodes? Would Billy even be welcome back to daycare? She'd have to tell him something.

Stepping inside the front door, Lyndsey put Billy down and yelled, "We're home!"

Billy sat down and crab-scooted along the floor. He reached the kitchen table and disappeared under it.

Lyndsey got down on all fours and peeked in on him. Billy had his arms locked around his knees. When he saw her, he growled.

She backed up, hoping he just needed some space and said, "You can come out when you're ready to."

"Prick, prick," Billy replied.

Her eyebrows shot up. She stared at him wondering if she'd heard him right.

"Trucking prick," he whispered and pinched his forearm. Big white welts sprung up on his arm wherever he pinched.

"Uh, uh." Lyndsey reached in to stop him. "Don't honey," she soothed. "You'll hurt yourself."

Billy jerked his arm away from her. He scooted farther back under the table, out of reach. His message was clear. Get away from me!

Not sure what to do, she hesitated. Should she yank him out from under the table? Should she just leave him there? Was it too late to give him back?

Dear God! Lyndsey blinked back the tears she'd been holding in all day. She couldn't remember feeling this overwhelmed in a long time. Deciding for the moment at least that Billy was okay, she went to find Drake.

Stopping in the hallway to straighten a picture, she heard his muffled voice coming from the bathroom door. She poked her head inside and stopped.

Drake leaned against the bathroom counter. He held up one finger and spoke into the phone. "I'm not cutting anymore from the building. You're nickel and diming me to death!"

She noted his brows knitted together and his wrinkled nose. A sure sign that he was pissed.

"No!" Drake barked, stabbing a finger into the air. "You're not listening to me!"

186

Closing the lid on the toilet, Lyndsey sat down. Might as well get comfortable. By the sounds of Drake's conversation, she could be there for a while.

Whoever Drake was talking to was loud. She could hear the man talking from where she sat.

Drake pulled the phone from his ear and rolled his eyes at her. "Look," he said, "We have a contract. I'm not changing it. If you can't honor it, I'll pull my guys off the job."

A dust bunny caught her attention. The floor needed washing. Lyndsey grabbed a hunk of toilet paper, dipped it in the toilet, and got down on her knees.

"I don't care what you say. I stand by our original contract. Take it or leave it."

She pulled more sheets from the roll and cleaned the area around the toilet. A brown muscled forearm reached down and stopped her.

Drake looked down at her. "I gotta go," he said and hung up.

His big brown eyes met hers. "What's wrong?" he asked, thumbing a tear from Lyndsey's cheek.

Susan's son, Lyndsey's ex-boyfriend, aka HIM, and the little boy that Billy had bitten, all jumbled together in her mind. Lyndsey blurted out, "Everything!"

Drake took the soggy paper from Lyndsey's hands and flushed it down the toilet. He wrapped his arm around her, steering out of the bathroom. "Let's talk," he said, and opened their bedroom door.

"I should check on Billy." She tried pulling away from him, but he held her in place.

He nudged her down on the bed and pulled up a chair beside her. "Billy's fine." His eyes narrowed. "Now what's up?"

What could she say? That she thought she saw HIM today and wondered if Susan's son was hers? Or that Billy almost chewed a kid's arm off? How about the fact she regretted taking Billy and wanted to give him back? Drake folded his arms across his chest and waited for her to talk.

Stalling for time, Lyndsey asked, "Who was on the phone?"

He shook his head. "It doesn't matter. Why were you crying?"

She shrugged and tried to smile. "I think I'm just tired."

"No," he shook his head. "It's more than that."

"I must be getting my period, I'm overly emotional." Lyndsey stared at the brown carpet below her feet. It needed a good vacuum. She fought the urge to bolt from the bed. There was something to be said about vacuuming. It drowned out the noise in her head. Even weirder, she found comfort in the neat lines it left behind.

Drake sighed. "Would you talk to me, please?"

She raised her head and met his eyes. "It's…g" she broke off and swallowed. Drake's love not only moved her, it made her feel unworthy. She still struggled with those feelings, especially when she felt like this.

"Um…" She shook her head.

"Linds, come on, you're starting to scare me!"

God, she was such an ass! Drake had been right. They should never have taken Billy on. She bit her lip. "You were right."

"Huh?"

She fingered a loose thread on the bed cover and rolled it underneath her thumb. "I mean about Billy," Lyndsey whispered.

"What about Billy?" Drake was clearly perplexed.

"He, ah, bit a kid at daycare. I don't think they'll take him back."

"He bit a kid?" Drake scratched his head. "How bad?"

"Bad!" She reached for Drake's calloused hand. "The poor little boy was sobbing."

"Jesus!" Drake shook his head. "They're not gonna sue us, are they?"

"No…" Lyndsey trailed off because honestly, it hadn't occurred to her that they might. "At least I don't think so."

"Was the kid bleeding?"

"No, but Billy bit him hard. I could see tooth prints in the little boys arm."

"At least he didn't break the skin." Drake swallowed. "I don't think they'll sue us. Not if he wasn't bleeding."

Lyndsey rubbed her arm and stuck it in Drake's face. "The little boy wasn't the only one Billy bit today."

"What?" Drake shot her a sideways look and touched her arm. He ran his fingers over the welts made by Billy's teeth. "That must have hurt!"

"It did," she admitted. "I've been thinking."

Drake groaned. She poked him before saying. "I think you were right."

"About?"

"About Billy." Lyndsey rolled her eyes at the door. "I think I made a huge mistake bringing him to live with us."

Drake got up from the chair and sat down beside her on the bed. He wrapped a flannel clad arm around her shoulders and whispered in her ear. "You don't know how badly I wanted to hear you say that."

Irritated, she cut him off. "I don't need you to rub it in my face!"

He smiled. "I'm not. Really Linds," he repeated, seeing the spark in her eye. "You didn't let me finish. What I was saying is, you don't know how badly I wanted to hear you say that in the beginning. Back when we first got Billy. Now I've grown to love the little guy."

"Oh?" Anger drained away to be replaced with exhaustion. Her shoulders slumped.

Drake rubbed her drooping shoulders and said, "Don't worry, we'll get through this."

"Yeah," Lyndsey snorted. "Well, one of us might have to stay home from work tomorrow and it can't be me."

Drake shrugged and grinned at her. "Maybe it's time Billy learned how to swing a hammer."

"Really, you'll look after him?"

"We'll figure something out. Compared to what we've gone through, this is nothing!"

Lyndsey grinned at him, feeling better. "You're right. We've been through far worse than this."

The phone chirped beside the bed. Drake frowned and looked at her. "I better get it. I've got some scheduling to figure out."

She shook her head. "No Hon, it's okay. Let me get it. It's probably Jan anyways." Lyndsey picked up the phone before he could, still smiling.

Her eyes widened as the smile slid from her lips. She covered the phone and mouthed, "It's Dee."

Chapter **31**

LITE-BRIGHT PICKED AT A PIMPLE ON HIS CHEEK AND whispered, "Is it gonna come back clean?"

Declan elbowed him under the counter and frowned. "Of course it's gonna come back clean," he hissed.

Tom dropped his pen on the desk and frowned. "Knock it off," he said to Lite-bright. "Go to the bathroom to do that." He shook his head and muttered, "Jeez! Some people's kids!"

Pete poked his head through the door. He glanced at Declan and said, "Tom, I need you to see this."

Tom sighed and pushed his chair away from the desk. He got up and pointed a finger at Declan. "Stay put!"

When Tom and Pete had left the room, Declan turned to Lite-bright. "Where's Gary?"

"Gary?" Lite-bright repeated, studying the gore hanging from the end of his finger.

Declan kicked him in his shin. His eyes went wide. "Ow! That hurt! What did you do that for?"

"Because," Declan spit out, "You're acting like a disgusting pig!"

"I… I…" Lite-bright stuttered.

"Look," Declan said, meeting his eyes. "I'm sorry I kicked you, but you were grossing me out."

Lite-bright wiped his finger on his leg, looking like he might cry.

Declan smoothed it over by saying. "I need your help."

Lite-bright blinked rapidly and swallowed. "You hurt me."

Fighting the urge to reach over and strangle this weirdo by the throat, Declan shrugged. "Like I said, I'm sorry. Now will you help me or not?"

Lite-bright appeared to be considering it.

Declan glanced over at the door. "Come on. We have to hurry. They'll be back any minute!"

Lite-bright reached for an unpicked pimple on his cheek and stopped. He dropped his hand back into his lap and nodded. "Okay," he agreed. "What do you need?"

"Atta boy." Declan grinned at him, and then got serious. "I need you to find Gary. Don't say anything to him when you do. Just come back and tell me where he is."

"Why do you want Gary?"

"I'll explain it later." Declan nudged him. "Hurry, go before they get back."

Lite-bright stood up and quickly scurried away. Declan glanced over at the pile of papers Tom had been signing. Curious, he picked one up and studied it. CARF Accreditation -- Step by Step. The words blurred before his eyes. He read a few lines, but the document was boring as hell.

Tossing the paper back onto the desk, he glanced around. Two guys sat in front of a muted TV, staring at the picture screen. A hockey game was on. Why didn't they turn the sound up? It was like going to a concert and wearing ear plugs. What was the point?

Further down the hallway, he could see Lite-bright open a door wide and peer into a room. He turned and caught Declan's stare. He shook his head and jerked a thumb at the ground.

Declan made shooing motions with his hands, hoping Lite-bright would catch on. Tom and Pete would be back any minute now.

Lite-bright motioned okay and returned his attention to the next door.

"Yeah!" The two guys on the couch jumped up and high-fived each other as their team scored, before settling back down again.

Declan lost sight of Lite-bright as he turned the corner. Just in time too. Tom and Pete strode across the room and reached the desk.

"You need to look through these," Tom said to Pete, pointing at the documents.

Pete shrugged. "It's all mumbo jumbo. I can't see the point. Why are we doing this?"

"You know why." Tom broke off as if just noticing Declan.

"Can I go now?" Declan asked the two of them.

Pete grinned, showing a row of yellowed teeth. "You're clear."

Getting up from his chair, Declan couldn't resist. "I told you so!"

Tom stopped shuffling the papers and frowned. "What? What did you tell us?"

"I told you I didn't drink hand sanitizer." Declan shook his head. "Jesus, do you guys really think I'm that messed up?"

"Yeah," Tom nodded. "We do."

Pete broke in. "You're no better than anyone else in this place, mister!"

Actually he was, Declan thought. He was a hell of a lot better than all of them. He wasn't anything like these guys. These dudes were chronic.

He wasn't. End of story. He stared at Pete and Tom, considering whether to argue the point.

Pete's cheeks puffed. "Just because your piss test—"

"Urine analysis," Tom said.

"Uh, right, urine analysis," Pete agreed and then continued. "Was clean doesn't mean you're less of an alcoholic than Gary is. When he was your age, he wasn't drinking hand sanitizer either."

Tom stroked his cheek and nodded. "That's right. Addiction is a chronic and progressive disease."

Disease? Why did they keep calling it that? It wasn't like Gary had cancer. These clowns didn't know jack shit!

"True," Pete said. "Hey Tom, do you remember what I was like when I first got here?"

Tom snorted and rolled his eyes. "Do I ever! You needed a straw to drink your coffee!"

"Yeah, and do you remember how sick I was? We didn't have all these cushy detox meds back then."

"Maybe it was a good thing. Personally, I think the meds make it too easy to forget." Tom scratched his head and glanced at Declan. "You know what I mean?"

"Yeah," Pete nodded. "I do. I'm not sure if I'da made it if I had it as easy as they do today."

Enough of this BS already! "Can I go now?" Declan asked, hoping to get away.

"I guess…" Tom trailed off and looked at Pete.

A round of groans erupted from the TV room. It looked like the hockey game was over.

Pete shrugged at Tom and gave Declan a sharp look. "We'll be watching you, kid," he warned.

That's good. Then watch me sail right on out of here. Of course, he didn't say it out loud. He feigned interest in the TV screen and backed away from the desk. Out of the corner of his eye, Declan spotted Lite-bright. He was waving furiously at him from across the hallway.

Chapter **32**

Dee glared at Charlie and snatched the phone from his fingers. Suddenly awkward, she stammered into the receiver, "Ah hi, ah Linds?"

"Dee?"

"Yeah, it's me."

"Jesus, Dee!" Lyndsey squealed. "Where are you?"

"I'm at Charlie's place."

"Charlie? Who's Charlie?"

"Um, you don't know him. He's an old guy." She glanced up at Charlie, wondering if she should have said that. He drummed his fingers on the tabletop, looking unaffected by her statement.

"Dee, is Charlie your pimp?"

"Ha!" Dee pulled the receiver from her ear and crowed. "Charlie, Lyndsey wants to know if you're my pimp!"

Charlie frowned and said quietly, "Finish your conversation."

"Dee? Are you there?"

"Yeah," Dee nodded and pressed the phone to her ear. "I'm here."

"Why are you calling me?"

"Well, I was thinking…" she trailed off.

"Yes?"

"I was ah, kinda wondering how Billy's doing."

"Well," Lyndsey blew into the phone. "He's adjusting."

"Adjusting?" Dee bit a fingernail and spat it out. "What does that mean?" A wet dish cloth landed on her lap. She glanced up. Charlie was staring at her, his arms folded tightly across his chest.

"Clean it up," he said, waving at her fingernail lying on the table.

"It means…" Lyndsey paused. "He's adjusting. Billy has issues. It's going to take a long time and a lot of therapy for him to get past all of this."

Swiping at the table, Dee frowned. "What'd you mean he has issues?"

"Wow, Dee! Are you serious?" Lyndsey's voice rose. "Do you remember your childhood?"

"Yeah…"

"Well, multiply that by a hundred!"

Dee squared her shoulders and sat up. "I'm not following you, Linds."

"Come on Dee! Billy has seen you tricking, for God's sake."

"No he hasn't! I only did it when he was asleep!"

"Yeah right, don't kid yourself! Billy is one messed up little boy!"

Hot tears gathered in Dee's eyes and she blinked. "I asked you to look after him while I was healing from getting beat up. I thought when I asked you that, he'd be safe. Is he?"

"He's safe, Dee. As safe as he can be."

"What do you mean?'

"I mean the damage Billy is facing isn't on the outside. I can keep him safe from exterior threats. It's his interior I worry about."

Dee rubbed her eyes with the dish cloth and set it down. Her head was pounding and her back ached. She covered the phone and looked at Charlie. "I need a pill."

Charlie shook his head. "You don't get the next one for another thirty minutes."

Something hot and sour rose in Dee's throat. She wanted to scream and throw the phone in Charlie's face. She did neither. Instead, she gripped the edge of the table so tightly her knuckles turned white. Think of Billy.

"Dee?" Lyndsey's voice jolted her from her thoughts.

"I'm here," she mumbled.

"Are you high?"

Dee laughed. "I wish!" she said.

"Look Dee, I don't have time for this right now. I gotta go."

Panic flared within her and she blurted, "Lyndsey, please! Don't hang up!"

"Okay," Lyndsey hesitated. "What do you want?"

"I want to talk to Billy."

"I need you to think about Billy. Just for a moment. Can you imagine how he must feel right now?"

Dee pictured Billy's dark, tousled hair. Her arms ached to hold him. She needed her baby! Why did bad things always happen to her? She shouldn't have given Billy to Lyndsey in the first place! What the hell had she been thinking? Angry and resentful, she spat out, "He's my kid, Linds. He's not yours. Now put him on the phone!"

"If I didn't know just how sick and pathetic you really are, I'd hang up on you." Lindsey's tone softened. "But I do know. I've been there. You're no good to Billy right now. Hell, you're no good to yourself! If you really care about Billy, get clean. Go to treatment. Get help!"

"I am getting help!" Dee screamed into the phone.

A long pause and then, "You are?"

"I am." Dee looked over at Charlie. "It's that old guy I was tellin' you about."

"Um, okay." Lyndsey didn't sound convinced. "How's he helping you?"

"I'm not really sure. He's giving me a roof over my head…"

Lyndsey broke in, "And what's that costing you?"

"Nothing," Dee paused. "Well, that's not true. I have to go to these dumb meetings with him every day." She laughed. "You should see them, Linds, a bunch of brainwashed people sitting in a circle and…"

Lyndsey interrupted. "Do you mean AA meetings?"

"Yeah," Dee shook her head. "I guess that's what they're called."

"Really? You're going to AA meetings with this Charlie guy?" Lyndsey snorted.

"Jeez, you don't have to act so surprised!"

"I am surprised. I'm not acting."

"Yeah, well, I don't see what all the fuss is about. It's just a bunch of dumb people sitting in a circle talking about their sorry lives."

"Dee, those dumb people are me. I go to meetings every week."

"Why would you do that? If Charlie wasn't making me, I sure as hell wouldn't go."

"I go because I need them. You know I'm clean. Where else am I going to hang out? When I first started going, I felt like you. I thought I was smarter than everyone in the room. I had nothing in common with those people." Lyndsey chuckled.

Dee smiled. "Do you remember the house parties we used to hang out at? Now that was fun!"

"Was it? You're forgetting. At one of those house parties, you were thrown out with the garbage. Your addiction has warped your mind. It's playing tricks on you. Your thinking is pathological."

Hairs on the back of Dee's neck stood up. She remembered the incident as if it was yesterday. She'd had way too much to drink and gone to bed with one guy, and woken up with another. But she hadn't been awake for long. After passing out a second time, she's woken up outside on top of the garbage.

"Seriously, Dee, how can you call what you're doing fun?"

"Well aren't you Miss High and Mighty!"

"You know what? If you can't talk to me with respect, then you can't talk to me, period. That's my last warning!"

A thick heaviness clogged Dee's throat. She longed to scratch out Lyndsey's eyes and hug her at the same time. She felt crazy. Sweat gathered above her top lip. She rubbed it away. God, she wanted her baby in the worst way! "Lyndsey, please," her voice broke. "I need to speak to Billy."

"Aww Dee, I feel for you."

She swiped at her nose and blinked back tears. Shit, she couldn't handle this. When someone was nice to her, it messed with her mind.

"I'm sorry, sweetie, I can't let you talk with Billy right now. It's too soon. But if you keep going to those meetings, I'm sure we can arrange something."

Dee's eyes widened and her nostrils flared. "Are you telling me I can't talk to my own fuckin' kid?"

"Jesus," Lyndsey whispered.

"Are you?"

"I'm telling you," Lyndsey paused, "that you can't talk to him right now. Go to a meeting. Call me tomorrow. If you're still sober, maybe we can work something out."

"Who the fuck—" The dial tone stopped her from finishing her sentence.

In disbelief, she stared at the phone. Noticing Dee was about to fling it across the room, Charlie reached over and plucked it from her fingers.

"Fuck!" she screamed. "What a bitch!" She jumped up and slung her purse over her shoulder.

There was only one person she wanted to see now. Doc. And she knew just where to find him. No more screwing around. She was done with Charlie and his group of morons.

Checking in her wallet, she fingered the one dollar bills. Ten dollars. It wasn't enough. Ready to do whatever it took to get high, she stared at Charlie and held out her hand. "I need some money."

"Okay," Charlie nodded.

Her eyebrows rose. Something wasn't right.

Charlie stood up and walked over to the sink. He reached into the cupboard and pulled out a glass. Filling it from the faucet, he placed it on the table and reached into his pocket. His eyes met hers as he twisted off the lid. "I don't carry money on me. We'll have to go to the bank machine. But first, it's time for your pill."

Suspicious, she snatched the pill from his outstretched hand. Not bothering with the glass of water, she chewed it between her teeth. The bitter taste made her wince.

Charlie smiled and said, "I hear it's like biting into an orange." He nudged the glass of water closer. "This will help."

Draining the glass in one swallow, she nodded. "Let's go."

Charlie picked up the glass and spoke into the air, "Oh, no problem at all, you're welcome!"

Heading out the door, she could almost taste it. Her nose ran in preparation. Knowing she was only minutes away from getting high was almost as good as the real thing. For the first time that day, she felt happy. Soon, all her troubles would be over.

Charlie smiled too. He, however, had a different plan.

Chapter 33

HOW DARE DEE COME ACROSS LIKE THAT! LYNDSEY paced back and forth in the darkness of their bedroom and seethed. Rubbing her ear, she thought back to their call. Had she done the right thing? Should she have let Dee speak to Billy?

Recalling the first time she'd seen Billy and the condition he was living in, Lyndsey didn't think so. Besides, it would be too hard on him. He wasn't old enough to understand any of this. Guilt churned in her belly as she chewed a thumbnail.

And seriously, was Dee really going to AA meetings? Oh my god! What if she'd just triggered her? Maybe she shouldn't have mentioned the party thing all those years ago. It was traumatic. Why had she even brought it up? Years of counselor training flew out the window. Anxious and unsure, Lyndsey went in search of Drake.

Halfway down the hallway she stopped. Oh Jesus… Billy! She ran to the kitchen and checked under the table. No Billy. She looked in the living room, but he wasn't there either. Flinging open Billy's door, she stopped. The room was dark, the shades pulled low. Billy lay in his bed, curled around his yellow blanket and stuffed duck.

A smile curled her lips. Thank God for Drake. By the looks of Billy's damp hair, he'd been bathed and put to bed. On tip-toes she backed out of the room, careful to shut the door quietly behind her.

Now to find Drake. Wondering if he'd gone back to his office, Lyndsey stepped outside the kitchen door. The light in the garage was on.

The night was cool and she didn't bother with a sweater or shoes. Running in bare feet, she reached the garage. Drake was there, bent over his work bench. The music was turned low. A steel mask with goggle-like eyes covered his head. Grasping a hissing torch, he sang along to the country song.

A large piece of metal lay flat on the work bench. Smoke curled from the torch and stung her nose. A small corner of the gray metal turned red and sparked underneath. Drake painstakingly sewed in a neat seam. Satisfied with his work, he stood up and stretched. He put the torch down on the bench and flipped up his mask.

"Nice job!"

Drake jumped and spun around. "Jesus, woman! When did you get here?"

"A minute ago. I didn't want to bug you while you were in the zone."

He pulled her by the hand, excited to show off his work. "What do you think?"

It was a big project. She eyed the steel fabrication he'd been working on. When he was finished, it would be a stainless steel tool box for the back of his truck. The piece he'd been working on was the lid. The seam was tight and neat. "It's beautiful, honey."

"Linds, toolboxes aren't beautiful. You on the other hand..." He smiled and pulled her close.

She inhaled him. God, he smelled good. Safe in his embrace, she relaxed, letting her body lean against his. They rocked back and forth, hips swaying to the beat of the music.

Drake's lips pressed hot against her ear. "We haven't given this shop its proper due. What do you say about a little christening, hmm?"

Meeting his eyes, Lyndsey grinned. "Honey, we don't have to sneak around. Our bed is much more comfortable than…" She eye-balled the work bench.

"Kill joy!" He grinned down at her.

The last thing on her mind was sex. Drake wasn't bothered by a head full of problems. At least his libido wasn't. She, on the other hand, needed to be in the right frame of mind. Which, at the moment, she was not.

Drake swatted her on the behind and stood back. He stared at her for a moment before reaching over to switch off the music. The sudden quiet brought with it a feeling of somberness.

The words just tumbled from her lips. "You know the baby I gave up for adoption?"

Drake's forehead wrinkled. "Say again?"

Lyndsey shook her head. "I'm not saying this right," she mumbled, leaning back against the workbench. "I was with one of our alumni today. She wanted me to come with her to visit her son. He's in a court mandated rehab."

Drake blinked. "That's a little out of your job description, isn't it?"

She nodded. "I'm sure I over-stepped a boundary, but this woman…" she trailed off, careful not to mention Susan's name.

"I don't get it. What does this alumnus have to do with the baby you gave up for adoption?"

"I'm not sure." Lyndsey eyed him. "Let me tell you what happened."

Drake folded his arms across his chest as Lyndsey blurted it all out. He waited a beat and then said, "You don't really think this is your son, do you?"

Here in the garage with Drake, the idea did seem kind of farfetched, and yet…

"Honey, I think the stress is just getting to you. I'm sure the boy you saw today wasn't the son you gave up for adoption. I mean, what are the chances?"

"I don't know. I was so sure," she whispered.

"Listen," Drake tilted her chin up. "Why don't we go away for a little holiday this weekend? We could find a nice hotel, right on the beach. Just me and you. We've been working way too hard. I think it's time to kick back and have some fun. What do you say?"

Was it possible she'd been wrong? Maybe all the stress was playing tricks on her mind? "But I was so sure," Lyndsey tried again.

Drake shook his head and pulled her close. "The chances of that boy being your son are a million to one. I think you'll see it straight after a weekend away." He jerked his head. The welding helmet lowered over his face as he turned back to the bench.

"I don't know." She shook her head and wrapped her knuckles on Drake's iron clad cheek.

Drake flipped the helmet up with a questioning look.

"We can't go away. Who's going to look after Billy?"

"Call the social worker. Didn't she mention something about respite?"

"Oh, I don't know."

"Linds." Drake jerked his eyes at the tool box cooling on the work bench. "I've gotta get this finished."

"I don't think it's a very good idea for Billy to go into a stranger's house. Do you?"

Drake shrugged. "I don't think it's dangerous, if that's what you mean. These people would have been screened, the same as us."

"I know he'd be safe. I mean, physically. I just think it would do more damage to him emotionally. Do you know what I mean?"

"Not really."

"Well…"

Drake interrupted her. "Linds, please, I have to get this finished." He flipped his helmet down.

She stared at his back, wondering what to do.

Drake switched the music back on and turned on his torch.

The idea of a weekend away was tempting. God, she'd love to get away from all of this, even if it was only for a few days. But what about Billy? Maybe she could meet the respite family first. She'd bring Billy with her and see how he interacted with them.

Yeah, right, Linds! And when are you going to find time to do that?

Back in the kitchen, she scrubbed the counters, not seeing them. Instead, she saw Susan's son.

Her eyes widened. She might be crazy, but she felt it in her gut. Determination squared her jaw. One way or another, she was going to find out if Declan really was her son.

Chapter 34

Declan yawned and slid off the chair. "I think I'll get some shut eye."

Pete's tanned arm shot out from behind the desk, wrapping around his wrist.

"What the hell?" Declan yanked his arm free from Pete's grasp.

"Wait a sec," Pete ordered.

"Jesus! What now?"

Pete thumbed through the papers in front of him. "I've got an assignment for you."

"An assignment?" Declan sneered. "What are we, in school?"

Pete's eyes went flat. "You know, it's no skin off my ass if you get booted outta here. Might even be a good idea." He glanced at the phone. "Yeah, a real good idea…" He trailed off and picked up the receiver.

His pulse kicked up a notch.

"What're the names of those two cops who brought you in?"

"Fine!" he blurted. "I'll do your stupid assignment."

Pete's mouth formed an O. One eyebrow arched high and he shook his head. "Nah, I don't believe you want to be here. It might take some convincing on your part." He grinned, revealing yellowed teeth.

"I said I'd do it," Declan argued.

Pete separated the sheets of papers into two piles. He picked up the first pile and waved it in Declan's face. "Yeah, but you didn't say please."

"Seriously?"

Pete didn't respond.

Through clenched lips, Declan said, "Please."

Crossing his arms in front of him, Pete nodded. "Okay. You convinced me."

Declan reached for the papers before Pete could change his mind. He nodded thanks and turned to go, when Pete stopped him.

"Aren't you gonna read it?"

"I will," he said, meeting Pete's eyes. "I thought I could concentrate better if I was in my room."

"Well," Pete wagged a finger, "That would be breaking the rules. Don't you remember? No isolating! Hanging out in your room is strictly prohibited unless it's lights out or you're getting changed or showered. Besides, you're gonna need some help answering those questions. Why don't you ask Nick over there to help you?"

"Nah, ah... I think I can figure it out." Declan glanced at the papers in his hand.

"Hey Nick," Pete shouted.

Nick was one of the guys on the couch. Declan hadn't bothered getting to know him. He didn't figure he'd be here long enough to make friends. Besides, these weren't his kind of people. Rehab was a place for freaks and nut jobs.

"What?" Nick yelled back.

"Come over here for a sec, would ya?" Pete pointed at the chair beside Declan.

Nick shrugged and sauntered over, his jeans slung low on his hips.

"Have a seat." Pete waved at the empty chair.

Declan snuck a glance down the hallway but Lite-bright had disappeared.

Pete lowered himself into the chair and turned to Nick. "As senior peer, I'd like you to mentor Declan here."

Declan's cheeks turned red. "I don't need help!"

Pete smiled. Nick just stared at him.

Nick's eyes matched the gray hoodie he was wearing. "You're wrong, man," he said. "We all need help."

Declan shook his head about to argue the point, but Nick beat him to it.

"It's okay, bro. You don't have to believe me. I don't expect you to. Let's just get this assignment done and then we'll talk."

Dammit! Declan was in a corner and he knew it. For the moment, he'd have to do as he was asked. Then he got an idea. "I need to get my pen, I'll be right back."

Nick reached into the pouch of his hoodie. "Here, use mine," he said, handing it to Declan.

Fuck! He couldn't catch a break!

"Tim, John!" Nick yelled at two guys sitting on the couch. He turned to Pete. "I think we'll head into the dining hall and work there."

Pete nodded. "Good idea."

Surrounded, there was no way out. Declan followed them down the hallway, his steps dragging.

The dining hall was empty. The tables gleamed, wiped down and readied for the next feeding. Salt and pepper shakers were lined up evenly on each one.

The smell of coffee was rich in the air. Nick grinned. "My new DOC," he said, pouring himself a big cup. "Hey Tim," he cocked an eye brow. "Who would have thought this shit was so good!"

Tim winked and said, "It's even better triple bagged."

John perked up. "You want me to make some triple bag?"

The energy changed. It were as if the three of them had just done a line of cocaine. Their eyes grew bigger, shiftier, as they checked out the coffee pot.

Declan took a step back, watching.

Tim eyed the door and nudged John. "Do it! The coast is clear. I'll cover you."

John glanced at the doorway and frowned. "Tim, man, you gotta swear…"

"Yeah, yeah," Tim muttered and shoved John.

Nick raised a hand. "Stop!"

Tim and John spun around. "What?" they said in unison.

Nick pointed at Declan. "We're supposed to be setting an example here."

As if the air had been sucked from the room, Tim's shoulders slumped. "Yeah," he mumbled. "Guess you're right."

Pushing the salt and pepper shakers out of the way, Nick sat down and laid out the papers. Tim and John sat down beside him. Trying to keep the smile off his face, Declan joined them. The Three Stooges. Watching these three was the most fun he'd had in ages.

"Okay," Nick started. He shoved the papers in front of Declan's nose. "What you need to do is answer these questions honestly."

John said, "You probably don't know how to do that yet. That's why we're here to help you."

"Yeah," Tim agreed. "We're here to keep ya honest."

Playing along, Declan nodded.

Nick cleared his throat. "Cost of addiction," he read the title on the paper. "This will help you see what your addiction has cost you.

Addiction? What addiction? He wasn't an addict. But there was no sense telling these bozos that.

"Number one," Nick continued. "Has your using ever hurt anyone else?"

Miranda's face flashed before him, and then his mom's. He pushed the images away.

Nick leaned over him. "Do you understand what this means?" he asked. "Have you ever hurt someone you love, just to get high?"

The kitchen disappeared. He went back in time. Miranda smiling, Miranda laughing, Miranda in the court room, pale as ghost.

"Well?" Nick repeated.

Chapter **35**

DEE STOMPED HER FOOT AND GLARED AT CHARLIE. "You promised!"

"I did," he nodded, removing the keys from the ignition.

They were parked in front of the big white church again. The same people she'd seen before were lined up outside the front doors. A cloud of smoke circled above their heads.

The car seat was soft. Dee leaned against it and relaxed. The pill she'd taken earlier was starting to work. The worst of her nausea faded and she felt strangely indifferent.

Charlie stuffed the keys into his pocket and turned to her. "Meeting first, and then we'll hit the bank machine."

"But –"

"Look," Charlie broke in. "I said I'd get you the money, I didn't say when. My meeting is starting and I don't want to be late." He reached over and opened the door. It swung wide.

Cold air rushed into the car and she shivered. "I'm cold."

"Yeah, well, it's warm inside. Come on!" Charlie said, and climbed out of the car.

Dee couldn't figure him out. Was he actually happy to be going to these stupid meetings? He acted as if he'd just scored or was heading to the bar.

The circle of people waiting at the front door began filing inside.

Charlie tapped on the top of the car and yelled, "Hurry up, we're going to be late!"

Dee reached over and grabbed the door handle. Might as well get it over with. She could always sleep during the meeting. The door slammed with a loud thud as she ran to catch up with Charlie, but he disappeared through the front doors without a backwards glance.

She halted in front of the big double doors. All she had to do was turn around. Cold crept up her spine and she shivered, huddling into her sweater for warmth. Her stomach made growling sounds. Was she ever hungry! The tantalizing smell of coffee wafted through the closed doors. At least it would be warm inside. Dee pushed through the doors and stopped.

Rows of chairs formed lines, with a podium up front. A lean, bald man stood behind the podium. He glanced over at her and smiled. Then he spoke into the microphone. "Welcome."

Necks craned. Dee's cheeks burned and she glared at the man.

The smile slid from his face as he turned to the audience. "Please join me in the Lord's prayer."

Still feeling embarrassed, Dee walked over to the table and poured a cup of coffee from the urn. A box of donuts got her attention and she helped herself to two. The chairs in the back row were all full. The only ones available were right up front. She stuffed a donut in her mouth and made her way over to one. The room was warm and reverberated with voices.

Our Father, who art in heaven.

Hot coffee sloshed onto her hand as she settled into the chair. "Fuck," she cried.

Hallowed be thy name.

The crowd was an interesting mix of characters. Dee looked around to see if there was anyone she could talk to, but all their heads were bent in prayer. They looked ridiculous, like they were on the nod and they weren't even stoned!

Thy kingdom come.

Thy will be done.

The lean man at the podium raised his head and looked at her. His eyebrows shot up and waggled hello.

Dee lowered her head. Idiots! They looked so goofy.

On earth as it is in heaven.

A big swig of coffee chased away the last of the donut. Charlie said these meetings weren't church, but he lied. Why else would these people be praying?

Give us this day our daily bread and forgive us our trespasses.

A memory came to her. Little Dee was kneeling beside her bed. Her flannel nighty trailed the floor behind her. Her palms were pressed together to form prayer hands. Her head was bent low as she whispered into her dark bedroom.

Dear God, can you bring my daddy back?

The door creaked open and her mother stepped through it. She flicked on the light. "Dee..." She stopped. Little Dee opened her eyes. She looked up at her mom. She noticed her mother's long brown hair, hanging in a wild tangle over one shoulder. Her eyes were red and mean.

"Are you praying?" Dee's mother laughed, as she marched over and yanked Dee up from the floor.

Little Dee's stomach flip-flopped and she flinched.

"Praying is a waste of time, Dee. There ain't no God. There's just you and me."

Little Dee climbed into her bed, scooting over as far as she could. Not wanting to cry, she prayed. Please, Daddy, come and get me!

Blood shot, red eyes drilled into hers. "What were you talkin' to God about?"

"Nothing," she whimpered.

A steel hand grabbed her by the chin and yanked it up. "Now Dee, don't you dare lie to me!"

Little Dee froze. Her mother's hand relaxed its grip on her jaw. Carefully, Little Dee inched back in her bed.

The bed sagged under her mother's weight as she sat down. "Welllll?" her mother asked, drawing out the word.

Quiet as a mouse, Little Dee wiggled further away. The silence was deafening. It was like a monster was breathing down the back of her neck.

Her mother whispered, "Don't make me ask you again."

The hairs on the back of Little Dee's neck stood up. She gulped, knowing if her tone was whiny, she'd set her mother off even worse than she'd already done.

In a matter-of-fact voice, she stated, "I was asking God if he could bring Daddy back."

"What?" her mother screeched, and reared up.

She stiffened, waiting for the smack. But it never came. Instead, her mother sneered. "You little idiot, he ain't comin' back!"

Tears stung the backs of her eyelids and she blinked. The memory faded as the room came back into focus. Embarrassed, Dee glanced around, wondering if anyone had noticed. But no one had. No one was paying any attention to her at all. Relieved, she closed her eyes and let loose a sigh.

As we forgive those who trespass against us.

Goosebumps broke out on her skin. Her mother's face flashed vividly before her. A creepy-crawly sensation squirmed loose in her mid-section. Her eyes blinked wide open.

Chapter **36**

"HI LINDS, IT'S KIND OF LATE FOR YOU TO BE working, isn't it?" Janet, the new girl at front desk, looked at her questioningly.

"Yeah, I forgot the paperwork I needed to finish up." Lyndsey shrugged.

Janet stood up from her chair and stretched. "Oh boy, do I ever need coffee."

Lyndsey picked up the clip board in front of Janet and scratched her name on it.

"How long will you be?" Janet said, eyeing her chicken scratch.

"Not long," she smiled. "Don't worry. I can let myself out."

"Okay." Janet yawned and wound a long strand of red hair around her finger. "It's been pretty quiet out here. I can barely stay awake!"

"Yeah, well, quiet is better than the alternative." She grinned. "Chaos!"

"True," Janet nodded. "Although a little chaos sure helps the time fly."

"Be careful what you wish for." Lyndsey eyed the interior of the building. All the lights were on. They were never off. Dark places weren't good for recovering addicts. Too many hidey holes and amorous bodies made the possibility for patients to have sex too easy. Which was never good, because sex in treatment was a dischargeable offence. By now, the patients would be in their rooms, getting ready for bed.

She dug her fob out of her purse and waved it in front of the little red light beside the glass door. When the red light turned green, she pushed open the door. "Have fun," Lyndsey said over her shoulder and gave Janet a little wave. Janet waved back and turned to the computer in front of her.

Now that she was in the front door, Lyndsey headed for her office. The only other time she was here this late was when she was working the weekends. When a patient was in crisis, she'd be called in for what could sometimes be an all-nighter. But there was no patient in crisis tonight. At least not that she was aware of. She was here to do something she'd never done before. She was going to take confidential information out of the building. Specifically, Susan's.

As crazy as it seemed, she just needed to know. She hadn't quite figured out what she might say if she found it. She'd have to just wing it as she went.

Out of habit, she glanced into each patient room that she walked past for monitoring purposes. Even though she wasn't actually working right now, it was hard to not to. Adrenaline made her heart beat fast. It wasn't like she was stealing state secrets, for crying out loud! She was just taking one phone number. It wasn't that big a deal!

Yeah, right Linds, keep telling yourself that and you might even believe it!

Luckily, no one else noticed she was there. Support staff would be busy counting heads and doling out night time medications.

Her hands shook as she inserted the key into her office door. A soft click indicated it was unlocked and she flicked on the light. Her desk was just as she'd left it. Papers squared off into a neat pile were ready for her to work on tomorrow. She guessed she could have avoided this late night trip by waiting to take Susan's file then, but it was too risky. There were just too many staff members around in the day time.

The door was open. She retraced her steps and glanced down the long hallway. The coast was clear. She had about ten minutes before support staff would come by to check the office.

The harsh glare of the fluorescent light overhead made her feel exposed. She thought about turning it off, but that would only alert the staff. With one eye on the door, Lyndsey turned to the dark brown filing cabinet and began searching for S.

Susan's progress notes and referral sheet would have enough information to help her get started. But what she really needed were the patient files from her stay in inpatient treatment. If she could get her hands on Susan's social history, she'd find what she was looking for.

With her legs curled under her, Lyndsey pulled open the bottom drawer. Her heart beat madly as she rifled through the cabinet. Her hands looked like little wild birds, they shook so badly. In spite of this, she continued to thumb through the files.

Come on, come on!

The papers weren't cooperating. They stuck together and she lost time trying to get them apart.

Get it together, Linds. Calm down. You can do this.

She took a deep breath and steadied her hands. Slowing down, she continued the search. Weird… Susan's file was missing. She looked again and stopped. The corner of a blue file poked out from underneath all the rest. Careful not to tear it, she pulled it free. Somehow, Susan's file had gotten stuck under the others.

Hungry for information, Lyndsey scanned the pages, noting the address, age, and any known allergies. She flipped to the back of the chart. There were notes scrawled in her handwriting, with Susan's patient number at the top of the page. With the ID number, she could boot up the computer, access her patient files, and get all the data from Susan's inpatient stay.

The file number was FP 136. Lyndsey memorized it and shoved the file back into the drawer. Just as she was closing it, she heard footsteps. Keys rattled in the doorknob as she flung herself against the wall, hiding beside the cabinet.

The door open and she held her breath. She was so screwed!

"Make sure you look inside each room or office," Sarah, the support staff supervisor said.

"But the door was locked," a female voice replied. Lyndsey didn't recognize the voice, likely a new staff member in training.

"It doesn't matter, it's still good practice to look," Sarah insisted.

"I guess…"

The door shut with a soft click, leaving the rest of their conversation unheard. Holy shit! That was close!

Lyndsey crawled over to the door and glanced out the window. Sarah and the new girl disappeared down the hallway.

Feeling like a criminal, she booted up the computer and waited for it to load. So far, she hadn't done anything she couldn't undo. But that was about to change.

Without a printer in her office, she'd have to send the file to the admin printer upstairs. The office was next to the support office. Lyndsey just hoped no one would get curious about files being printed at this time of night.

Oh well, she'd cross that bridge when she came to it. She hit the send button and turned off the computer. The phone in her purse vibrated and she jumped. She snatched it up before it could ring again. The call display read Drake.

'Hello," she whispered.

"Linds?"

226

"Yeah,"

"What are you doing? I thought you were getting us ice-cream?"

"I am. I'll be home in a minute."

"Where are you? Won't the ice-cream be melted by now?"

"I haven't got it yet."

"Why are you whispering?"

"Jesus, Drake! I can't talk right now. I'll explain when I get home."

"Linds?"

"Gotta go, babe, be home in a minute." She clicked off the phone and shoved it back in her purse.

Great Linds, you're not only a thief, now you're a liar. What are you going to tell him when you get home? Huh?

Now wasn't a good time to develop a conscience. Lyndsey pushed her thoughts aside and left the office. The hallway was empty. She resisted the urge to run, walking quickly instead.

When she passed the men's lounge, she glanced inside. Three men watched the late night news. One glanced up and spotted her. She smiled and waved. He waved back. The patients didn't know if she was supposed to be here or not, but her coworkers would.

As she passed the support staff office, Lyndsey ducked, then inserted her key into the admin door. It was the only door in the whole building without a window in it.

The printer began to spit out papers just as she closed the door. With the door closed, she felt a little safer. The papers were still warm as she began to read. Her eyes devoured Susan's story, looking for any signs of the little boy she had adopted.

Halfway through, Lyndsey found it.

Chapter **37**

Declan squirmed in his chair. For all the comfort it offered, he might as well be sitting on a block of concrete.

Nick smiled. "They don't make them very comfortable, do they?"

"Yeah," John joined in, "they don't want us feeling comfortable. We might want to stay."

Tim snorted. "Not bloody likely!"

Declan reread his answer to the question in front of him, and then scratched it out. "Are we done yet?"

Nick pointed at the paper. "There are twenty one questions on that assignment. You're only on number two."

Declan's brows knit together as he stared at Nick. He couldn't figure him out. He said he didn't work here, but he sure as hell acted like he did.

Tim yawned. "I'm grabbin' another cup of coffee. Anyone else want one?"

John thrust his mug forward. "I'm in."

"Me too," Nick said.

Declan rolled his eyes. "Aren't you guys hitting the coffee hard? You'd better be careful, you might get addicted to it."

Nick shook his head. "You weren't here yet, so you missed the lecture on addictive substances. Coffee isn't one of them. You can become caffeine dependent, but not caffeine addicted."

"Aren't you just the Funk and Wagnall of information," Declan sneered, throwing down his pen. He wished they would leave him alone.

He didn't like this assignment. It was bringing back memories of Miranda and a time long ago. A time when his family had been happy.

Nick tapped his finger on question two and read it out loud. "To what lengths have you gone to obtain your drugs and/or alcohol? Be specific. For example, did you steal from your family? Did you commit crimes and break the law? Did you cheat on your partner? Did you lower your moral standards? Did you physically hurt yourself or someone else?"

Nick pushed the paper across the table towards Declan. "This is your opportunity to get honest, pal."

What was it with this place? This Nick guy clearly worked here, and yet said he was a patient. Nick reminded him of Twitch. Was he a narc?

"Well?" Nick poked Declan in the arm.

He slapped Nick's hand away and watched Tim.

Tim was clutching three mugs of coffee. He never spilled a drop as he placed the cups in front of Nick and John. He took a loud slurp from his cup and sat down beside Declan.

Tim sat too close to him. Declan scooted his chair over and frowned. He didn't like thinking about his past, but he'd give it a try. He picked up the pen and scrawled a few lines, then stopped. This was bullshit. It wasn't making him feel good at all. Tears stung his eyes. Christ, he felt like a little kid again. He swallowed the lump in his throat.

"Can I read it?" Nick asked.

Declan shook his head and growled, "I haven't finished yet."

Nick help up two fingers as a peace offering. His face flushed. He picked up his cup and hid behind it.

It was weird. It was as if none of them knew what to do without a bottle in their hand. Sobriety sucked. It was awkward as hell. It was intense, and Declan was pretty sure he wasn't the only one feeling it. He looked down at what he had written. *I lied to my mom, and stole her money. I lied to my girlfriend and almost got her fired.*

A sudden urge came over him. He wanted to rip the paper in two. His face got hot and he flung down his pen. "I'm not doing this!"

John pushed his coffee cup away and leaned back in his chair. He met Declan's eyes. "I hated doing it too."

"Yeah, well." Declan dismissed him. "I don't give a shit what you hated. We're not in school anymore. There's no point in digging up the past."

"Actually," Tim said, "there is."

Declan shook his head. He didn't agree with these bozos at all. Where the hell was Lite-bright, and why hadn't he found Gary yet? Declan stared past Tim down the hall. Patience had never been his best virtue and the urge to bolt was strong.

"Just give it a try," Tim urged. "Don't worry, we're not going anywhere. If you get stuck, ask us for help." Declan bit back a retort. Maybe if he played along, they'd leave. He scanned the paper and thought back...

It was Sunday afternoon and they'd spent the day in bed. He wasn't sure why, but when he was hung-over, he was horny as hell. "Promise me, baby," Miranda said, her big brown eyes shimmering with tears as they locked on his.

He'd laughed and pulled her close. She was warm and soft and...

Fuck!

Declan rubbed his eyes. He'd made her so many promises. The thing was, he'd had every intention of keeping them. Well, most of them, anyway. What had happened? How had it gone so wrong?

Now he was stuck here with these idiots and Miranda wouldn't even pick up the phone. A flash of anger erupted in his chest. He bet it was her parents' influence. They didn't like him from the start. Oh well, it didn't matter. The feeling was mutual. Declan didn't like them either. He'd never felt like he was good enough for their precious daughter. His brow wrinkled when a new thought entered his head. Maybe Miranda had gone home to her parents'? Nah, he didn't think so. Declan couldn't imagine her not waiting at their place, but then again, he never imagined that she wouldn't answer his calls either.

He chewed a thumb nail. He needed a smoke. Ah, hell. What he really needed was Miranda, but if he couldn't have her, getting shit-faced wasted would have to do.

His mind raced as he thought up ways to get rid of Nick, Tim, and John. He hit upon one and patted his pocket. "I need a smoke."

Nick nodded and the four of them rose. Tim and John high-fived one another, mouthing in unison, "Smoke break!"

Shit! Now what? In his most sincere voice, Declan said, "I really appreciate your help. It's very kind of you, but I don't want to keep you any longer. Dudes like you have important things to do. I got this." He smiled a stiff grin and pocketed his pen.

Tim bumped his shoulder. "Anytime, bro!"

Declan bit down on his lip to stop the smile from appearing on his face.

Nick, appearing to have changed his mind, thumped the table with his fist and sat back down. "You can smoke later. Quit procrastinating. Now let's get this done."

"Well I…" Declan trailed off as a better idea came to mind. "I guess I could use your help." He slid the paper over in front of Nick's face and tossed him the pen.

Nick caught it in mid-air.

"Because you already did this assignment, why don't you just answer the questions for me?"

"I could," Nick agreed, "But then they'd be my answers, not yours."

"Nobody would know," Declan argued.

"You would."

Declan smirked. "I don't care!"

Nick shook his head and sighed. "That's the problem, you don't care. You don't care who you hurt or screw over. It's all about you."

"Fuck you! You don't even know me! How the hell can you say that?"

Nick snorted. "I know your addiction. It's the same as mine. It's a selfish bastard that says me, me, me. It doesn't give a shit about anyone else."

"Bullshit!" Declan shouted, shaking his head. "You might be a selfish bastard, but I'm not. I love my family, I don't hurt them." His cheeks burned. What he'd said wasn't quite true. He'd hurt them. Big time.

"Have you ever held them hostage?" Nick asked.

"Huh?" Declan stared at him. "That's crazy, of course not."

"You know, like have you ever threatened to kill yourself, or told them the dope dealer will hurt you if they don't give you money?"

Declan's eyes widened. How the hell did Nick know that?

"Well?"

"I might have said it a time or two. But I was hurting. I was dope sick. But I didn't take them hostage. I'm not a fuckin' terrorist."

"Yes, you did," Nick said, "and yes, you are."

Imagining handcuffs and blindfolds, Declan shook his head. "You're wrong, dude!"

"No, I'm not," Nick argued back. "You did take them hostage, and in the worst possible way."

"You're not making any sense." Declan took his paper back from Nick. "You guys are a bunch of morons. I don't need your help."

"We're not morons," Tim said.

Nick smiled, but it didn't reach his eyes. "Don't take it personal, Tim. Declan knows the truth."

The urge to get wasted was intense. Declan pictured an ice cold beer. He tasted it sliding down the back of his throat. Oh, it was good…

"Breathe," Nick interrupted Declan's craving.

Declan blinked and came back to the room. "Holy shit!"

Nick placed a warm hand on his forearm. "Pretty strong, hey?"

Declan nodded, feeling weird. He could taste the beer on his tongue.

"It happened to me too," Nick said. "For the first few weeks, I could taste coke in the back of my throat. I'd see a spoon and start to crave. It was wild."

Declan looked at Nick with interest. "You did coke?"

Nick snorted. "That and a lot of other things."

"Nick was one of the biggest…" Tim broke off, seeing Nick's dirty look.

Maybe there was something for him here after all. Declan re-evaluated the situation. These guys might know where he could score. He slid his hand across the paper straightening out the creases, and picked up his pen.

Not wanting Nick to have the last word, Declan said, "I'll do the assignment, but I'll never agree that I held my family hostage. That's just ludicrous."

"Uh, uh." Nick shook his head. "You held them hostage just as surely as if you put a gun to their head. Worse, the gun you were holding was pointed at their heart."

"You're crazy!"

"No, I'm not. You took them captive. You held them hostage, emotionally." Nick turned to face him.

Declan pushed back from the table, but Nick grabbed him.

"Face it, Declan," he said. Nick's eyes filled with sorrow. "You did the most damaging thing possible. You manipulated them by using their love for you against them."

Stunned, Declan reeled back in his chair. Nick's words rang painfully in his ears as he sucked in air. Holy shit! Declan thought he might puke.

Chapter **38**

THE TIP OF HER CIGARETTE TURNED CHERRY RED.
Dee's cheeks drew in as she sucked; the nicotine burned going down
her throat. Not able to get any more in, she blew out. A great gray
cloud of smoke billowed from her mouth.

Miriam coughed and waved a hand in front of her face. "Inhaling that
thing isn't going to make it go away, you know."

Dee looked at her blankly.

"You're using that cigarette like a baby uses a pacifier. Only unlike a
pacifier, that cigarette will kill you."

What a dumb ass! She shot Miriam a dirty look and took a final drag.
She threw the butt on the ground and stomped it beneath her heel.

Miriam pointed at the sign on the wall. Please discard your cigarette
butts in the can. "Do you have trouble taking suggestions?"

Already craving more, Dee fished in her purse for another smoke and
looked around for Charlie.

"Because if you do," Miriam continued, "it will make our time together
much more difficult."

That caught Dee's attention. "Our time together?"

"Yes," Miriam frowned. "Didn't Charlie tell you?"

"No…" Dee trailed off, wondering what Miriam was talking about. She had absolutely no intention of spending another minute with this crazy old bat.

"Well, it doesn't matter. I can tell you just as well. Charlie asked me to be your temporary sponsor. I'm going to lead you through the steps."

"Steps?" Dee pictured a large hill with steps leading up the side.

"Yes," Miriam sighed.

Dee flicked her lighter and lit up. Her cigarette package was almost empty, only two left. When Charlie paid her, she'd get him to stop at the store. Then what? For the first time in a long time, she wanted food. Her need for heroin had temporarily worn off and she was starving.

A big fat juicy steak would taste so good. Her mouth watered. She'd get Charlie to pick up a steak with her cigarettes. Oh, and ice cream. Double fudge, yum!

The old lady was still blabbering on about something. Dee pushed a strand of her from her face and asked, "where's Charlie?'

"Haven't you been listening to me?"

Dee met Miriam's eyes and gave her a cold stare. The woman didn't flinch, or look at her like she was crazy. Instead, she stared back.

Not getting the response she hoped for, Dee tried another approach. "Um, I'm not feeling well. I'm not interested in exercising."

"Exercising?" Miriam was clearly confused.

"Yeah," Dee smirked. "You know, the kind you get when you climb stairs."

"Oh!" Miriam's eyes grew big and round. Her painted lips parted wide. Her head tilted back and she laughed.

Great! The woman wasn't just a huge pain in the ass; she was also a raving lunatic. Where the hell was Charlie? The crowd had thinned out. The church doors were closed. His car was still parked where he'd left it. What was he doing in the church, anyway?

Miriam pulled a Kleenex from her purse and wiped her eyes. "Why, I haven't laughed like that in years. Thank you, dear."

The clasp on her purse snapped open and closed as she played with it. "You're welcome," she mumbled, still not following.

"I'm sorry for the misunderstanding. We won't be exercising today, although it's not a bad idea." Miriam chuckled and stuffed the Kleenex back into her purse. "The steps aren't about exercise. They're not physical, they're…"

Hot pokers burned up and down Dee's arms and legs. She had that twitchy feeling again, like she couldn't stand still. One leg bounced up and down. If Charlie didn't get her soon, she'd go over and start beating on the door.

"Emotional!" Miriam trilled, having found a word that suited her.

"Look," Dee started. "I'm sure your steps are nice and all, but right now I just want to find Charlie and get the hell out of here."

Miriam's brows joined together and she shook her head. "Honey," she said softly, "Charlie isn't coming. He's gone for coffee with the men. You're coming with me. He'll stop by my place later on to pick you up."

"What?"

"Sweetie," Miriam's eyes grew damp and she blinked. "Give yourself a chance."

Dee's hand automatically reached for another cigarette.

Miriam put an arm around her. "You can't smoke those feelings away. That's why we're going to start working on the steps. You won't stay clean without them."

"Who says I want to stay clean?"

"You wouldn't be attending these meetings if you didn't."

"For your information," Dee huffed, "I don't want to attend these meetings. They're stupid and so are the people going to them. If Charlie wasn't making me, I wouldn't be going!"

A lopsided smile curled Miriam's lip. "It's been said that God works in mysterious ways."

Dee curled a fist. She never wanted to hit someone so badly in her life. She'd slap the smile right off Miss Miriam's face. But she didn't hit her. Instead, she retorted, "There ain't no God! Don't you know that? I learnt it a long time ago. There ain't no God, there's only assholes, bastards, and idiots like you!"

Miriam flinched and withdrew her arm. "I won't take what you just said personally. I know you're hurting."

Dee's fist unwound. She clasped her hands together and held tight.

"I used to think like you," Miriam smiled. "I believed this world was filled with rotten sons of bitches, and that nothing good would ever happen to me. When my uncle raped me, it only confirmed what I'd already known. This world was a messed up place."

Dee looked up from her hands. "Your uncle raped you?" she whispered.

Miriam's head bounced up and down. "He did," she confirmed. "And I nearly drank myself to death over it."

"Of course you did. Who could blame you?" Dee thought of all the johns she'd been servicing regularly. How she hated them. They were rotten, cheating bastards. All of them.

Miriam held out one hand. "Let's finish this conversation in my car. It's cold out here."

Dee stared at the church door, not sure if she should believe Miriam. "Is Charlie really gone?"

Miriam nodded. "He's gone for coffee, but he's not gone for good. He'll be back to pick you up. Now let's get in the car."

Dee's feet dragged and scattered pebbles as she walked beside Miriam. They crossed the parking lot and stopped in front of a bright green Jeep. Miriam fished the keys from her purse and thumbed the fob. The doors opened with a chirp. Miriam climbed up onto the side-step and jumped in.

She rolled down the window and smiled at Dee. "Didn't your mama ever tell you, you'll catch flies with your mouth hangin' open like that?"

Wow! Dee eyed the tricked out Jeep. The chrome rims must have cost over a grand! "Whose truck is this?"

"Mine," Miriam smiled. "Stay sober and you'll be driving one soon too. Come on, let's go!"

Dee threw her purse strap over her shoulder and jumped in.

The interior of the Jeep was tan. The seats were made of soft black leather. The inside was just as spotless as the outside. Dee ran a finger over the dash, loving the way it smelled.

Miriam said, "I think I have OCD, I like things clean. Dirt bothers me."

Then what are you doing with me in the car? Dee didn't say it, but it crossed her mind.

"Anyway," Miriam started up the car and turned the heater on high. "To finish our conversation, I never told anyone about my uncle. I tried to put it out of my mind, and I did, for a while. But then I began having flashbacks. By this time, I was older and married. I was a mess. I'm afraid my poor husband didn't realize what he was getting into when he said 'I do'."

Why was this woman telling her this? She fidgeted opening her purse and caressed the cigarette pack. It was strange sitting with Miriam. With guys, it was easy. She knew what they wanted. But she hadn't figured out Miriam's angle yet.

"I couldn't…" Miriam faltered. Her cheeks grew red and she whispered, "act like a real wife. I felt so dirty."

Dee stared at Miriam, startled by her confession. This woman had felt dirty too?

"I started drinking heavy then. It got bad. I'd go to work and come home and drink. Poor Tom." She turned to Dee and added, "Tom was my first husband."

Dee nodded to let Miriam know she was following along. The air coming from the Jeep's vent was warm. The heat felt so good. Dee relaxed back in her soft chair and listened.

"It got so I was drinking before I went to work and after. Then one night I woke up around three a.m. and had a drink. Pretty soon, I couldn't sleep through the night without one. By this time, the booze was running my life. I wasn't in charge of it anymore. I, ah…" Miriam broke off and stared out the window.

The sky had turned an ominous gray. Fat raindrops splattered against the windshield. "I always hated the gray." She shook her head and turned to Dee. "Can you relate to any of this?"

She could, the dirty part. But for some reason, she found herself unable to tell Miriam that.

"Doesn't matter," Miriam continued. "I was a mean drunk. It might have been different if I wasn't so mean. Poor Tom… I killed him."

Dee craned her neck and stared at Miriam, wondering if she'd heard her right.

"I'd been on a binge. I was drunk for three days straight. Tom was so worried about me, he hadn't slept or ate. His heart wasn't good, and in looking after me, he'd forgotten to take his medication."

This was heavy. Should she be saying something? She squirmed in her chair feeling helpless and not sure what to do.

"I screamed at him. I called him a rotten, pitiful husband. I told him he was useless and that I wished I'd never married him. I blamed every single thing that was wrong in my life on him," Miriam sobbed. "I even wished him dead. It was right after that he made strangling noises and put a hand to his heart. At first I thought he was being dramatic, but when he fell to the ground, I knew something was wrong."

Tears flowed down Miriam's cheeks, unchecked. "The paramedics told me he was dead before he hit the ground."

Dee suddenly felt the need to help Miriam feel better, and not able to think of anything else, blurted, "It wasn't your fault. You didn't kill Tom. If he'd taken his medication, he'd still be alive."

Miriam smiled. "That's kind of you to say, honey, but it's not true. I might not have murdered Tom with my hands, but I killed him just as sure as I'd stuck a dagger into his heart. He died from living under severe stress. His heart was weakened and he was codependent. It wasn't until much later on that I learned Tom was just as sick as me. He didn't drink like I did, but he was consumed, anyway. He was obsessed with me, so much so that he put my needs before his. Sadly, it cost him his life. Even sadder still, he didn't help me with his sacrifice. All he did was allow me to drink longer than I could have on my own."

"Well, then…" Dee faltered. "Isn't that good? I mean, he loved you, right?"

"Yes," Miriam nodded. "Tom loved me alright, but it was a sick kind of love. Our love was toxic. He almost loved me to death and it killed him."

"I wish someone would love me like that," she said wistfully.

"No, you don't." Miriam shook her head sadly. "That wasn't love, it was addiction."

"You sure don't look like you've been through all that. I mean…" Dee trailed off, not wanting to offend her.

But she wasn't offended. She just threw back her head and laughed.

Dee couldn't stop the smile from spreading to her face and joined in. It was kinda crazy sitting here in this tricked out Jeep, talking with this old woman. She'd never had a conversation like this one before.

Miriam dabbed her eyes and turned to Dee. "Oh honey, you're good for me."

"I am?" Now Dee doubted Miriam's sanity.

"Yes, you are," Miriam replied, putting the Jeep into gear. "Now enough talk. I'm starving! We'll eat first and then we can work on step one."

"How many steps are there?" Dee had no intention of hanging out with Miriam all day.

"Twelve," Miriam replied.

Hmm, twelve, that shouldn't take long, Dee thought to herself.

Miriam checked her side mirrors and backed around the parked cars like an old pro. She roared out of the parking lot, flinging gravel with her tires.

Dee sat back and buckled up. She glanced back at the church and broke out in goose bumps.

She was one week clean today.

Chapter **39**

LYNDSEY WOKE TO THE SHRILL SOUND OF THE ALARM clock as it blasted its annoying 'beep beep beep' from the table next to her. Her hand shot out and hit the off button. Rolling over in bed, her fingers searched for Drake. The spot he occupied was empty. Squinting, she sat up and looked around.

Beams of sunlight squeezed through the horizontal blinds as they danced against the far wall. The light coming from their bedroom window said it was way past time to get up. She must have slept right through the alarm! Worried, she leapt out of bed.

With a quick tug to the covers, she tidied the bed and headed to the kitchen. Lyndsey plugged a pod into the coffee maker and stood back waiting for it to brew. Her head was thick and heavy. She felt like shit. She considered calling into work to say she was sick, but just as quickly dismissed the idea.

As the kitchen filled with the rich aroma of coffee, last night's events came to mind. Her heart kicked up a notch and she ran back to the bedroom to search for her purse. She passed Billy's room and stopped.

Billy was babbling to one of his toys. She hoped he hadn't been awake for too long. She should probably go in and get him, but the need to reread Susan's file was too strong. Her overstuffed purse hung off the chair she had flung it on last night. Retrieving the crumpled file, Lyndsey retraced her steps back into the kitchen.

First a sip of coffee! She filled her cup to the brim and sat down to read. Her eyes scanned the pages until she came to the spot she was looking for.

Shit! She hadn't imagined it! Sweat broke out on her forehead. She felt nauseas as she stared at the date. July 16, 1995. Declan's birthday was the same day as her son's.

Oh my god! It couldn't be. Could it? Lyndsey chewed a thumb nail and thought back.

A knife-like pain had awakened her. It stopped for a minute, and then started again. The pain was more severe than anything she'd ever experienced in the past. She had held her breath as hot pincers stabbed at her pelvis, ripped through her stomach and raced up her spine. Her back felt like it was on fire. Getting out of bed, she'd waddled up the stairs. Her stomach was like one large, seized muscle. Moaning with pain, she was sure she was dying. She'd looked down at herself, afraid of what she would see. It felt like the baby was being ripped out. She thought she must be sitting in a pool of blood. But neither had occurred. She couldn't see anything but her large, grossly distorted stomach, which blocked her from getting a closer view.

As the pressure began to build again, she called for her mom, gritted her teeth, and doubled over. Wave after wave of contractions pulsed through her pelvis and up her back. Another wave hit and she held onto the bed post, riding it out as best she could. Strange noises came from her throat. She clutched a tiny blue outfit in one hand. Her bag was on the dresser ready to go. In it was a snugly plush teddy bear and soft blue baby blanket.

As she glanced around the room, she wouldn't let herself notice the missing crib or baby toys. She refused to think about returning with empty arms. Instead, she'd imagined cradling her tiny bundle. She thought she could keep him safe. As if love was all that was needed to be a good mother.

It wasn't an easy delivery. It was horrible and traumatic. She was in labor for hours. The hospital room was scary and cold. Strange looking equipment beeped beside her bed. There were no pictures or bright colors; just the opposite. The walls were sterile and stark white. The room smelled funny. Like a dentist office. In a thin blue hospital gown, she'd huddled under a sheet on the bed.

Other than her mother, no one knew she was here. She thought she might lose her mind. She wondered how anyone could possibly be sane after an experience like this. She had wished for a gun, and she would have used it too. Anything to escape the torture she'd been in.

The labor was long and hard. They'd asked her to push and she had. She pushed so hard she thought her veins might burst wide open. She'd screamed, babbled, and grown mute. Then mercifully, she passed out.

Lyndsey blinked away tears and took a sip from her cooling coffee. She noticed her hand was shaking as she put the cup to her lips. The first time she saw him, she thought something was wrong. Her baby's head looked deformed.

She asked the nurse what was wrong with her son, but the nurse assured her nothing was. The cone at the top of his head was a result of her long labor. The nurse told her it would smooth out in a few days. Of course, she didn't have a few days. She only had minutes. So she plopped the little blue knitted cap she'd brought for him on his head. The cone disappeared and she stared down at him in awe. Pulling him close, she held onto him as if she never had to let him go. He was beautiful! His pink face scrunched up and he stirred in her arms. His lips pursed and his blue-gray eyes opened wide. His forehead wrinkled as he peered up at her. Her heart stopped, she would have sworn it. When it started beating again, it didn't belong to her. It belonged to him. His tiny body was so soft and warm. He smelled of innocence and undiscovered possibilities. A million images ran through her mind. His first tooth, his first birthday, his first day at school, his first kiss, his first heartbreak…

Of course, she wouldn't be there for any of them. A scream welled up in her throat. It was so big, she couldn't get it out. Instead, she choked on it. Her arm tingled. She could still feel him there, in the crook of it. He'd been so small and helpless.

Like she had been.

Woodenly, Lyndsey drank from her cup. Billy yelled from his room. She forced herself up and away from the table. On stiff legs, she walked towards Billy's room. God, she was tired. Exhaustion added extra pounds to her body. This was one of those days where she wished she could crawl back into bed and pull the covers up high.

Pushing open Billy's door, she pasted a smile on her face. "Good morning sweet..." Her sentence broke off as she took in the room.

Red and black crayon scribbles covered the wall by Billy's bed. But it wasn't the new artwork that held her attention. Billy sat on the floor among his dismembered toys. A ball of white stuffing leaked from his teddy bear. His stuffed turtle was mutilated.

"Bad!" Billy scolded, as he used the scissors she'd bought to do crafts on the stuffed tiger he held in his hand.

"No Billy!" Lyndsey ran across the room and grabbed him by the arm. She took the scissors carefully from his hand, saving Tigger just in the nick of time.

Billy wasn't happy with the rescue. His lower lip thrust out, a sure sign a massive temper tantrum was in the making.

More to distract him than anything else, she pointed to the wall. "What a beautiful picture," she forced gaiety into her voice even though truthfully, she felt like throttling him.

With the scissors tucked into her pocket, she wondered how he'd managed to get his hands on them. Billy wasn't going to be distracted, however. His lower lip hung out so far, he was at risk of tripping over it. He screwed his eyes closed and took in a huge breath.

Lyndsey braced for it. Her spine stiffened and her jaw clenched.

The color of Billy's face changed from pink to red and finally, to purple. His screams were ear piercing as he thrashed around, beating the floor with his fists and legs.

He reminded her of a patient she'd seen at work. This person had been having a grand mal seizure. With seizures, you don't do anything but make sure the person is safe. She decided the same would apply for Billy. So instead of trying to make him feel better, she stood back and let him go at it. Maybe she was tired, or maybe it was intuitive, but she didn't think she should be rewarding or paying attention to this type of behavior.

As if Billy weren't having a meltdown in front of her, Lyndsey hummed a song under her breath and bent to pick up the pieces of stuffing all over the floor. Billy's screams escalated. She hoped he wasn't doing harm to his vocal cords.

Calmly, she turned to him and said, "When you're ready to talk, I'll listen. Now please help me clean up this mess."

If only it was that simple, Linds. The old familiar sarcastic voice jeered in her head.

Not listening to the voice or Billy, she went to work restoring the room. By the time Lyndsey was finished, so was Billy. He looked spent! His eyes were puffy, and his cheeks were blotched as he sat in the middle of the floor, hiccupping.

Still not reacting, she looked around the room. It was tidy again. Billy's bed was made and the surviving stuffed animals sat by his pillow. The wall was a different story, however. She'd need to paint it, or maybe Drake would. Or maybe they would just leave it.

Lyndsey glanced at her watch and froze. There was no way she was going to make it to work on time. Jesus, what a morning!

Her life was becoming more complicated by the minute. First there was Billy, then the pilfered file she'd stolen last night. Not to mention Susan's son, who she strongly believed was hers. And now to top it all off, she was late.

Billy tugged on her arm and whined. "Hungry."

"Okay sweetie." She scooped him up. Billy sagged against her and nestled his head into the crook of her throat.

Hot tears blurred Lyndsey's vision as she held him close. Yes, her life was complicated. But there sure were some sweet moments.

Hugging Billy close, she walked to the kitchen and reached for a bowl. She opened the cupboard door and pulled out two boxes of cereal. "Which one do you want?"

Billy raised his head from her collar bone and pointed to the box with yellow corn puffs on it. Once he was in his booster seat, Lyndsey loaded up his bowl. Billy ate breakfast as if nothing unusual had just happened. She supposed in Billy's world, dismembering stuffed animals, biting children, and seeing your mother on drugs and prostituting herself wasn't unusual. It was just another day in the life of little Billy.

The clock struck eight thirty and she winced. There was no way she was going to work today. But what could she tell her supervisor?

Um, I stole a file last night and found out an alumni's son is actually mine? Nope. That wouldn't fly. How about saying she was sick? It was kind of true…

Billy coughed and Lyndsey got an idea. She crossed the tiled floor and picked up the phone. Five minutes later, she hung up. Now she wasn't just a thief, she was also a liar.

Strangely, the thought didn't bother her that much.

Chapter **40**

A WHITE LIGHT SHINED DOWN, ILLUMINATING A CREAM-colored mound of fluffy powder. Beside the mound, lined up and ready to be snorted, was a nicely chopped line. A rolled up bill and razor blade lay next to the pile of heroin.

Out of the darkness his arm and hand appeared, seemingly disembodied from the rest of him. His fingers fumbled to pick up the bill, but they were clumsy and wouldn't grasp it. The room faded to black. The weirdly glowing heroin and his detached arm were all he could see.

In the bowels of darkness Declan wondered, am I dreaming? The light began to move slowly away from the pile of heroin and trailed off across the room. The corner, which had been previously invisible, lit up.

He gasped.

A bedraggled woman sat tied to a chair with her legs splayed wide open. In her mouth was a gag and she was blind-folded. Her wildly mussed hair was the same color as Miranda's.

Declan wanted to cross over to her, but his legs wouldn't work. He looked down fearing what he might see, but he was invisible. Only his dismembered arm was visible.

The light circled around the woman's head once and moved back across the floor. It lit up the heroin. He could smell it. The slight sweet sour smell was like music to his nose. Saliva pooled, his mouth watered. His nostrils flared open, preparing to inhale. Just then, the light went out. He blinked, blinded by the darkness.

The woman in the corner moaned. Sounds of terror escaped her gag. His hair stood on end.

"Miranda?" he called, but the word stuck in his throat like a wet ball of cotton.

The light clicked back on, revealing the strange but familiar woman. He watched helplessly as she thrashed in her chair. Not able to move or speak, Declan willed himself to wake up, but couldn't.

The light bounced between the woman and the pile of heroin. It flickered on and then off, gaining speed as it went. As if in a mad house, it jumped dizzyingly between the two. He felt sick and thought he might throw up. The room spun crazily around him, growing smaller and smaller with each turn.

In turn, Declan spun with the room. Gravity pulled him towards the floor. His dismembered arm shot out to break the fall. But it didn't touch hard concrete. Instead, his hand landed in the fluffy pile of heroin. He raised his fingers to lick his hand, but realized he had no mouth. The woman in the chair reached over and grasped his leg, which just moments before hadn't been there.

A large butcher knife appeared above his head. It floated in mid-air slithering like a snake, and then moved to the woman's throat. She screamed and thrashed wildly in her chair. A loud buzzing sound filled the room. A fan appeared before his eyes. The fan rotated, floating in the air, and then aimed itself at the pile of fluffy powder.

"No!" Declan screamed. The words echoed inside his mind as he had no lips, tongue, or vocal chords with which to express them.

Just in time, he jumped in front of the powder and saved it. The air blew coolly against his belly, as the woman's shrieks grew louder. He craned his neck and his eyes bulged. The knife that had been resting across the woman's throat was sawing back and forth. One droplet of red ran down her neck, then two.

The room continued to spin at a sickening speed. The fan whirred back on and took aim at the pile of heroin.

Oh! Now he got it. The message was clear. Declan would not be able to save them both. His dismembered arm shot out and grasped the fan, flinging it into the darkened corner.

The thrashing noises ceased and the knife fell, clattering to the ground. Not wanting to see what he knew he was about to, Declan turned his head and looked at the woman he thought was Miranda.

It wasn't pretty. She was slumped over in her chair. "Noooo," he screamed, and tried to pick her up.

A door banged closed in the room next to him and Miranda disappeared. The dream dissolved and he bolted up in bed, blinking. His heart beat wildly in his chest. He ran a shaky hand through sweat drenched hair.

Holy shit! What the fuck was that? "Just a dream," he muttered, answering his own question.

Declan knuckled his eyes, trying to get rid of the hideous image. The last time he'd had a dream as wild as this one, he'd been trying to quit smoking. He'd gone to bed with a patch on his arm and woke up screaming. He slumped against the headboard and looked around. Where was everyone? The bed next to his was neatly made. The noises outside his door said he'd slept late.

He thought back to last night and frowned. The questions he'd answered on that assignment had made him feel sick. Maybe that's why he'd had such a weird dream? And he wasn't feeling much better this morning either.

Declan got out of bed and grabbed for his towel, hoping a hot shower would help. He washed away the cobwebs and stepped out of the shower. He was starving!

The blackboard in front of the cafeteria read, 'Good Morning! Today's breakfast is oatmeal.'

Shit, he hated oatmeal. Declan grunted hello at the old man serving the slop. Four heaping teaspoons of brown sugar later, he took his tray and crossed the room. He saw Lite-bright and a couple of other guys at a table and turned in their direction. "Hey," he said, using his foot to pull out the chair. It scraped along the floor, ending the conversation. Lite-bright wore a neon orange colored Tee-shirt. It clashed with the green in his hair.

Declan placed his tray on the table and reached for the orange juice. There was a brief silence before the conversation started up again.

"Hey," Lite-bright grinned at him.

"Any luck on tracking down Gary?"

Lite-bright's spoon stopped in mid-air and his eyes lit up. "Yeah," he nodded. "Didn't I tell you?" he frowned.

"No?"

"Oh, thought I did." Lite-bright shoved the spoon into his mouth. The side of his cheek bulged like a hamster's when hoarding food.

Declan took a long pull on his glass of orange and drained it. He set the glass back down and shook his head. "I'm sure you didn't tell me," he insisted, "You must have gack-brain."

"But…"

"It doesn't matter," Declan interrupted. "Where is he?"

"Well…" Lite-bright dragged out the word and smiled widely.

Declan fought the urge to punch him in the face. The guy was such a dork. Jesus!

"He's in the infirmary."

"Shit! How am I gonna get in there? Don't they keep it locked?"

"They do." Lite-bright grinned. "But some of us can get in anyways!"

Declan's eyes narrowed. "I'm not following you."

"They switched my duty, that's how I found him."

"Your duty? What has that got to do with anything?"

Lite-bright putted out his chest and said, "You're looking at a senior peer." He chuckled. "That's why they gave me this new duty. I guess they figured I could handle mopping floors in the infirmary and seeing all the needles and shit in there."

"Oh?"

"Yeah, and that's how I found Gary. He was in one of the beds and I sidled up to him when no one was looking. He says to give you a message."

"What's the message?"

Lite-bright shoveled another spoon full of oatmeal into his mouth and chewed. Declan drummed his fingers on the tabletop and waited.

Lite-bright made a show out of cleaning his bowl and licking the spoon before he laid it down. A sly look crossed his face. "So what's it worth to ya?"

"Huh?"

"You know," Lite-bright responded, "I have something you want. Now what will you give me for it?"

A fat fuckin lip if you don't watch it. But he didn't say that. Instead, Declan asked, "What do you want?"

Lite-bright touched one finger to his lip and said, "How about twenty bucks?'

"Twenty bucks! I don't have twenty bucks," Declan lied.

"Okay," Lite-bright met his eyes. "What do you have, then?"

Declan thought fast and pulled his cigarettes from his shirt pocket. He opened the pack and showed it to Lite-bright. "There's ten left. How about I split them with you?'

Lite-bright looked at the cigarettes and then back at Declan. A smile lit his face and he stuck out his hand. "Deal!"

Declan counted out five cigarettes and passed them over.

Lite-bright took them and said, "I would have done it for free, ya know."

"Don't fuckin' get me started," Declan warned. "Now what did Gary say?'

"He said," Lite-bright rolled his eyes around the room as if he was a spy instead of a junkie, and whispered, "He got what you wanted."

"Okay," Declan fought to keep his face blank. "Did he give it to you?"

A frown creased Lite-bright's forehead. "Give what to me?"

Declan almost blurted out 'the money' but bit back the words in time. Careful not to give it away, he replied, "Did he give you anything for me?"

"Nah," Lite-bright shook his head. "He says he has what you want, but you'll have to go and see him for it."

Declan spooned a bite of oatmeal into his mouth and thought. "How can I get in there?"

"I can get you in."

"Yeah? How?"

"I'm scrubbing the floors in there this afternoon. I'll find a way to leave the door open, but it'll cost you."

"Jeez," Declan played along. "You drive a hard bargain."

Lite-bright's chest puffed out and he nodded. "I do," he agreed.

They made plans to meet back in the cafeteria at three-thirty that afternoon. Declan scraped his bowl and ate the rest of his cold oatmeal as he watched Lite-bright swagger from the room. He grinned. By his calculations, he only had six more hours to go and it was adios to this place!

Chapter 41

THE TEA WAS GOOD. JUST THE WAY DEE LIKED IT, sweet and hot. She couldn't remember the last time she'd enjoyed a cup this much. The warm mug felt nice in her hand. She looked around, curious about Miriam.

Miriam didn't decorate her house like an old lady should, in Dee's opinion. There were no lace doylies or crocheted pillow covers. Instead, there was a large white marble fireplace with a beige leather chester-field across from it. On top of the chesterfield was a plush, chocolate colored throw blanket. Big plump cream colored pillows decorated each end.

Opposite the chesterfield were two leather La-Z-boy recliners. Dee reclined on one and Miriam sat upright on the other.

Old Miriam sure must have hit a jackpot! Dee wasn't an interior designer, but she didn't have to be to know this stuff was expensive.

Careful not to spill, she set her mug down on the sturdy oak side table next to her and said, "Miriam, your husband must have been awfully rich!"

Miriam picked up her mug, her long, knobby fingers curled around it. She rested the mug against her cheek. "I guess some people might have considered Tom to be rich." She gave Dee a curious look and continued. "It all depends on your perspective."

Dee stared at Miriam's knobby fingers and wondered if they hurt. Then another thought crossed her mind and her heart sped up. Why, she'd bet anything that old Miriam here had pain pills in her medicine cabinet. The thought brought a warm rush, which travelled from her fingertips to her toes. It was almost as good as if she'd just fixed! The itch was on!

"Why do you ask?"

"Oh, well, no reason really."

"Oh?" Miriam stared at her, confused.

Switching subjects, Dee said. "I have to go to the bathroom. Where is it?"

Miriam gave her an odd look before raising one long twisted finger and pointed down the hallway. "Third door to your left," she replied.

Dee cautioned herself not to leap off the recliner and said, "Be right back."

As she hurried down the hallway, she wondered if Miriam had an ensuite bathroom. If so, chances were the medication would be there. But she wouldn't know for sure until she checked out the main bath.

In her haste, the bathroom door banged shut behind her. Dee jumped, on edge. Not wasting any time, she flung open the cabinet door. A toothbrush still wrapped in cellophane occupied the lower shelf. Next to it was a pink razor and toothpaste. A bar of soap and a bottle of mouthwash were on the top shelf. There were no medications of any kind in this medicine cabinet. Irritation prickled her. Why call it a medicine cabinet if you weren't going to put medicine in it?

She bent down and opened the cupboard underneath the sink. There was toilet paper and cleaning supplies, but no medications.

Dee turned in a circle to see if she missed anything. The green walls and the brown floor tiles spun before her eyes. Unless old Miriam was hiding her pills in the toilet, she didn't think there was anything here. But just to be sure, she lifted the lid off the toilet tank and peered in. The water was crystal clear. The inside of the toilet tank was sparkling clean.

Miriam was either a neat freak or she had a large cleaning crew. Dee didn't think she'd ever seen a house this spotless. Reminding herself to be quiet, she lowered the lid on the tank and crossed the floor. She listened at the door for any sound of Miriam.

The house was quiet. Maybe Miriam had fallen asleep in her recliner?

She crept out of the bathroom and turned down the hallway. The dark hardwood floors gleamed under her feet. There were three white doors, all of them closed in front of her.

Dee opened the first door and poked her head in. A midsized room, with light gray walls and a large mahogany desk said this was Miriam's office. Or maybe it was her dead husband's? Her mind raced with possibilities. If it was an office, wouldn't Miriam have her checks here?

Torn, she hesitated. Should she go for the money, or for the drugs? She wanted both, but knew there wasn't enough time. Or maybe there was? What if Miriam really had fallen asleep out there? After all, she was old. Really old! Isn't that what old people did?

As far as Dee could tell, Miriam had a good thing going here. She lived like a queen and had more than her fair share of wealth. Dee just bet that Miriam had a fat stack of cash in one of those desk drawers, too. Intending to come back later, she closed the office door and continued down the hallway.

The next door opened on a bright yellow bedroom. A large queen sized bed was center in the room. Under it was a beige and rose colored throw rug which covered the dark hardwood floor. A fluffy white goose down quilt with big green and white checkered pillows dressed the bed. A chair, bedside table, and armoire were the only other pieces of furniture in the room.

The bedroom was bare of any personal items or family pictures. She didn't think this was Miriam's room, but rather her guest bedroom. She closed the door and turned to face the remaining one.

Before opening it, she stopped to listen. If Miriam wasn't sleeping, she'd be wondering where she was by now. Dee hoped the old gal's etiquette kept her from snooping.

The house was still quiet as she turned the knob. If Miriam did come looking for her, she could always say she'd got lost. Playing dumb was something she did well.

The door opened soundlessly and Dee entered the room. One look and she knew it was Miriam's. A king sized bed with canopy took up most of the space. On it was a gold and cream colored duvet. The duvet looked like a big cloud resting atop the bed. Just like the other bed, it was dotted with decorative pillows.

How did people sleep on beds with so many pillows?

The walls in Miriam's room were pale peach. They looked nice with the dark bedroom furniture. It wasn't the bed that told Dee she'd found the right room, though. She knew it was Miriam's room because the room smelled like her. Taking in all the opulence, she was pissed. Life was so unfair! Why did Miriam get to live like this and she was, well, stuck at Charlie's place?

Fuck it. She'd do what she'd always done. She'd even the odds. She'd learned that trick a long time ago. If she wanted something, she'd take it. There wasn't anyone going to give it to her if she didn't.

Determined to score, Dee marched through Miriam's bedroom, no longer afraid. She wasn't going to pussyfoot around anymore. If Miriam heard her and came looking, she'd be sorry!

Miriam's ensuite bathroom was just as luxurious as the rest of her house. Dee stopped to take it all in. The white marble on the living room fireplace continued in the bathroom on the countertop. The vanity had two sinks, with gleaming chrome facets and a large oval mirror above each. It ran the entire length of the bathroom wall.

Dee's reflection looked out of place in the room. The pale gray walls, the white and gray marble countertops, and the image of her there in the mirror made her cringe. For the first time in a long time, she stared at her reflection.

God, she looked like shit!

She was skinny. Her face hollow and pitted. Meth scars dotted the surface of her chin and nose. Dee's eyes locked on her nose. It was too big for her narrow face. She'd always hated her nose. As a kid, she had tried covering it with her hand when people looked at her. But it only made things worse. She bet that with Miriam's money, she could afford a nose job.

All the bad things she'd ever felt came rushing back. It felt intense, ugly, and hot. Her fingers curled into a ball. She wanted to put her fist through the mirror and shatter the image before her. But she didn't. Instead, Dee uncurled her fist and turned to the medicine cabinet. She wrenched open the little door, praying she'd find what she was after.

She hit pay dirt! Unlike the other medicine cabinet, this one was jammed full of bottles. Jesus! Miriam was a walking pharmacy!

Dee grabbed the first bottle she saw and pulled it out. She read the label, 'Zaroxolyn, take one tablet in the morning.' What was Zaroxolyn? She wondered if it would get her high. Not sure, she placed it on the counter and pulled out the next bottle.

Potassium. This one she knew wouldn't get her high. She pushed it aside and scanned the bottles next to it. Baby Aspirin, and nitroglycerin.

Hmm. Old Miriam must have heart problems.

A label caught her eye. Dee shoved the rest of the bottles aside and reached for it. OxyContin 80mg tablets! Holy shit, she'd hit the motherlode!

Wow! She couldn't believe her luck. She scanned the label, ignoring the cautionary warning about drowsiness, and looked for the tablet count. The prescription had been filled a month ago, but Miriam must not take many, the bottle was full. Dee's eyes narrowed as she read. According to the label on the bottle, there were a hundred and forty of these little beauties!

How the hell did Miriam score OxyContin? She thought they weren't prescribing it anymore. She'd heard doctors were prescribing Oxycodone instead. It was nowhere near as good as OxyContin, because of the time release mechanism thingy they'd built into it. Of course, any good addict could still get around something like that, but still.

"Dee?" Miriam pounded on the door.

Shit! The old lady was awake! Dee turned on the faucet and yelled, "Just a minute!"

Miriam continued to knock so Dee turned the tap on full and twisted the cap off the bottle. She shook out a tablet into her palm.

The round green pill stamped 80 was a beauty to behold. Finally, her luck had turned! She picked up the crystal water glass and filled it from the tap. The pill felt good in her mouth. The glass was halfway to her lips when she stopped.

A little voice whispered inside her head. Don't do it! What about Billy?

Dee plucked the pill from her mouth and stared down at the dampened orb. She'd be blowing a week of clean time if she did this. She couldn't remember the last time she'd gone this long. Not to mention thinking of getting Billy back. She wanted that in the worst way possible, but her brain wasn't wired for waiting. It was wired for now.

Before she could change her mind, Dee put the pill back in her mouth and bit down. Fuck the water; if she chewed it, it would work faster.

Miriam knocked again as she eyed the bottle. Should she just take half and leave Miriam some? Nah, she couldn't do it. She needed all of them. With her decision made, she plunged the whole bottle deep into her bra and closed the medicine cabinet door.

Then she flushed the toilet for good measure and turned off the tap.

"Dee," Miriam yelled, "You open up this door right now!"

With the water off, Dee could hear Miriam clearly. The poor old thing was getting hoarse. Dee yanked open the door. "Cool your jets."

Miriam glared at Dee from the other side of the door and looked anything but happy to see her.

Chapter **42**

COME ON, YOU'RE MAKING THIS MORE DIFFICULT THAN IT HAS TO BE. Lyndsey eyed the phone trying to work up her nerve when a sudden thought stopped her. There was no way she could call Susan from home. What if she had call display? How would Lyndsey explain why she was calling from home?

No, it would tip her off. Susan would know something was up, and Lyndsey wasn't ready for that. Nervous tension drove her out of the chair. She paced the kitchen and tried to come up with a new plan.

Maybe she could make the call from Drake's office? But then Drake's work number would show. That wouldn't work either. Maybe she could call block her phone? But she'd never done it before and didn't know how anyway.

And how would she explain wanting to meet away from work? This whole thing was becoming complicated. Maybe Lyndsey should just tell Susan the truth? But wouldn't that be professionally unethical? After all, Susan was a past patient and Lyndsey had stolen her file.

Without even realizing it, Lyndsey swiped at the crumbs on the countertop. After cleaning it, she turned to the wall and scrubbed it too.

She had her head in the microwave, eyeing the interior, when she caught herself. Stop it! Lord knows she'd much rather be cleaning than doing what she was about to do, but if she wanted information about her son—and she did—she'd need to stop putting off the inevitable.

As she put away her cleaning supplies, Lyndsey reached a decision. She'd get Billy ready and take him to the park. On the way there, she'd look for a payphone. After they'd finished at the park, she hoped Billy would be tired enough to sleep in the car, and then she could chat with Susan.

She didn't have all the details worked out just yet, but at least it was a start.

Billy was right where she'd left him, in front of the television. He loved TV and she was okay with that. Because she worked in the field of addiction and was a recovering addict, she was on guard for any behavior that could be interpreted as addictive. But honestly, sometimes she was a little too vigilant. It was easy for her to turn anything into an addiction. Drake had said she better watch out for that, and Lyndsey had agreed with him.

She picked up the remote and Billy's eyes followed it. His face foreshadowed the storm sure to come. Turning off the television would cause another outburst., which she just wasn't up to today.

Maybe bribery would work? Before Billy could get himself worked up, Lyndsey said, "Hey Billy, you want to go to the park?"

Billy loved the park. It was a big treat. The storm clouds disappeared. He grinned and jumped down off the couch as she clicked off the set. He danced circles around her legs. His joy was contagious and she grinned with him.

"We go park!" Billy squealed.

Lyndsey scooped him up. "We're going to the park," she corrected.

The grin slid from Billy's face to be replaced by a frown. Whether he understood it or not, he knew he was being corrected.

Great. Why did she have to be such a killjoy? Screw it; she needed to lighten up. Putting a finger under Billy's chin, Lyndsey met his eyes. "We go park," she conceded.

Billy grinned and clapped his hands. "We go park! We go park!"

"Yes," she nodded. "We go park. Now go get your coat on!" She put Billy down, smiling, as he raced off in the direction of his bedroom.

Relieved to have avoided a tantrum, she gathered up her purse and keys. Billy roared down the hallway shouting, "Park! We go to park!"

Lyndsey grinned, wishing she could get as excited about the whole thing.

Billy flung himself at her legs. "Go! Go!" he insisted. His Sponge Bob raincoat was inside out and hung crookedly on his little frame.

As she picked up Susan's file, she resisted the urge to fix Billy's coat. Instead, she opened the door and he scooted through it.

The park was deserted. Billy had it all to himself, which made it a much more fun place for her to be. With one eye on Billy, Lyndsey scanned Susan's file, wondering if there was anything she'd overlooked last night.

"Look! Look me!" Billy screeched as he slid down the slide.

She smiled and waved at him. He waved back and ran over to the swings.

She flipped through the pages, but couldn't find anything new. Doubt made her wonder; was she crazy to be doing this? Why did she keep sabotaging the nice life she and Drake had made for themselves? Taking on Billy and now this.

"Look Nin!"

Lyndsey closed the file and stuffed it back in her purse. Billy hung upside down from the swing. She got up from the park bench and walked over to him. "Are you having fun?" She gave him a little push as he hung upside down.

Giggles confirmed that he was. Billy shouted, "You too, Nin!"

She eyed the swing and thought, why not? She gave Billy another push and then lowered herself onto the swing next to him. Pumping her legs hard, she swung high into the sky.

"Me too! Me too!" Billy shouted from below.

Then Lyndsey did something she hadn't done since she was a child. She let go of the chain handles and launched into mid-air. She landed on the ground beside Billy.

He stared at her wide eyed. "Wow!" he said, letting go of his swing and running to hers.

"Careful!" She grabbed the chain and stopped it from hitting him. She picked up Billy and sat back down on the swing with him in her lap. She turned him so that he was facing her. "Are you ready?"

He nodded and Lyndsey pushed off, pumping as hard as she could. "Hold tight," she warned.

Billy's fingers went white as he held tightly to the chain. His laughter was like sunshine on her face. It warmed her all over. For a while, Lyndsey forgot about everything except the moving ground beneath their feet, and the dancing sky above them.

They swung for a long time. She was almost out of steam and she'd stayed much longer than she'd planned too. It was going to be a fight trying to get Billy in the car.

Oh well, you've already bribed him once today, a little voice in her head nagged. Using her feet as breaks, Lyndsey slowed the swing.

Billy stiffened in her arms and demanded, "More, Nins."

The swing stopped and she lowered him to the ground. Billy scowled up at her, his forehead wrinkled. He stomped his foot, crossed his arms, and stuck out his lower lip.

Before he could escalate further, Lyndsey said, "Ice cream."

His arms opened wide and he jumped up and down. "Scream, scream, me want scream," he agreed, racing in circles around Lyndsey's legs.

Jesus, she'd better watch it! She was rewarding bratty behavior with ice cream. Not a good idea at all! Preferably, he would fall asleep in the car so she could make the call before stopping for ice cream.

After she buckled Billy into his car seat, Lyndsey drove to the nearest mall. She circled the parking lot but couldn't see a pay phone. There was a Chevron gas station across the road. She'd try her luck there.

Glancing in the rear-view mirror, Lyndsey noticed Billy's head drooping. So far, so good! She pulled into the gas station and spotted a pay-phone on the wall right next to the door.

There was an empty parking spot beside it which she claimed. She glanced in the rear-view mirror again and sure enough, Billy was out. She left the car running, not wanting to chance waking Billy up, and took Susan's file and some change from her purse.

The phone booth was covered in graffiti. Whoever Renee was, she wouldn't be happy when she saw what was written about her.

Come on, Linds. Quit stalling!

Opening the file to the front page, Lyndsey memorized the number. She took a big breath, dropped in a quarter and listened for the dial tone.

One ring, two. She swallowed, trying to wet her dry mouth. The phone was heavy in her hand. She wanted to hang it up but couldn't.

On the third ring, Lyndsey remembered to breathe. Maybe Susan wasn't home. God she hoped so… God she hoped not!

What if her voice mail came on? Should she leave a message? But then what if Susan called her back at work?

"Hello," Susan answered.

A big knot lodged in Lyndsey's throat and she squeaked, "Hello."

"Hello?" Susan's voice turned sharp. "If this is a sales call, I'm not interested."

Lyndsey willed herself to speak.

"Who is this?" Susan demanded. "If you don't tell me your name right now, I'm hanging up!"

"Don't hang up!" Lyndsey blurted, finally able to get the words out.

"Lyndsey? Is that you?"

"Yes, it's me."

"Did you hear about Declan?" There was panic in Susan's voice.

Lyndsey hoped to sound reassuring. "No, at least..." she faltered. "I don't think so, but, ahh, I'd like to talk to you. Do you have a minute?"

Chapter **43**

A DROPLET OF SWEAT LANDED ON THE FLOOR IN FRONT of him. Declan swiped it away with his mop. The floor gleamed from his efforts. He rinsed the mop in the bucket Lite-bright had left out for him and took another pass at the floor. The infirmary had smelled of piss when he first walked in. But thanks to his efforts, all Declan could smell now was bleach. He put the mop back in the bucket and looked around.

The two beds in the infirmary were occupied by patients. On the first bed was a very skinny man. His long, matted gray and brown hair poked out from his sheet draped body. One thin, long arm hung down over the side of his bed. It ended in yellow nicotine-stained fingers.

Declan dismissed the skinny man and dragged his mop over to the next bed. Gary was propped up on it, gazing out the window. He looked like shit. Worse than shit, actually. Gary's face was green; even stranger, the whites of his eyes were yellow. His pock-marked face was shiny and his oily hair stood up on end.

"Gary," Declan whispered.

Gary dragged his eyes away from the window and looked at Declan. "Huh?"

"Jeez, Gary, I've been looking all over for you."

Gary frowned and shook his head. A lock of hair fell down and landed on his nose. With a shaky hand, he smoothed it back in place. "Huh?" he asked again.

A thin tube snaked into Gary's wrist. He stroked it absently and then turned back to gaze out the window.

What the fuck? Trying a different approach, Declan whispered, "Hey Gary, it's me, Declan."

"Stop talking!" the skinny man from the next bed moaned.

Gary turned to Declan and stammered, "Deck, deck. Whaa kind a name isss that?"

What the hell? Was Gary playing with him? He eyed the bag hanging from the aluminum IV pole. With Gary this wasted, Declan expected to see hydro-morphine or Demerol written on the bag, but it was neither. It looked like Gary was bombed on saline.

This didn't make any sense. Gary was in worse shape than when he'd last seen him. "Gary," Declan tried again and shook Gary's shoulder.

The skinny man in the next bed threw off his covers, sat up, and glared at Declan. Declan smiled at him and hoped he would lie back down.

No such luck. The skinny man pointed a finger at him. "You're not supposed to be in here!"

He thought fast. "I'm filling in for Lite-bright. He's not feeling very good today and Pete didn't want him passing his sick germs on to you."

"What's wrong with the kid?" the skinny man snickered, "I mean other than the color of his hair, that is."

"Ah," Declan stumbled. "I think it was something he ate."

"Jesus, you kids nowadays are sure soft. When I was your age," he peered over at Declan. "How old are you anyway?"

274

"Twenty-one," Declan lied.

"Well, like I was saying, you boys need to toughen up. Take a guy like me, for instance. I've been using heroin since you were in diapers."

"You say that like it's a major accomplishment or something."

One scraggly eyebrow rose and he snorted, "It is an accomplishment! How many old junkies like me do you see around the streets these days?'

This was stupid. Declan didn't come here to talk. He glanced over at Gary, but he appeared to have fallen asleep.

"Well?"

"Um," Declan stalled for time.

"None!" The skinny guy cackled. "It takes a lot of smarts," he said, tapping the side of his head, "To make it as far in life as I have. Most of my friends are dead. You know why? Because they were just too dammed soft and didn't know how to play the system!"

Jesus, this guy was nuts!

"What'd you say your name was?" The skinny guy looked suspiciously at Declan again.

"I didn't."

"Never mind, it doesn't matter anyway. My name is Mike, but they call me Felix."

Baffled, Declan wondered how you'd get Felix from Mike, but that was one story he didn't want to hear. Declan noticed that when drug addicts were bored, they liked to talk shit. He stayed silent, hoping Felix would shut up and go back to sleep.

"Shouldn't you be working?" Felix pointed to the bucket and mop.

Shit! Declan didn't come here to work, or talk. He came here for the money Gary was supposed to be holding for him.

When he didn't move, Felix asked again, "Are you sure you're supposed to be in here?"

Declan nodded. Maybe Felix wasn't as dumb as he first appeared. He picked up the mop and swiped around Gary's bed.

"Yeah, like I said, Pete told me to take Lite-bright's place," he explained.

"Oh?" Felix scratched his head and then jumped down from his bed. "Well if Pete knows about it, then I guess it's okay."

"Yeah, it's cool," Declan agreed.

Felix crossed the floor with his backside exposed. The white hospital gown hung off his skinny frame, showing off his hairy back and flat ass.

"I gotta take a leak," Felix said over one shoulder. "Be right back."

Oh please, take your time! But Declan didn't say it. Instead, he just grunted and turned to Gary. Expecting to see him asleep, Declan jumped.

Gary grinned at him and winked. "That guy's got jack shit on me, huh kid?"

"Jesus Gary! You scared me. What the hell are you doing?"

"Keep your voice down," Gary warned. "Ole Felix will be back in no time."

"But I thought..." he stopped. "Were you just playin' me?"

"Nah," Gary laughed. "I got nothing against you kid. The way I figure it, if I have to be here, being in the infirmary is the best place to be. They bring me my medications and meals, with none of that group bullshit you have to go through."

"Gary, where..."

"Why are you still here?" Gary interrupted him. "Didn't you say you were leaving?"

"You bastard! We had a deal."

"What deal?" Gary stared back, his eyes big yellow eyes all innocent.

"Jesus, Gary!"

"Ha, ha," Gary slapped his thigh. "I'm playing with ya, kid. Lighten up!" He glanced at the door way and got up.

Declan shoved the mop and bucket out of the way and leaned up against the wall.

Gary pulled his mattress up and felt underneath. "We done good kid," he said, dropping the mattress and climbing back into the bed.

Declan lowered his voice and asked, "How much?"

Gary fanned the bills out in front of him. "Four hundred bucks."

"Is that all?'

"Is that all?" Gary frowned at him. "What the hell's that supposed to mean? Where I come from, four hundred bucks is a lot of money. Way I see it, your share's gonna be a hundred, and I'll take the rest."

"No way, I should get half!"

"Uh uh," Gary shook his head. "I broke into the safe. It was me taking all the risks."

"That's not—" But Declan never got to finish his sentence.

Four men burst into the room. One was Pete, the other Tom. But it was the other two men with them which caused Declan's stomach to curl.

Gary gasped, "What the hell?"

Tom looked on solemnly. "The gig's up, boys."

Pete just shook his head sadly.

Declan stared at the door and wondered if he should make a run for it. As if he'd just read his mind, Hawkface held an open pair of handcuffs and snapped one on his wrist.

Fat cop, AKA Officer Wilkes, stepped forward and said, "You have the right to remain silent…"

Declan panicked. He pulled his arm away, but the steel cuffs circling his wrist wouldn't budge.

"Just a minute," Pete waved at Hawkface. He looked at Gary and Declan. "Tom and I have been watching you two for some time now. We knew it was you who broke into the safe. We hoped you'd come forward and admit your mistake, especially you, Declan. I was impressed with the progress you were making on your assignments. I thought you were starting to come around."

Tears stung Declan's eyes. "I am! I swear it, Pete, I am! If you'd just give me another chance, I'll do anything you ask."

Tom shook his head and blew out a breath. "Sorry boys. I hate to say it, but you're all out of chances."

Chapter **44**

"WHAT WERE YOU DOING IN THERE?"

"Nothing! Jesus, Miriam, chill!" Dee huffed, and pushed her out of the way.

Miriam tottered after her, muttering to herself.

If Dee wanted the old gal's money, she'd better hurry. It wouldn't be long before her eyes would start to droop, and then Miriam would be on to her.

"Jeez!" She turned to face Miriam. "Can't a girl have a little privacy?"

"Hmm." Miriam cleared her throat and looked at her suspiciously. "Let's go into the kitchen. We might as well get started."

As they entered the kitchen, Dee noted that Miriam had been busy. On the table was a pen, paper, and the Big Blue Book.

"Take a seat," Miriam ordered, waving at a chair.

Dee eyed the blank paper and wondered if she should just grab the money and run.

Miriam pulled out the chair across from Dee and sat down. She opened the book and said, "We should start on step one, but I've got a feeling we need to go bigger than that, so..." Miriam trailed off, seeming unsure. She looked at Dee and made up her mind. Miriam let out a breath and continued. "We're going to skip steps one through three and start on four."

As she doodled on the sheet in front of her, Dee tried to plan her next move. With the bottle of oxys and a couple of bucks, she wouldn't have to pull any tricks for days. Hell, she might not even pick up H. Maybe she'd just rent a nice room to relax in and finish off the bottle of pills. She could watch TV, have a bubble bath, and order in a nice big juicy steak.

"I'm probably going to get in trouble for this," Miriam broke in, and thrust the Big Blue Book at her. "I want you to turn to page forty-two."

To pacify Miriam, Dee flipped through the pages.

"All I'd like you to do is to listen. Okay?" Miriam's eyes met hers.

Dee nodded and let her mind drift. If she stuck to her plan, she wouldn't be hurting anyone. Besides, if the pills were prescription medication, and they were, it wouldn't be as bad as using heroin.

"This might seem kind of overwhelming at first." Miriam tapped a long, bent finger on the thick pad of paper. "You'll be doing a lot of writing, and then we're going to talk about what you've written down."

Dee looked past Miriam's head out of the kitchen window and noticed it was growing dark outside. "Shouldn't Charlie be back by now?"

"Don't worry about Charlie. He'll come by when I call and tell him to."

Dee wasn't worried about Charlie. It was probably a good idea for her to leave before he got here. Miriam and Charlie together would only get in her way.

"Step Four," Miriam announced, reading from the blue book.

The way Dee saw it, heroin was the enemy. If she didn't use that, she'd be fine. Pills weren't a threat. They were her friend. She could already feel their warm kiss in her skin.

"Made a searching and fearless moral inventory of ourselves," Miriam's words drifted over to her on a soft cloud.

"Mmm." Dee felt better than she had in a long while, and sighed with pleasure. Why had she ever stopped using? Well, truthfully, she guessed she hadn't. If it wasn't for Charlie, she wouldn't even be sitting here.

"Do you know what that means?"

The cloud broke apart and Dee raised her head. "Huh?"

"Step four. Do you have any questions?"

Dee's eyelids felt heavy. She fought to keep them open.

"What's wrong with you?"

Her head jerked up and she blinked.

Miriam's lips twisted downwards and she frowned. "Why are you so sleepy?"

"I'm not," she lied.

"Yes, you are." Miriam eyed her shrewdly.

Under Miriam's frosty glare, some of Dee's fuzziness wore off to be replaced with anger. "You know Miriam, you're really a bitch. You invite me here, and then ask me to work on some stupid…" Dee glanced at the pen and paper, confused, "…I don't even know what! And to top it all off, you follow me around and accuse me of being high!"

Miriam's brow wrinkled. Then she smiled. "I have been known to come across a little too strong," she admitted.

In control again, Dee relaxed against her chair. "Well," she frowned, "If you don't stop it, I'm gonna leave. I don't need this kind of…"

"It's okay, Dee," Miriam broke in and squeezed her hand. Her grasp was surprisingly strong.

Dee's hand lay limp in Miriam's. She felt weird. Should she jerk her hand away, or leave it there?

"I was wrong." Miriam's eyes welled up with tears.

A strange flutter moved deep in Dee's chest. She hoped it didn't rattle the pill bottle nestled inside of her bra. "Never mind," Dee replied, and pulled her hand free. "It doesn't matter."

"Yes, it does," Miriam argued. "The last thing I wanted was for you to feel unwelcome in my home."

"Well, I…" Dee didn't know what to say to that. She just needed to get Miriam's money and go. Only now, she felt like a big shit for thinking about it.

"Will you forgive me?" Miriam's voice quavered as she met Dee's eyes.

Guilt weighed heavily on Dee. It was horrible and suffocating. She wanted to run and hide. She really did. It took everything she had just to remain in her chair. It was the money that kept her there, and the thought of stealing it made Dee want to bolt.

Double jeopardy. That's what Dee called it. It was a terrible place to be. She wanted the hotel room and bubble bath. She wanted the sweet release that the little beauties nestled inside of her bra would bring. She wanted the juicy steak and soft bed. She wanted to be left alone.

But there were things she didn't want too. Dee didn't want to hurt Miriam. But she could see no other way around it. Her recent stay at Charlie's had softened her. She'd better get it together.

With the choice made, Dee doubled over and moaned.

Miriam was at her side in a flash. "Are you all right?"

Dee tucked her head between her knees and gasped, "Stomach cramps."

"Would a hot water bottle help?"

She raised her head and shook it. "Uh, uh, I need to use the wash-room again."

Miriam linked her arm through hers and helped her up.

"I can walk," Dee assured her, not wanting Miriam to follow her down the hallway.

Miriam wrung her hands. "I'll add some ginger to our tea. It helps with stomach ailments."

"Good idea," Dee said, and headed in the direction of the bathroom.

When she rounded the corner, she stopped and listened. Cupboard doors opened and closed. Good, Miriam was busy.

Making a bee line for the office, Dee opened the door and stepped through. She hoped she was right! The desk drawer opened silently. Inside it she could see a stapler, rubber bands, and paperclips. She closed it and moved on to the next drawer.

This time she wasn't so lucky. The drawer stuck, jammed from the inside by a jumble of papers. Dee pulled hard and winced as it came open with a loud grating sound. She reached in and yanked a handful of papers free from the drawer. Not bothering to look at them, she dropped them on the floor. The drawer was stuffed full. There were stamped utility bills, and an odd assortment of pens and pencils. Damn it, no cash! But there was one good find.

An embossed, black leather cover stamped 'Miriam' caught her eye. Dee bet anything Miriam's checks were inside. She reached in and flipped open the leather covering. She grinned; sure enough, there they were. Even though she didn't find cash, this was almost as good. She'd just write herself a big fat check and drop in the bank machine, and then it'd be smooth sailing.

As she closed the desk drawer and shoved the check book down the front of her pants, Dee glanced at the mess she'd made. She couldn't leave it like that. She crammed the papers back into the drawer and backed out of the room.

"Dee?" Miriam called from the kitchen. "Are you okay?"

Good, she wasn't coming to check on her. "Yes, I'm fine," Dee called back. "I'll be out in a minute."

The check book scratched her belly. She shoved it farther down her pants and looked in the mirror, hoping it didn't show.

The mirror wasn't her friend. Dee glanced at her flat, lifeless eyes and looked away, deciding it was time to go. As her hand reached for the doorknob, she stopped. Might as well take another pill. She wouldn't be around long enough for Miriam to notice anyways.

Dee pulled the bottle from her bra and twisted off the cap. She wished she had her syringe handy. Surprised at the thought, she pushed it away and shook a pill into her palm. She tossed it into her mouth and bit down. It tasted nasty. A bitter chalky paste filled her mouth. She ground her teeth together and swallowed.

Years of altered brain chemistry as a result of her addiction had taken its toll. The urge to get wasted was strong. Dee eyed the bottle and shook out another tablet.

Fuck it. With her tolerance, one more wouldn't hurt.

Chapter **45**

"WHAT DO YOU MEAN, YOU DON'T THINK SO? ISN'T that why you're calling me?" Susan screeched.

"What? I'm not following you. Please Susan, slow down." Lyndsey's fingers clenched the phone so tightly, they hurt. Flexing them, she took a deep breath.

Not slowing down but speeding up instead, Susan blurted, "Is there any way he can come to you? I don't want him going back to jail. Oh God…" she broke off in sobs.

A heavy blanket of dread unfolded in Lyndsey's chest. Something must have happened to Declan!

"Lyndsey, you have to help us!"

She forced herself to stay calm and said, "I need you to start from the beginning, and go slowly."

Susan stuttered, "What? I'm confused. You wouldn't be calling if you didn't know, right? How did you find out, anyways?" Susan stopped talking and blew her nose.

Lyndsey pulled the phone from her ear and tried to come up with a good explanation. "I don't know what you're talking about. I was calling to see if you were coming to our alumni luncheon," she said, thinking of an upcoming event.

"The alumni luncheon? Nobody told me about a luncheon."

"Never mind," Lyndsey said. "What happened to Declan?"

"Oh my god, you wouldn't believe it! I just got a call from Tom, over at the government facility where—"

"Yes, yes, I know where Declan is," she said. "I went to visit him there with you, remember? What happened?" Dee nearly shouted the last sentence. She'd better keep it together. It was a lot easier when she thought Declan was Susan's child. When it was your own child that was in trouble, it changed everything.

"Like I said, I got a call from Tom. Apparently," sarcasm dripped from Susan's voice, "Declan stole money from the rehab facility and now his parole conditions are revoked."

Poor Susan, she had such a tough time believing her boy was capable of these things. Now she was beginning to understand why.

"When Tom called you, what did he say? Did he say they were taking him back to jail, or trying to find another facility for him?"

"They hadn't decided yet. That's why I was going to call you. Can you please call Tom? I bet if you tell him Declan can go to your facility, they'll take him there instead of talking him to jail. God, Lyndsey," Susan begged, "Please! I don't want him to go to jail. He's not a criminal!"

Actually he is, but Lyndsey didn't say it. Every drug addict was a criminal. When you took illegal drugs, what else would you call yourself?

Even when the drugs were prescribed by a doctor, if you were an addict, you would eventually find reasons to increase the dosage. Still, Lyndsey more than anyone knew that drug addicts and alcoholics weren't bad people. But they were sick.

"Lyndsey, are you there?"

"I'm here, I was just thinking."

If she got involved with this, how would she explain why she was calling in about a new admission when she'd just called in to say Billy was sick?

"Well, think fast, because we're running out of time."

"You know, if Declan comes to us, you'll have to pay. Do you think your ex would chip in?"

"I don't know. We're not on very good terms. And you know I'm on the verge of bankruptcy. Still…" Susan trailed off.

Lyndsey wondered if they could get Declan into treatment on a scholarship. Normally the participant needed to be involved, and show their commitment by phoning in and doing all the paperwork. She didn't even know if Declan wanted to go into another rehab facility.

She would be breaking all the rules by doing what she was considering. But there was an upside to this. She wanted to know where Susan adopted Declan. What town and what hospital? She had the date. If Lyndsey filled out the application form with Susan, she could find a way to get those answers.

"I might have an idea," Lyndsey said. "But a lot of it would depend on Declan."

"What idea? What do you mean?"

She ran through the scenario with Susan, emphasizing Declan's need to be willing to attend treatment in order to be accepted for scholarship.

"That would be fantastic! How soon will you know? Where do we go from here?"

"Give me Tom's number and I'll call him. He might not be able to give me much, due to confidentiality rules, but I'll get what I can. Then I'll call you back. Between us, we might come up with something."

"Do you think you could pull some strings?" Susan asked hopefully.

"I wouldn't put it that way," Lyndsey said. But wasn't that exactly what she was doing?

"I'll be forever in your debt if we can pull this off," Susan promised. "I'd be so happy for Declan. I never thought much of that government rehab he was in. It looked, well, shabby."

"Susan," Lyndsey reminded her, "Declan was lucky to have the opportunity to attend there. Someone took a big chance on him, and he's blown it by the sounds of it."

"You don't know that!"

"I'm not going to argue with you, and I doubt the center made up those facts. I need you to be on board with me or I can't help you. Going back to your old ways of enabling won't help Declan, they'll only enable his addiction," Lyndsey warned.

"You can say that, but no one knows my baby like I do."

Losing control, Lyndsey snapped, "He's not a baby, and you're not helping him! If you continue to make excuses for his poor choices, we might as well throw in the towel right now!"

"Easy for you to say," Susan snapped back. "But you wouldn't say that if he was your child. I don't care how many times you tell me. You can't possibly know how hard it is to turn your back on your baby, especially since you've never had one."

Susan had a point. Truthfully, she was beginning to see how hard this whole mess was. When it came to matters of the heart, it appeared logic came in second place.

"You're right," Lyndsey agreed, "It is easy for me to say. So let's work together on this."

Susan readily agreed. "I'm sorry. I know I'm reverting back to old behaviors, but I'm scared. You know nothing good comes from going to jail."

"Not true," Lyndsey argued. "Sometimes jail is exactly what's needed. People do get clean in there. But," she hurried before Susan interrupted her, "In this case, I think our facility is Declan's best chance."

"I agree. So what do we do now?"

"I'll call Tom and see if I can get Declan transferred to us. But first, I need to see if we have a bed available. And if we do, I'll meet with you and Declan to go over the scholarship papers."

"Okay, what do you need me to do?" Susan asked.

Lyndsey thought for a second. "I need you to wait by the phone. And Susan?"

"Yes?"

"Now would be a good time to pray."

Lyndsey hung up and blinked. Her heart was heavy. She was riding a runaway train that could derail at any second. A little voice whispered in her head, *everything happens for a reason*. Very soon, she may have the answers she'd been seeking for the last twenty years.

She shivered and plucked a quarter from her wallet. Ready or not, it was time she found out.

Chapter **46**

Tom pulled the phone from his ear and turned to Officer Wilkes. "Can you boys hold up a minute? His Mom," he craned his neck in Declan's direction, "says she thinks another rehab facility will take him."

"Nah," Officer Wilkes shook his head. "I don't think mommy is going to fix it this time."

"But—" Declan stopped as Tom shook his head.

The other cop had taken Gary into the next room. They'd separated the two of them before Declan could get his hands on the money. It was right there in plain sight when the police had entered the room. Declan was so busted. His mind spun, trying to come up with a plausible excuse.

"She might," Tom chuckled. "Never underestimate the power of mothers."

"It's cut and dried. The kid," Officer Wilkes jerked a fat finger in his direction, "is in violation of his parole."

Declan's eyes darted between Tom and Officer Wilkes. If he wasn't mistaken, Tom was on his side. Why, he had no idea. But if that was the case, why had Tom phoned the cops in the first place? It didn't make any sense. Was he missing something?

"Maybe not," Tom shook his head and strode over to the gray metal filing cabinet leaning against the far wall.

"This is a waste of time!" Officer Wilkes argued.

Declan got the feeling Tom didn't like Officer Wilkes much.

Tom shrugged. "Think of all the overtime you'll get on your next check." He pulled open the gray metal drawer and peered inside.

For the first time in ages, Declan was looking forward to seeing his mom. He'd expected to hear her crying on the other end of the phone when Tom called, but he didn't hear anything at all. Which was weird. On her last visit, something was different about her. She'd rambled on about starting a new life and said she'd sought help. Why, he didn't know. As far as he could tell, the only problem she had was his dad leaving all those years ago. He didn't think she needed rehab for that.

Officer Wilkes sighed. "I don't have all day, you know."

Declan felt more confused than ever. He couldn't get a read on Tom's face, and he wasn't sure what was going on.

"Yeah, yeah," Tom pulled open the next drawer down and muttered, "It's in here somewhere."

Officer Wilkes blew out a breath and waddled over to the chair. He eyed it, probably wondering the same thing as Tom. Would he fit? The officer backed his large ass up to the chair and lowered himself down.

It was a tight squeeze. The cop dwarfed the chair and fat bulged through the arm rest. The chair under him groaned in protest.

"Hey Tom, can you turn on the AC?" Officer Wilkes swiped at the drops of sweat rolling down his red face.

"No can do," Tom replied, turning around. "Budget cuts from the mayor. AC was the first thing to go."

Declan stared at the floor and bit his tongue. Officer Wilkes didn't need AC, he needed liposuction!

Thumbing through a red file, Tom stopped. "Ah, here it is." He used his elbow to close the metal drawer, crossed the office, and sat down behind his desk.

"Well?" Officer Wilkes struggled to sit upright.

"Just a minute." Tom frowned and scanned the papers in his hands.

Declan stared at the red folder Tom held. What was in it?

"Ahem," Tom cleared his throat. He pushed his glasses up on his head and nodded "I thought so. See here." He turned the file so it faced Officer Wilkes and shoved it across the desk at him.

The cop made to get up and stopped. He turned to Declan. "Pass it over to me, will you?"

Glad to be of service and to earn a few brownie points, Declan jumped up from his chair. Resisting the urge to read what was there, he picked up the file and placed it in the cop's outstretched hand.

"You'll find his parole order on the last page," Tom advised.

Officer Wilkes opened the red folder and placed it on his lap. He thumbed through the pages, and stopped halfway. Marking his place with a finger, he raised his head and looked at Tom. "What's an A and D?"

"It's nothing you need to concern yourself with." Tom looked at the cop and then he looked away. "If you must know, it's a term we use for an alcohol and drug history. It was going to be Declan's next assignment."

"Oh?" Officer Wilkes shrugged and turned back to the file in his lap. He thumbed through a couple more pages and stopped. His eyes narrowed and he frowned. Yanking a single paper free of the folder, he held it up and looked at Tom. "That says he has to go straight to jail!" he exclaimed, and pointed at the third paragraph.

Tom looked at Declan before turning to the cop. "Do I have to spell it out for you? The court clerk left a big loophole when writing this up."

"What do you mean?"

"Yeah, what do you mean, Tom?" Declan asked.

"This legal document says Declan here has two choices. He can go to rehab or, if he refuses to go, he goes back to jail."

Officer Wilkes snorted. "We knew that already. It's why we brought him to you in the first place. Now he blew it, so guess what?" He smiled and looked over at Declan. "You're going back to jail."

"But that's not what it says." Tom pointed at the document. "You don't have to be a lawyer to understand it. The order is clear, and the way I see it, as long as Declan agrees to go to another treatment center, he doesn't have to go back to jail."

"Jesus Christ!" Officer Wilkes pushed himself up from his chair. "Are you telling me I don't know how to do my job?" The cop waved the file at Tom. "That's nuts! This kid can't create a stink wherever he goes, and get himself kicked out of one rehab facility after another. Are you're saying there's nothing we can do about it?"

Holy shit! Was this true? Declan hid a grin when Tom cut in.

"Oh there's something we can do about it, all right." Tom slapped his desk.

"What do you have in mind?" Officer Wilkes asked.

"Well," Tom replied, and slid the glasses back on his nose. "We're going to make a little change to the document."

Somewhat smugly, Declan shook his head. "Can't alter a legal document," he argued.

"True," Tom grinned. "That's why your mom is bringing her lawyer here. Officer Wilkes and your mom's lawyer can take the document back to court and ask for an alteration. The alteration will read: 'If Declan leaves prematurely or is discharged from rehab, he will proceed immediately to jail."

The cop scratched his head and looked at Tom, then at Declan. He appeared to be softening. "I can take him right now, but I guess one more chance wouldn't hurt."

Tom turned to Declan. "Your mom's lawyer will go before the court to make the appeal while you're getting settled into your new surroundings."

Declan didn't like this new alteration at all. The courts had screwed up. It was his get out of jail free card. He shot from his chair outraged. "You can't do that!"

Tom looked at him with sorrow. "Oh, but I can," he disagreed. "If you don't want to play my way, you're going back to jail. You can sit there while the lawyers figure it all out."

"Yeah right! My mother will never go for this!" Declan insisted.

"Oh, but she will." The sad look on Tom's face changed to a smirk, as he added, "She was the one that suggested it."

Chapter **47**

"HERE LOVE, DRINK THIS. IT WILL HELP." MIRIAM thrust a fresh cup of ginger tea in front of her and said, "Do you feel well enough to go on?"

Dee took a sip of tea and set the cup back in its saucer. Her fingers felt rubbery. Come to think of it, so did her neck. The tea warmed her throat and slid into her belly. She sighed. It was better than being under a thick, fuzzy blanket.

"If not," Miriam said from far off in the distance, "I can put it away and we can try again tomorrow."

"Tomorrow, tomorrow, I love you tomorrow," Dee sang and giggled.

"What?" Miriam looked at her, confused.

"Nothing," Dee said. "It's just a silly little song I used to sing to my son."

"Oh?" Miriam halted.

"I'll get him back. You'll see."

"Hmm," Miriam shook her head and looked serious. "You need to work on your fourth step. You have a lot of work to do before you'll be fit to raise your son."

"Head and shoulders, knees and toes…" Dee floated back to the hotel room and was giving Billy his bath.

Miriam nudged her on the shoulder. Dee's head jerked up.

"You're not making sense."

The room spun and Dee blinked. "Whoa!" She held onto the kitchen table.

"Are you dizzy?"

Her head bobbed up and down, and she grinned. The room spun out and she was on the merry-go-round. "I am!" she laughed.

"You don't have to sound so happy about it." Miriam frowned.

The merry-go-round cracked beneath her feet and Dee fell to the ground. Tears stung her eyes and she whispered. "I'm sorry. I'll be good."

Miriam's forehead puckered. "There's nothing to be sorry about, Dee. I know whatever brought you to this point in your life wasn't entirely of your own making."

Billy grinned up at her from his towel, freshly scrubbed and toothless. A sob caught in her throat.

"Oh sweetie." Warm arms wrapped around her shoulders. Miriam whispered in her ear. "Let it all out."

"I miss my little boy," Dee wailed.

"Of course you do," Miriam crooned.

They rocked together, and she was on a see-saw. She went up. She came down.

"You're doing the best thing you can for him."

The see-saw vanished and she was back in Miriam's arms.

"Little boys need healthy mums. I should know. My drinking damaged my kids. They're still paying for my mistakes."

Blah, blah, blah, Dee didn't want to hear it. Miriam was ruining her buzz. Dee squirmed, wanting free from Miriam's embrace.

Miriam picked up on her cue and let go. "I know it's not fun to talk about this." Her eyes narrowed and she leaned in close. "But it's necessary. You can't heal what you continue to avoid."

The walls in the kitchen shifted, like they were attached to a big wave. Dee thought she might be sick.

"Still not feeling well?"

The table rolled up and down in front of her. The room spun. She lowered her head and her eyes fluttered shut.

Warm fingers stroked her brow. "You poor wee thing, you're really not well."

"Mmm," Dee agreed.

"Why don't we put this away for now?" Miriam shuffled papers and snapped the book closed beside her.

The kitchen disappeared and Dee was on the beach. The blue sky overhead was gorgeous and the sand was white and hot beneath her feet. Her eye lids burned, swollen and heavy.

Miriam's question reached her beach. "Do you want me to call Charlie, or would you rather lie down in the guest room?"

The beach dissolved back into the kitchen table and Dee fought to stay awake. "Want to stay here," she mumbled.

Miriam helped her up. "A good night's sleep is what you need. I'll phone Charlie and let him know you're staying here tonight."

Dee nodded, holding onto Miriam's arm as she led Dee down the hallway.

They entered the guest bedroom and Miriam flicked on the light switch. "Don't worry about your clothes. I can loan you one of my nighties."

Dee giggled. Nightie. Miriam was so cute. She leaned over and placed a wet, sloppy kiss on her cheek.

Miriam patted her on the hand and then turned to pull down the bedcovers. "I'll be right back with your nightie. There's a fresh towel and face cloth on the shelf in the guest bathroom. Just help yourself."

Silly, I already did! Dee almost blurted it out, but caught herself just in time.

The opiates in her bloodstream worked faster than she thought they would. She felt a warm glow, like sweet honey circulating within her. She wanted to give Miriam another kiss, but managed to hold back.

Love, love, love! She loved it!

An electric hum buzzed inside her head. If her skin could sing, it would have. Fragments of songs from her past came to mind. She sang off key and stumbled to bed. Crawling in, she pulled the covers up to her chin. The song changed and another one took its place. The music turned off and a long, dark tunnel opened up in front of her. Not fearing the dark space, she entered.

The bedroom disappeared and she was back on the beach playing in the warm tropical ocean. Sea salt residue stuck to her arm and she giggled, getting water in her mouth. She tried to spit it out, but inhaled more in the process. Deep, wet coughs exploded from her, and she floundered. Her arms flayed and her feet thrashed as she choked on the ocean.

A large wave picked her up and she rode it, skimming the surface. The water held a powerful undertow. It took all her efforts just to stay on top of the wave. She skimmed along the surface for a few more seconds before being dragged under beneath the waves.

The ocean pushed and pulled her. Numbness set in. She could no longer feel her body. She became one with the ocean. She was water, salt, softness, and bliss.

Her breathing grew shallow and slowed down, and then everything went black.

Chapter **48**

"A<small>RE YOU SURE YOU WANT TO TAKE HIM ON</small>?" T<small>OM</small> asked incredulously.

Lyndsey nodded and then realized he couldn't see her. "Yes, I'm sure."

"Do you mind me asking why?"

As she twisted the phone cord around her finger, she thought, *yes, I do! It's none of your damn business.* But she didn't say it. Instead, she repeated herself. "Like I said, Declan's mother was a patient of mine. She asked me to facilitate his transfer into our care."

"Oh?" Tom blew out a breath. "Still, it's kind of unusual, don't you think?"

Buddy, you wouldn't believe it if I told you!

"Not that I'm disagreeing or anything," Tom continued. "Just between you and me, I've grown fond of the little shit." He laughed. "He's not doing anything I wouldn't have done at his age. Course, that's what landed me in rehab. And it's a good thing it did because…"

"Excuse me, Tom," Lyndsey cut in.

"Oh, sorry," Tom apologized. "I'm rambling, aren't I?"

"A little," she agreed.

"Well," Tom sighed into the receiver. "There's a little matter of the two cops from the sheriff's department, which might not be that big a problem, now that I think about it. The kid has a court mandate to be in treatment, or back in jail. The document didn't say which rehab facility he had to attend, just that he had to attend one."

"That's good. I don't think the courts will argue with where he's going, just as long as he gets there."

"I don't know…"

"Think about it. This time it's not on the taxpayer's dime."

"True, I guess. It might take some convincing, though."

"Don't worry," Lyndsey said. "I'll advise Susan to seek legal counsel. She can sign anything you want. She'll take full legal responsibility for any of the fallout."

"I'm sure we can handle it. I'll get Pete to print out a release of transfer."

This was all great, but she wasn't even sure she could get Declan a bed. If he'd used in the rehab facility he was in now, there was no way her center would take him. They wouldn't want to put their patients at risk.

Shit! Why hadn't she thought of this before? Lyndsey fought to sound calm. "Are you sure he's still clean?"

"Yeah, I'm sure. He never got his hands on the money and we drug tested him to be certain. It came back negative. He's clean."

Relief swept over her. One less hurdle to deal with, she sighed. "That's good. We couldn't have taken him if he wasn't."

"Oh, believe me, if he wasn't clean, we wouldn't be having this conversation. He'd be going straight back to jail."

"Why did you test him? Was it random? Isn't that expensive?"

"No, it wasn't like that. His roommate got into the hand sanitizer. He and Declan partnered up to pull off a little robbery. We had to make sure Declan was clean, so we used a urine drug test kit."

"They're not as conclusive as blood," she said, worried.

"I know, but I was with him. He was stone cold sober. Took the kid forever to take a leak." Tom chuckled.

Not wanting to go there, Lyndsey switched topics. "So what do we have to do to make this happen?"

"I need to talk with the two cops here. They'll be escorting Declan to your facility."

Shit, she hadn't thought about that either. Joanne, her clinical director, would not be impressed with the chaos cops were sure to bring to the inpatient population.

What a mess! And it was getting worse by the minute.

"Okay, so why don't you talk with them, and I'll call you back? I have one more call I need to make before we can make this happen."

"If," Tom warned, "we can make it happen."

"Right," she agreed. "If… I'll call you right back."

She hung up the phone and chewed on her thumb nail. Things were about to get very messy. She'd have to lie through her teeth if this was going to work. So much for her program of honesty. She just hoped she was doing the right thing. Lyndsey closed her eyes and said a silent prayer. With a deep breath, she plucked another quarter from her wallet and punched in numbers.

In a disguised voice, she asked the receptionist for Joanne's line. Luckily, she picked on the third ring. "Joanne speaking," she said crisply into the phone.

She cleared her throat and began. "Hi Joanne, its Lyndsey."

"Hi Lyndsey, how's Billy feeling?'

Guilt washed over her. She was such a jerk! "He's okay. I think it's just a stomach bug. You know kids." She paused, because Joanne didn't have kids, and it was a sore subject. "Anyway, I think he's feeling better, but that's not why I'm calling."

"Oh? What's up?"

"I was wondering if we have a bed. I have a possible admit coming in today."

Joanne laughed. "No you don't, you're not working today. You phoned in, remember? Now focus on Billy, we can talk about this tomorrow. See you then."

"Joanne, wait! Don't hang up!" Lyndsey cried in alarm.

"Now you're scaring me. What's so urgent that you're calling me about it from…?" Joanne trailed off.

Lyndsey's heart beat fast. She could imagine Joanne glancing at the phone's caller ID. She held her breath and waited.

"Where are you calling from?" Lyndsey's heart sunk. "The caller ID says it's not your home number."

Old habits die hard. The ease with which she lied was scary. Thinking on her feet, Lyndsey came up with a doozie. "I just took Billy to the doctor. While I was waiting, I realized I'd dropped the ball on the new admit, so I stopped at the nearest payphone. That's why I'm phoning you now. I wanted to make sure we had a bed while it was still on my mind."

"Remind me to talk to you about boundaries," Joanne scolded.

"I know, but I wouldn't feel right if this kid didn't get in on account of me."

"Okay," Joanne sighed. "Fill me in."

Ten minutes later, Lyndsey hung up the phone. Everything on her end was in place. Now it was up to Tom and his two cop friends.

As she glanced at the car, she saw that Billy was still asleep. When he woke up, he'd be ready to go again. She'd call Drake to see if he could watch him for a couple of hours while she met Susan and Declan at her office to start the paperwork.

Then she would find a way to work into the conversation more details on Declan's adoption. Of course, she'd have some explaining to do about why she was coming to work, when anyone in admitting could just as easily admit him.

There were still a few loose ends to tie up, but Lyndsey was pretty sure by the end of this day, she'd have her answer. A shiver of excitement ran through her. She broke out in goose bumps.

This could only go one of two ways. She just hoped she still had a job when it was all done.

Chapter **49**

TOM, OFFICER WILKES, HIS MOM, AND THE LAWYER huddled together. The four were deep in conversation, giving Declan the perfect opportunity to check out the new lawyer, John. Declan thought he was a much improved version of the older one. John's suit appeared custom made and his black shiny wing tips probably cost a fortune. He bet the guy made a bundle.

Declan turned his attention away from the lawyer and studied his mother. He noted she looked different, younger maybe. Her hair was different too. Her gray roots were gone and her hair was a lighter brown, streaked lightly with blonde. It was longer than he remembered and hung down in a shiny wave that rested on her shoulders. She appeared to have gained a little weight too. Not in a bad way. The extra pounds looked great on her, making her sharp features more rounded. She looked softer and prettier.

Declan's mother spoke to Officer Wilkes, who laughed in response. He turned to the lawyer and nodded. Tom picked up the red folder and removed a piece of paper from it. His pen made scratching sounds as he scribbled his name across the sheet.

It was weird; they weren't paying attention to him. He wasn't sure if this was a good or bad thing. Tom finished writing and handed the paper to his mom. She used Tom's pen to sign it.

Declan cleared his throat and asked, "Do you need my signature?"

Tom shook his head, dismissing him.

His mom never even looked at him. She sat down in the chair across from him and talked quietly with Tom and Officer Wilkes. Frowning, Declan noticed her voice sounded different too. Less whiny, more... He couldn't think of the right word.

He fidgeted in his chair, trying to get her to look at him. Something was wrong. Usually she'd be fussing all over him. He had always been the center of her world. But this time, she barely glanced in his direction. He couldn't tell if she was pissed with him, or just indifferent. Confused, he stared at her. Rehab had definitely changed her. He was still wasn't sure why she had gone. She wasn't a junkie and she didn't drink much. Oh sure, maybe the odd glass of wine, but that was all. Just because she took a few pills didn't mean she was a drug addict.

That was the thing with rehab centers. You would think it was just the junkies who went to treatment, but nowadays it seemed everyone was going. He could understand why guys like Gary needed it. I mean, Jesus, the guy drank hand sanitizer. Now that was messed up! But his mom sure as hell didn't need rehab and neither did he. If only he could get her alone, he was pretty sure he'd be able to make her see it his way again.

Thinking back, Declan winced. He'd been a stupid kid. He'd made a ton of mistakes. No wonder he got caught. But he wasn't a kid anymore. He'd learned a lot in jail. Life was a game and the one with the most money won.

No matter what anyone said, he didn't think his using drugs and booze was a problem. Okay, maybe he'd gotten a little carried away, but the real problem hadn't been what he was using. His problem was getting caught and then losing Miranda. Sure, there were plenty of other chicks out there, but Declan didn't think any of them could make him feel the way she did.

Before the pills got the best of him, they'd had some good times together. At least, he thought they had. Miranda was like cocaine to him, and he couldn't get enough of her. Weird though, he couldn't remember her favorite color, or what kind of flowers she liked. Come to think of it, he'd never really listened to her either. Oh sure, she talked a lot, but he'd tuned her out, too busy thinking about what he wanted. If they weren't having sex, he really hadn't paid much attention to her at all.

Now he wasn't even sure if he loved her, or the way he felt when he was around her. Declan shook his head, trying to clear her from his mind. Weird shit was happening to him. Maybe it was the assignments that were making him think this way. He wasn't sure what was happening but he didn't like these new thoughts. They made him look at himself in a way he'd never done before and it didn't feel good at all.

Deep in thought, Declan jumped when cool fingers tapped him on the hand.

"Well?" his mom asked, standing in front of him.

Tears wet his eyes and he felt like a little boy. He was such an ass. "I'm sorry," he blurted.

Susan's nicely shaped brows knit together and she bent down to look him in the eyes. Her hand covered his, warm and reassuring. He blinked back tears and swallowed the lump in his throat.

She gave him a brief hug and whispered, "We can talk later." Then she released him, crossed the room and sat down.

"Do you understand?" John asked.

Rather than admit he hadn't been listening, Declan asked, "Can you run it by me again?"

"Sure," John nodded. "We've made an alteration to your court document. The old one stated you were to be placed in a rehab facility or jail. We've amended it to say that if you're discharged or walk out of the facility you're about to enter, you will proceed straight to jail."

"But that's not right!" Declan argued. "Is this legal? You can't just change a document like that!"

Officer Wilkes jerked a thumb at him and sneered, "Now you're worried about legalities?"

Tom cut in. "It's either that or jail. You might not believe it, but we're doing you a favor."

"A favor? Are you out of your mind?" Declan stared at Tom, perplexed. "With the new changes, I could end up in jail! How's that doing me a favor?"

Susan spoke up. "It's better than the alternative, honey."

"What alternative?" Declan shouted. "What are you talking about?"

"Declan!" His mother said, this time with a little more grit in her tone.

He fought the urge to pout or bolt and sat up straight, staring at her. His eyes sent a message his lips were unable to, because of the other people in the room. He let her see how angry and disappointed with her he was.

In the past, Susan would have looked away. But this time she didn't. Instead, her eyes hardened and she said, "The alternative is death. And while I can't stop you from making stupid choices, I can make it more difficult for you."

"What the hell happened to you?" Declan shot back. "What kind of game are you playing?"

"Declan..." Tom warned.

He ignore Tom and glared at his mom. She glared back.

Tension filled the room. Tom cleared his throat. "What we've put in place for you are preventative measures. No addict can recover without them."

Declan bit back his first thought. *I'm not an addict!* "Preventive measures, what the hell is that supposed to mean?" he said instead.

"It means no wiggle room." Mom blew out a big breath. "You've learned to do things the easier, softer way. I take responsibility for a big part in that."

"But Mom," he whined.

Susan shook her head. Declan felt like he was ten years old again.

"Declan, I've always given in to you. I was more worried about your liking me and not wanting you to feel upset than I was about being a good parent."

Wow! He had never heard her talk like this before. Why was she telling him this shit?

"That's in the past and I can't change it," she continued. "But I won't participate in helping you stay sick any longer."

"I'm not sick!"

Susan's lip trembled and she shook her head. Tears shimmered in her eyes. One rolled down her cheek, but she didn't seem to notice. Her voice shook as she met his eyes. "Yes honey, you are sick."

Declan wanted to scream and argue back, but he couldn't speak. So he sat mute in his chair, feeling like a helpless little kid.

"And it isn't just you," Susan admitted. "We both are."

Chapter **50**

"DEE!" CHARLIE SHOOK HER AWAKE.

"Go away, Charlie," Dee moaned, and pulled the covers over her face.

"Dee!" Miriam added to the noise.

Anger swept the fog from her mind and she shot up. "What the fuck!" she screeched at them. "Charlie, what the hell are you doing here?"

Charlie eyed Miriam and sighed. "Miriam asked me to come over," he said gravely.

Her head felt like a cotton ball. She knuckled the sleep from her eyes and peered out the window. What time was it? What had happened? Confused, she thought back. She'd fallen asleep after… the pills!

Shit! Where had she put them? She reached for her bra and stopped.

Charlie and Miriam looked at her like they'd seen a bad car accident. What the hell was going on? For privacy, she pulled the covers up to her throat and touched her bra. Relieved, she felt the hard, tubular shape enclosed within it.

"We need to talk," Charlie said, and crossed the room to retrieve a chair.

Dee touched the bottle and wished she could take another one. But first, she wanted Charlie and Miriam gone. Dee was offended. How dare they come in when she was sleeping! "Are you people insane?" she pointed her finger at them. "You don't just come in here and wake me up like that! Talk about rude!"

The nightie Miriam had offered to loan her draped off the chair Charlie had pulled up. He plucked it from the chair and handed it to Miriam.

"Look," he said. "Like I told you, Miriam asked me to come over."

"Well now that you're here, you can just leave!" Dee insisted.

Charlie frowned. "Not until I've had my say." He stared at her for a second and added, "And then I can assure you, one of us will be leaving."

Dee bit back her words and held her tongue. Although she wanted to bolt, she didn't. She'd be leaving soon enough, but there was more she wanted to take with her.

Dee didn't know what the hell had gotten into these two old buzzards, but it looked like she'd have to wait them out. As soon as she could, she'd get rid of them. Then with Miriam's checks in her purse and her pills in her bra, she'd find a nice motel to hole up in.

It didn't mean she was giving up on Billy. Just the opposite. She'd have one last hurrah, and then commit to going straight. One hundred percent. No more excuses. She promised to do whatever it took.

But first, she had to get rid of these two.

"Cut to the chase, Charlie," Dee snapped.

Miriam swayed as she held onto the edge of Charlie's chair. The old gal didn't look so good. The harsh look on Charlie's face faded as he looked at her. "Miriam," he said, all gentle and nice. "Please have a seat. I can stand."

Charlie placed a gnarled hand over Miriam's and gave it a squeeze. "Sit," he ordered.

Miriam smiled at him. The smile changed her face and Dee caught a glimpse of the beautiful young woman she had once been.

It just occurred to her that Charlie and Miriam were in love. Wetness dampened Dee's eyes and she blinked. Why couldn't anyone love her like that? The thought unleashed a thousand poor-me's.

It wasn't fair. Her life sucked. Everyone else had more than she did. When would she get her big break? She wouldn't. That was the hard, cold truth of it. All her life she'd never had one, not even one lousy little break. Nobody had been there for her. And everyone Dee had ever loved had hurt her. Even Billy had left, although she knew it wasn't really his fault. If she wanted things, she'd learned to take them. She was the only one she could count on, and it was still like that.

Charlie cleared his throat and caught her eye.

"What?" Dee insisted.

"This is how it's going to go," Charlie said, without a hint of a smile.

Dee eyed him, noting this was a new Charlie and not one she had seen before.

"Miriam and I have a few things we need to say to you. We're going to make you an offer, and then you get to say a few words. But," he wagged a finger in front of her face, "not until we're done. Do you understand?"

Jesus Christ, Charlie was talking to her like she was some kind of fuckin' moron or something. What the hell? Was he trying to play big shot in front of Miriam?

"Jeez—" she broke off when Charlie placed a finger on her lips and shook his head.

"Not a word," he insisted.

"Honey," Miriam turned to Dee. "You need help. The kind of help that Charlie and I just can't give you."

"What she means," Charlie added, "is you need professional help."

Dee's mind spun, trying to keep up. Professional help? What were these two old farts suggesting?

"So," Miriam continued, "after careful consideration, Charlie and I would like to pay all your expenses if you are willing to attend a residential treatment facility. We've made the call and found one that could really help you."

"Dee," Charlie said, the steel gone from his voice. "This is your chance."

Miriam smoothed a strand of her hair back in place and said, "They can take you today."

Today! Were they crazy? Dee wasn't going today. She had big plans for today. As if she could just drop everything and go to rehab. Besides, she didn't need residential treatment.

"Uh uh." Dee shook her head.

"Don't say no just yet," Charlie warned. "You haven't heard the rest of it."

The bed sagged when Miriam sat down. Dee moved closer to the wall and bunched the bedcovers between her fingers. She pulled her knees to her chest, hoping to protect her hidden treasure.

"This is hard for me," Miriam admitted. She looked sad. Dee wanted to cry just looking at her. Instead, she swallowed her tears and waited for Charlie to finish.

But it wasn't Charlie who spoke next. "Dee," Miriam hesitated and looked at Charlie.

Charlie reached over to pat her on the shoulder. "Go on," he urged.

"Dee," Miriam tried again. "I know you took my pills."

Dee bolted up in bed, on the defensive. "How dare you accuse me of stealing from you!"

Miriam blanched.

Dee took power from it. Anger fueled her words. "You pretend to care about me and then you accuse me of stealing? Quit playing your nasty games. Seriously, what kind of person does that?"

Charlie interrupted her. "It's not Miriam who's playing games, Dee. It's you. And it's time to stop."

On a roll, she pointed at Charlie. "And you, Charlie. You pretend to care, but you're nothing but a dirty old man. I see the way you look at me."

Dee snickered. "I bet you didn't know that, did you Miriam?"

Miriam got up off the bed and backed away from her.

Dee flung the covers off, preparing to go after her.

Charlie pushed her back down. "This offer expires in five minutes," he said calmly. "Then if you don't accept it, Miriam will call the police and press charges against you."

"For what?" Dee snorted. "You have no proof!"

Charlie just stared at her, not saying a word. The room filled with tension as she struggled to take it all in. She sat back against the headboard to break eye contact and to buy some time. There was no way these two old buzzards would call the cops on her. They were just blowing smoke up her ass. She'd learned that what people threatened to do and what they actually did were two different things. Charlie and Miriam might talk tough, but she seriously doubted they'd follow through with it.

Charlie let her sit there for a minute, then picked up where he'd left off. "You can state your case to the police officers when they get here. Now," Charlie tapped his watch. "Your time's up. What's it going to be?"

"Fuck you, Charlie! I'm not going to rehab! Are you crazy?"

Charlie turned to Miriam. "Call the police."

"Stop it, Charlie! She's not gonna call the cops."

Miriam picked up the phone on the night table and punched in three numbers.

They were bluffing. They had to be. They were nothing but a couple of old fools. She pushed herself up from bed and tottered on wobbly legs. She didn't feel so good. No matter. The fix was in her bra, and she wasn't waiting a minute longer.

A tinny female voice rang through the receiver gripped in Miriam's hand. "911, what's your emergency?"

Miriam's voice cracked. "We've just apprehended a thief. Please send the police."

Dee grabbed her purse from the end of the bed while Miriam gave the operator directions to her home.

For a second she stared at Charlie and Miriam in shocked disbelief. Her lips trembled and she felt a sincere sense of loss. Her arms ached to hold onto them, but the urge to punch them in the face was just as strong. Torn, she did neither.

With no time to waste, Dee slung her purse over her shoulder. "I knew it," she sneered. "You're just like everyone else who pretends to care about me. You're both fake! If something happens to me out there, it's on your shoulders!"

As Dee flung open the door, she looked at them one final time. "Thanks for nothing!" she cried, and took off running.

Chapter 51

"BUT I DON'T UNDERSTAND." DRAKE STARED AT HER, his big brown eyes were perplexed.

Lyndsey picked up the foam ball from the floor where it had landed by her feet and rolled it towards Billy. He squealed and whooped with glee before snatching the ball up and tossing it back again. Not yet fully coordinated, his right arm jerked and the ball landed behind him.

Billy opened his hands and asked, "Where's it?"

She pointed behind him and he turned, spotted the ball and raced off after it.

"Linds?"

"Honey," she sighed, and curled a piece of hair around her finger. "I wouldn't call you away from work in the middle of the day if this wasn't important to me."

"I know it's important to you," Drake sighed. "But is it sane? Jeez, Linds, you don't even know for sure if this is your kid or not."

"I know it must sound crazy, huh?" She reached for his hand.

"Crazy doesn't begin to describe it!" He snorted.

Lyndsey tried to be patient and not snatch her hand away from his. She felt a sense of urgency and wasn't sure how long it'd be before

Declan showed up at the rehab facilities front door. She wanted to be there for him when he did. "I know what I'm doing," she insisted.

"I'm not sure you do." Drake withdrew his hand and tapped his fingers on the table. It was a sure sign that he was worried. "Things have been going so good for us. Please don't sabotage it."

"I'm not sabotaging anything, Drake. Jesus! You don't have to be so dramatic about the whole thing."

"Dramatic!" His eyebrows raised high on his forehead. "Is that what you call it? How about the truth? Can you handle that, Lyndsey?"

"Come on, don't be such an ass! You're not being fair." She breathed through her nose and tried to calm down. Getting angry about things wouldn't help and she didn't want to frighten Billy.

"*I'm* not being fair!" He poked a finger in front of her nose. She fought the urge to bite it off.

Billy toddled back into sight and yanked on Drake's jean-clad leg. "Frow ball!" he ordered.

Drake took the ball from Billy and tossed it far into the other room. Billy took off running after it. "Whether you like it or not," he drummed his finger into the table to make his point, "you can't argue the fact that you're putting your career in jeopardy. The same career, I might add, that you fought so hard to get."

Lyndsey's stomach burned and her head hurt. And Drake's finger tapping was driving her nuts. "Look," she blurted, reaching over and grabbing his hand. "The truth is, I don't know if I'm doing the right thing or not, but it sure feels like it."

"Yeah, well, you can't always make decisions based on the way you feel. Is that what you're going say to your boss when they catch you? Oh, gee. I'm sorry I stole your file and lied, but it felt like the right thing to do?" He shook his head. "That doesn't cut it, Linds."

"Well," the sound of breaking glass stopped her from further conversation.

They jumped up from the table and started running. Drake rounded the living room corner first and swore under his breath. "Shit!"

Only a second behind him, she noticed Billy at the fireplace. "Don't move," Drake warned as he marched over to Billy and scooped him up.

With Billy out of the way, Lyndsey could see the damage. The crystal picture frame that they'd had their wedding photo engraved into lay smashed on the fireplace mantel.

"Oh, no!" Tears blurred her vision as she bent to scoop up the pieces.

"Careful you don't cut yourself," Drake warned.

"Me bad!" Billy wriggled out of Drakes arms.

Drake set him down and said, "Stay back, Billy."

She picked up a piece of Drake's eye, and her lips, noting the picture was too far gone to be repaired. God, she hoped it wasn't an omen.

Just then a loud knock came from their front door. "Oh, great," Drake muttered. "This day just keeps getting better."

Before he even had the chance to yell 'come in', the door opened wide. Her father stood in the entrance way. He eyed the three of them standing in the living room, then closed the door and walked over to them.

"Better and better," Lyndsey agreed.

"What?" her father yelled. Old age had hindered his hearing. He was almost deaf, but too proud to do anything about it.

"Nothing." She shook her head.

"What the hell's going on in here?" He waved a hand at the broken glass scattered about.

"Oh, Billy just had a little accident," Drake explained.

"Billy bad," Billy stated.

"Yes, you are," her father agreed, and shook a finger at him.

"No, he's not," she said. "He just made a mistake." Lyndsey locked eyes with him and dared him to argue. She was in the mood for a good fight and she wouldn't be taking any of her father's shit today.

Before either of them could say anything else, Drake said, "Billy, stop it!"

Breaking eye contact with her dad, she looked down at Billy.

Billy was making growling noises and his teeth were buried deep in his forearm.

"No, Billy!" She ran her finger under his lip and tried to speak calmly. "Let go, honey." Careful not to do more damage than he had already done, she tugged gently on his arm. "Come on," she repeated. "Let go."

"Something's seriously wrong with that kid!" Her father snorted. "He never should have been born!"

Rage heated her cheeks and Lyndsey thought, *you're no expert on kids, Mister. You sure fucked up the ones you had!*

With a wet plop, Billy let go of his arm. She took in the damage, noting his teeth hadn't broken through his skin, but there were great big red welts from them. Plus, his teeth had made indents on the flesh of his forearm.

Billy's slapped his chest and repeated, "Me bad!"

"Oh, baby," she murmured as she scooped him up in her arms and carried him over to the couch. "You're not bad."

"Don't baby him, for God's sakes. You don't reward children for breaking things."

"Um, sir?" Drake interrupted, having noticed the sparks in Lyndsey's eyes.

Years of intense dislike wedged in Lyndsey's throat. She choked on it. With Billy cuddled in her arms, she stared up at her father in disgust.

Sadly, his children had become far better people than he ever would. What did one do when they'd outgrown their parents? Luckily, she didn't have to think about it for long.

Drake scooped Billy out of her arms and said, "You better hurry."

"Hurry?" her father repeated. He was completely oblivious to the tension he created.

"Yes." Drake winked at her and turned away.

Lyndsey got up from the couch and walked past her father, not making eye contact with him. Her purse hung off the back of the kitchen chair where she'd left it. She pulled it free and slung the strap over her shoulder, checking inside to make sure her car keys were there.

"Where are you going?" her father asked.

Away from you! Lyndsey thought.

Drake cut in, "Lyndsey has an emergency at work. She needs to go now."

"But I just got here," her dad complained. "We haven't even had time for a visit."

"Oh you can stay." Drake stepped into the kitchen, kissed Lyndsey's cheek, and pushed her to the door.

He turned back to her dad. "I'll put on a pot of coffee and you can help me clean up the mess."

Lyndsey couldn't help grinning as she opened the door. She could still hear her Dad stuttering as she closed it.

Chapter **52**

Officer Wilkes sat on the bed opposite from Declan, scratching a pimple on his chin. He caught Declan watching him and frowned. "Get on with it," he instructed.

Declan turned his back on the cop and shoved the few clothes he had into a black garbage bag. He eyed his roommate's hoodie. It was sick. Dope designer name, and expensive. It was his kind of clothing and he wanted it. He rationalized the other dude already had two other dope hoodies and wouldn't miss it, so he tossed it into his bag with the rest of his belongings.

The black garbage bag was embarrassing. His few meager belongings inside were pitiful. It sure was a far cry from how he used to live. Feeling sorry for himself, Declan wondered what to do next. All he really wanted was to get his old life back. There he was king, but here, he didn't know what he was. Things were changing for him fast and he didn't like it at all. A pang of guilt gnawed at him as he thought about the hoodie he'd just stolen.

Maybe he could leave a note to say he'd borrowed it. He would leave his number and as soon as he was out, he'd get some money off his mom. Then he might even go out and buy the dude a nicer one than the one he'd just borrowed. Now that he'd thought it all out, he felt better.

Declan pulled open his desk drawer. Two pens and his last assignment were shoved into the corner. He eyed the assignment, wondering if he should bring it with him. The last question he'd been working on was to give an example of the dishonest thinking he'd had since coming into treatment.

Shit! He wished he didn't know the answer to that one. It was so much easier to get away with stuff when you could justify doing it.

Heaviness pressed on Declan's chest. Unfortunately, he knew what that was too. Guilt. It was a heavy motherfucker. Yeah, he had dishonest thinking alright. He just rationalized a bunch of shit in thirty seconds flat. His conscience directed him and he reached into the black garbage bag and pulled his roomie's hoodie from it.

Declan hung it up on the back of the chair where he'd found it and returned to his drawer.

"What are you doing, kid?"

"Huh?"

"You're supposed to be packing, not unpacking." Officer Wilkes jerked a thumb at the hoodie Declan had just hung up.

"Oh, that," Declan confessed. "It isn't mine."

Officer Wilkes' eyes narrowed. "Then why'd you pack it in the first place?"

"I was gonna wash it. My friend loaned it to me and I wanted to make sure it was clean before I gave it back to him. Then I realized I might not see him again, so I put it back."

The cop's eyes grew squinty as he stared at Declan suspiciously. Declan met his stare without flinching. Neither blinked. It was a stare off until the thin cop entered the room.

Wilkes grinned at him and said, "You're not the brightest lightbulb in the box, are you kid?"

Declan grinned back, thinking it might go easier for him if the cop thought he was just another dumb kid. Relieved to have avoided another theft charge, he stuffed his assignment along with the two pens into the black garbage bag. He figured he might as well finish the assignment. It might even earn him some extra brownie points.

"Got everything?" Officer Wilkes asked.

Declan looked around the room and nodded.

"Let's go then." The cop jerked his head at the door.

Declan nodded and followed them out of the room. They walked down the hallway and into Tom's office. He was relieved to see that his mom was still waiting for him there. Susan looked up as he entered the room and gave him a small smile.

"Have a seat," Officer Wilkes said, and squeezed into the chair next to Declan.

Declan looked at his mom. An idea had just occurred to him. He wondered how long the cop was going to stick around. Was he following them to this new rehab place?

"Hey Mom," he said. "Can we stop by the house to pick up some of my things?"

Even though he hadn't lived there much the last year, his mom kept his room the way he'd left it, except now it was clean.

Susan frowned and shook her head. "We won't be stopping at the house, Declan. We aren't going anywhere together."

"But, I—" Declan broke off, confused.

His mom reached across the small space that separated them and squeezed his hand. "You're not going with me. You're going with Officer Wilkes."

"What!" Declan snatched his hand away, feeling hurt, and stared at her.

"Don't worry," she said. "I'll meet you there."

"I don't care if you meet me there!" His voice rose.

"Declan!" Susan's voice turned cold. "This isn't about what you want. This is about what you need. You're lucky to be getting this chance."

Before he could get a word in, Officer Wilkes spoke up. "We can always take back the offer. Maybe a nice stay in prison is just what the boy needs."

Susan shook her head. Her eyes looked big and filled with worry.

Mixed emotions warred inside Declan. He hated not getting what he wanted. He was frustrated and couldn't stand feeling so powerless. He didn't want to go back to jail, nor did he want to go to rehab. After years of getting his way, it seemed he was out of options.

They were all looking at him when the phone strapped to Officer Wilke's black leather belt beeped. He picked it up. "Yup," he said, raising his eyes.

Susan mouthed, "Don't blow this, honey. Please."

Declan stared at the cop and hoped what was going on inside of him didn't show in his eyes.

"Okay," Officer Wilkes replied and removed the phone from his ear. He reattached it to his belt and got up from his chair. "Time to go." He nodded at Declan.

"Now? But don't I get to say goodbye to everyone?"

A sneer crossed the cop's face. "Oh yeah, Declan wants to say goodbye." His face hardened as he looked at him. "You should have thought about that before you ripped this place off."

It didn't take much to figure out this cop hated him, or that he was skating on thin ice. As Declan got up from his chair, he did the smartest thing he'd done in a long time. He pressed his lips together and shut his mouth.

Chapter **53**

Ha! It had been easier than she'd thought. The first thing Dee did after leaving Miriam's house was to write herself a five hundred dollar check from the checkbook she'd pilfered. She'd experienced a bad moment when she had deposited it into the bank machine. The hairs on the back of her neck had stood up as she had waited for the cops to come running up and arrest her. But they didn't. All that had happened was the machine had spat out her bank card, and the five hundred dollars with it.

She still couldn't believe it. No cops and a purse full of money.

She had almost blown it when she had dropped the money, but she couldn't help it. She had been so shaky, it had just happened. It seemed weird that no one had given her a second glance. One young man had even helped her to pick up the cash. As she had exited the building, she had made herself walk, not run, out the door. No one yelled 'thief!' Although that's what she was, for sure. Oh well. Old Miriam had more than enough money, anyway.

Dee's legs were shaking so badly, she stopped to sit on the bench just outside the bank. It wasn't the best place to sit, but she needed to take a minute to stop this shaking. As she sat there, she stared across the street. There was an old motel over there that, if she remembered right, wasn't too picky about the kind of clientele it housed. She had stayed there before. It wasn't the Ritz, but it was clean.

Her stomach churned. She felt sick. Her legs bounced up and down. She wanted to get going, but her body wasn't cooperating. A drop of sweat landed on her folded hands. Her legs slowed and finally stopped. The warm buzz she'd been experiencing was replaced by an itch, one that started deep down inside of her. It was the kind of itch you couldn't scratch. At least not with your fingernails.

Dee opened the bottle of pills, shook out two, and then screwed the lid down. There were enough in there to last her quite a while. But she wouldn't be out for long. She thought she'd give herself two days. After this weekend, she'd call Charlie and tell him she was ready.

Ignoring the bitter taste, she chewed up the pills and swallowed them.

The little voice that never shut up inside her head continued to scheme. Just one more big bang and she'd go straight. Well, maybe not straight, exactly. She'd probably still smoke pot or do something like that, but she'd swear off opiates.

As she contemplated the idea, she lit up a smoke and took a deep drag. Smoke burned her throat and filled her lungs. She blew it out, leaned back against the bench, and sighed. Might as well sit here until the pills took effect. She closed her eyes and waited. It didn't take long.

It was pure magic. Her aching muscles stopped hurting. Her shoulders relaxed. The joints in her knees and elbows didn't throb anymore. But best of all, the noise in her head went away. She smiled. Better. Much better.

Time to go! Dee got up from the bench and grabbed her purse. She took a final drag from her cigarette and tossed it on the ground. She stomped the butt beneath her heel, took two steps, and stopped.

She opened her purse and frowned. "Fuckin Charlie," she mumbled.

Damn! She forgot that he had cleaned out her purse. Now what? If this was her last big shebang, she wanted to do it up right, and Charlie had cleared out all her rigs.

Pissed that she couldn't check into her room just yet, she studied the strip mall in front of her. There was a Shopper's Drug Mart inside. Still none too steady, she marched in through the north entrance. Sometimes the clerk could be a real bitch. Dee didn't think the woman bought her story about diabetes, but hey, what could she really do about it?

Not only did her legs not hurt anymore, she was starting to lose feeling in them. Her bones felt like they had been replaced with rubber. She was careful to put one foot in front of the other. The funny thing with oxy was, you had to get it just right. Not enough and you would still be hurting, too much and you'd be on the nod.

Right now, she didn't want to do either.

She was lucky there weren't many people in the store. Dee made a mental list of all the items she would need. First on her list was shampoo. She stopped to pick up a bottle and put it in her cart. She spied the bubble bath and helped herself to one.

A big grin broke out on her face. She couldn't wait to take a hot bath and soak for hours. With money in her purse and dope in her blood, it didn't get any better than this, at least not without a syringe.

Happiness buzzed where despair had been. If she was a cat, she'd be purring. Dee laughed at the idea and thought she might purr anyway.

A bottle of bath salts got her attention. She added it to her purchases. Dee turned the corner and came across the perfume aisle. The bottles were beautiful, each one a work of art. She stopped to spritz herself from a pink bottle. Orange blossoms scented the air. Nice! She put the perfume in the cart and decided it was time to get down to business.

Two aisles down, she found what she came for. There were many different sizes to choose from. She picked up a package and read the fine print on the back. She was looking for a fine tip syringe. She figured she could use one multiple times before it became blunt. Now that her veins had time to rest, she should be good to go. She pictured her veins in bed under a white duvet cover and giggled.

The package in her hand wasn't quite what Dee was looking for. She stepped up to the pharmacy counter, thinking she might find it there.

A woman with white curly hair and glasses resting low on her nose looked over at her. "Can I help you?"

She pushed back a giggle and told herself to straighten up. Dee cleared her throat and looked serious. "Um, I'd like a box of 1 cc BD ultra-fines, please."

The old woman pushed the glasses up her nose. The big round frames made her look like an owl. She peered at Dee and asked, "Are you a diabetic?"

"Yes, I am."

The woman paused. She opened her mouth to say something, but the phone rang. Her eyes darted back and forth between Dee and the phone. "Oh dear!" she said and bent to look at the shelf below.

The phone rang a second time before her white head appeared. She answered it, "Pharmacy," and pushed the package of syringes across the counter at Dee.

The woman appeared flustered. Dee thought about adding her items in the cart to the syringes on the counter, but worried it might upset the woman. Right now, the woman was distracted by the phone but when she hung up, she wouldn't be.

She decided to ditch the rest of her purchases and settled on the syringes.

The woman spoke into the phone and punched a button on the till. She looked up at Dee and mouthed, "Thirty-five dollars, please."

Dee dug into her purse and pulled out the cash.

The woman placed the receipt and syringes into a white paper bag and turned her attention back to the phone.

Dee picked up the bag from the counter and waltzed out of the store, making her way across the street. After checking into her room, she sat on the queen sized bed and opened her purse. First she'd fix, then she'd bathe. She might even try to call Billy later on.

Dee hummed with pleasure and shook out five tablets. She wouldn't shoot it all. The two pills she'd taken earlier had taken the edge off, but she wanted to get wasted, so wasted that she couldn't think.

With the pills in her hand, she sat at the desk and picked up the drinking glass. She pulled the sanitary wrapper from it and tossed it on the ground. Then she turned the glass upside down and ground all five pills under its base.

Lucky for her, ole Charlie boy hadn't taken her little silver mixing tray. He would have, if he'd known what it was for.

With the end of the syringe, she stirred the ground-up powder together with a few droplets of water. Her hands shook with excitement. Holding a needle was like holding your first penis. It both repulsed and excited you at the same time.

Her hand steady now, Dee placed the tip of the needle into the filter she'd torn from her cigarette and drew the liquid into the syringe.

She set the syringe down and opened her purse. Dee pulled out a large elastic hair band and wrapped it around her left arm twice. She stared down at her vein. It bulged nicely.

Oh, this was gonna be so good! Dee picked up the syringe and held it over her arm. It was a little like foreplay and the ritual was part of it. But before she could poke it in, she stopped.

A little voice inside her head whispered, *don't*.

She saw Billy. Then Lyndsey. Charlie's and Miriam's images joined them. Torn, Dee hesitated.

For a moment, she could have sworn Billy was sitting right next to her on the bed. She could smell him. Her arms longed to hold him. Hot tears scalded her eyes.

It was so unfair! Lyndsey should never have taken her baby from her. A little voice argued, *but you gave him to her.*

Anger and delusion warred within her chemically altered brain and Dee argued back. *No I didn't. I only asked her to look after him. She wasn't supposed to take him away from me.*

Hatred darkened her eyes. *Fuck you Lyndsey*, Dee thought, and slipped the needle into her vein. As she drew back the syringe, it filled with blood.

She spoke to the empty room with a vengeance. You'll see! I'll show you all! I'm going to get straight and I will get my son back!

Dee stopped talking and pushed the plunger forward. She shot 0.1 ml into her vein and waited. Nothing happened, so she pushed lightly on the plunger and shot another milliliter.

Now that she'd decided to give going straight everything she had, she was eager to be done with this. A little voice responded. *Pull the needle out now. You can end this. Swallow your pride and call Charlie. Tell him you're ready.* But her thumb had a mind of its own and continued to press down on the plunger.

Her syringe was half empty when she stopped pressing. Dee looked at the needle in her arm. It should have repulsed her, but it didn't. Just the opposite in fact—she felt aroused and excited to see it there. She spoke out loud to the room once more. "I solemnly swear this time will be the last time I ever stick a needle in my arm."

She looked around the room, wondering if she should add anything else to her vow, but nothing came to mind. Without further ado, she emptied the syringe into her arm.

Her fingers tingled and grew clumsy, making it difficult for her to remove the needle from her vein. Whoa. Was she ever high! Sweat broke out on her upper lip and she barely managed to get her head over the side of the bed before she puked all over the carpet.

Whoa!

Dee gripped her knees and rode the wave. Her head drooped and jerked back up. The room blurred before her eyes.

Whoa!

She threw up once more and crawled to the middle of the bed. Dee hugged the pillow and curled into a ball.

Billy was there. He grinned at her with his funny smile. She tried to pick him up, but her arms wouldn't work. Her eyes closed and her breathing grew labored. She fought to stay awake. Her eyes flickered open a final time, but didn't see. The room faded to black.

Everything was quiet. The only sound came from the ticking clock and her labored breaths.

Thirty minutes later, only the clock ticked.

Chapter **54**

THE BATHROOM DOOR CLOSED WITH A THUD BEHIND her. Lyndsey ran to the toilet, praying she'd make it in time. She flipped up the lid and hung her head over the porcelain rim. A wave of vertigo made her dizzy as another bout of nausea rolled through her. Oh shit, here it comes! Vomit shot from her mouth and into the toilet. What the hell? She'd been feeling perfectly fine just a few minutes ago. Well that wasn't quite true. She was anxious, but anxiety had never made her throw up before.

Lyndsey shuddered and got up off her knees. As the toilet flushed, she watched the last nasty bits of her lunch swirl away. She looked at herself in the mirror and winced. God, she looked like shit! Her face was so pale, even her lips appeared bloodless. She pinched her cheeks to restore color, and thought she must be very stressed out. Her stomach was usually made of cast iron, but lately it had been feeling upset. Did she have the stomach flu? Or maybe she'd eaten something that didn't agree with her? She hoped it wasn't food poisoning! She made a mental note to call Drake to see if he or Billy were feeling sick. Thinking back, she realized she'd been awfully tired lately. Never one to nap, she'd caught herself nodding off twice in the past few weeks. When was the last time she'd gone for a medical checkup? Certainly, she was long past due. When things settled down a little, she'd call her doctor's office and schedule an appointment.

The taste in her mouth was awful! Unfortunately for her, there were no Dixie cups in the room. Not wanting to put her lips to the tap, she cupped her hand and filled her palm with cool water. Lyndsey swished the water around in her mouth and spat it out into the sink. Even the tiny amount of water she swallowed made her feel sick again.

Dear God! What was wrong with her!

Butterflies tickled her stomach before morphing into seagull wings. Oh jeez! Lyndsey fought the urge to vomit again by taking deep breaths through her nose. The cool granite counter-top felt good against the palms of her hands. She rested her head against the mirror, waiting. After a few minutes the nausea passed. But just to be sure, she turned on the faucet and ran cold water in the sink and plunged her wrists into it.

An image of her dad standing in their front room with his mouth hanging open came to her mind, and Lyndsey giggled. Poor Drake, she'd left him there to deal with him all alone. Come to think of it, maybe Billy wasn't such a handful after all. Compared to her dad, he was a piece of cake. Billy was young, and had good reasons for his temper tantrums. Her father on the other hand…

She pushed aside the image and dried her hands. Susan and Declan should be here any minute. God she was nervous! But at least she didn't feel sick anymore.

Back at her desk, Lyndsey squared off a pile of papers and read through the messages that were left in her absence. As she read, she noted a former patient had phoned to tell her she was getting married. Wow! Shelly shouldn't even be alive, yet here she was getting married. Lyndsey remembered when she had first met Shelly four years ago. The former patient had come through the front doors in severe psychosis. She'd been under the illusion that God spoke to her and told her things. Apparently, God had told her to shave her head and both her eye brows. To say she looked strange was an understatement. Shelly looked like a Q-tip. She was all skin and bones with a big bald head. Without eyebrows, she appeared alien. Her bizarre behaviors had earn her the nickname 'crazy Shelly,' and it wasn't far from the truth. Shelly hadn't had an easy go of it. After several sessions with the psychiatrist, she was put on mood stabilizers. Seroquel had kept her psychosis in check and the inability to get her hands on crystal meth had helped tremendously. Shelly stopped picking at herself and began to fill out. The medication kept her calm, and talking in group helped her decipher what was real and what wasn't. She learned to ignore the voices inside her head, and over a period of a few months, they began to fade. Shelly was one of the lucky ones. She'd been given enough time and help in rehab to recover. Crystal meth was a serious drug and many weren't as lucky.

Lyndsey smiled as she put Shelly's message aside and picked up the next one. When she saw who it was from, the smile disappeared.

Recently Lyndsey and Drake had been getting a lot of pressure from the child welfare agency to change their status with Billy. Instead of fostering him, the agency wanted them to adopt him.

If they did adopt Billy, Lyndsey was worried they'd lose the resources he was sure to need going forward. Although they both worked full time, Billy was going to need a lot of help. At the very least, he'd need counseling and a thorough pediatric evaluation. Then there were his dental needs. She didn't know if he would need glasses or braces. It was likely he'd struggle with addiction himself in the future because of the high genetic predisposition he probably inherited from his family of origin. Although Lyndsey didn't know Billy's biological father, she suspected he was an addict too. No, there was just no way that she and Drake could afford all the services he was sure to require. The idea of adopting him bothered her a lot and she was hesitant to do it. Not because she didn't love Billy—she did—but beside the monetary issue, there was a little part of her that held onto the idea Dee might finally get her shit together. If they did adopt Billy, it would be difficult and expensive to reverse parental rights.

In Lyndsey's mind, the best thing for any child was to be with their parents. As long as the parents were healthy, that's all that mattered. But Billy hadn't had that luck. Instead, he'd been born to an addicted mother and had likely been born addicted himself. A flash of anger went through her at this thought. Dee better be getting her shit together! Come to think of it, Lyndsey hadn't heard from her in a while. She scribbled a note to give her a call later. The last time they spoke, Dee was going to meetings. She sure hoped that was still the case.

Lyndsey shoved the note in her purse, straightened her desk, and looked around the room. Pictures of her and Drake and more recently, Billy, lined up on the shelf beside her desk. She got up and ran her hand over the shelf, noting it needed dusting.

She looked around the office trying to spot anything that might be confidential and saw a patient file laying out. Glad for something to do, she picked it up and filed it alphabetically with the others. At least now she needn't worry about Susan or Declan seeing something they shouldn't. A grin broke out on her face at the irony of it. Yeah, right! Who was she kidding? With what she'd been doing lately, breaking confidentiality would just be one more thing to add to her long list of wrongdoings.

Lyndsey paced around the room hoping to walk off some nervous energy. Her eyes caught the picture she'd hung up years ago. It had become a talisman of sorts, one from her earlier years.

The bright colors were faded now. Luckily, she'd thought to laminate the drawing when she noticed the edges were starting to crack. As usual, it hung on the wall beside the desk, crooked.

Seriously, she probably should have taken it down years ago. It didn't go with anything in the room, but Lyndsey kept it up anyways. Although it looked out of place, it was part of her story. When she spoke at events or went into high schools to talk with the students, she took it with her. Whether for good luck or just to back up her words, she was never sure. But the sight of the drawing was still comforting and Lord knows, she could use a little of that today.

Anticipation quickened in her belly. Lyndsey gnawed the edges of skin around her thumb nail and spied a piece of lint on the carpet. On her way over to pick it up, the phone on her desk beeped.

"Hello," she said.

"Um, Linds?" Trish from front desk asked.

"Yes?" Lyndsey didn't like the way Trish sounded.

"We might have a little problem here."

"Like what?"

"Well," Trish blew out air. "Like the big cheese—AKA our boss—just met your guests at the front door, and Linds?"

"Yes," she said softly, fearing what Trish would say next.

"She wonders why no one thought to tell her the new admit was coming in a police car. You know how much she hates that. She thinks it will freak out the rest of the patients and all."

Shit! She'd forgotten that part.

"Something else you should know," Trish went on.

"What is it?" Lyndsey croaked, barely able to get out the words. She held her breath waiting to hear: you're fired!

The stairs beside her office thumped with the sound of running feet. She stared at the door and felt sick.

But Trish didn't say she was fired. Instead she said, "They're on their way down to see you right now!"

"Okay, thanks." Lyndsey put the receiver in its cradle and took a deep breath. She straightened her shirt and prepared herself for what was about to unfold. Any second now, she would find out if Declan was her son, and if she still had a job.

As she crossed her fingers, she realized her whole world was about to change based on either answer.

Chapter **55**

IT WAS LIKE DÉJÀ VU. AS HE RODE IN THE BACK SEAT of the cop car, Declan stared at the back of the cop's neck. Three fat pink rolls bulged above his collar just as he remembered them. But unlike the last time, Officer Wilkes wasn't eating anything or saying much.

The same black garbage bag holding his clothes, just a little fuller, was nestled beside him. Declan craned his neck and looked out the window hoping to catch a glimpse of his mom. She was back there somewhere, following behind them in her car.

Sadness flattened his other emotions. It was like a hundred tiny cuts pricking him in places he had never felt before. He shook his head and sighed. There were so many things he'd taken for granted. Like driving, for instance. Why had it never occurred to him that he was lucky to be getting behind the wheel of a car and driving anywhere he wanted? Not to mention the car. Not only had it been free, a gift from his mom, but she had also paid for his gas, maintenance on the vehicle, and the insurance too.

The thought crossed Declan's mind that there wasn't much she hadn't paid for. There was this one time he remembered just after his mom and dad had a big fight. He had overheard them shouting at each other. His mom wanted to buy him a video game he'd been bugging her for but his dad had said no. He was pretty sure his mom was more pissed at his dad for saying no than he'd been. His dad had said if he washed the car, he would buy him the video game. Then his dad had given him a lecture about money not growing on trees. Declan had gone outside to wash the car but hadn't even got the hose turned on before his mom showed up beside him. She gave him a sideways grin and took the hose from his hand.

The car was almost clean when his dad popped his head out of the front door and noticed Declan sitting on the steps watching his mom wash the car. This started another fight and Declan had wandered back into the house. It wasn't long before his mom had showed up beside him with his new video game in her hand. He couldn't think of one thing she hadn't done for him, and he couldn't remember ever saying thank you, even once.

His shoulders drooped and his heart was heavy. Declan squirmed in discomfort as something tight and restricting filled his chest. He closed his eyes and swallowed the big lump in his throat. It occurred to him then that you could be blind, but still able to see. He'd had it all. A sweet gal, fine clothes, a nice ride, a loving mom, and a roof over his head. He'd never had to work a day in his life for any of it. He'd been given everything a guy could ever want and he hadn't appreciated it at all. As a matter of fact, the more he got, the more he expected.

Come to think of it, there wasn't a time Declan could remember feeling satisfied. Okay, maybe when he was getting laid or had just scored dope, but it was fleeting.

A frown crossed his face. Was there something wrong with him? Maybe he a psychopath? What drove him to cheat, lie, and steal? And why was he happier being stoned than he was being sober?

Weirder still, why was he even thinking like this?

Maybe somebody should just take a big black felt marker and write 'Loser' on his forehead. He snickered and looked around. Who was he kidding? Riding in the back seat of a cop car, it appeared somebody already did. Had he been a loser all along? Could everyone else could see the writing on his forehead but him?

"What's so funny?" Officer Wilkes craned his head around and looked at Declan sideways.

Declan shook his head and mumbled, "Nothin'." It was true. There wasn't anything funny about what was happening to him now. As matter of fact, it was sad and pathetic. The truth was, he'd been given everything a kid could ever ask for, and instead of being happy with it, he always wanted more.

More candy, more video games, more money, more clothes, more girls, more stuff, more dope, more, more, more! Give-me, give-me, give-me…

Ah, fuck!

It hit him like a truck. He was a piece of shit. Declan stared out the window, not noticing the scenery as it whizzed passed him. Images from his childhood played out before him. His dad grinning and holding out a teddy bear to him. His mother covering his face with kisses as he squealed trying to get away from her. Trips to Disneyland. Eating ice cream on the beach.

Where had it gone wrong? He thought back. Had he always been a selfish little prick? Surely, he didn't get this way from using?

The car slowed and turned into the parking lot. Officer Wilkes cranked on the steering wheel and pulled up to the front door. Declan looked out the window at his surroundings. The new place was a definitely an upgrade on the old one. He picked up his black garbage bag and shuddered. He might be a selfish little prick, but he was still vain. The garbage bag in his hand was just another reminder of the low life scum he'd become. He didn't want anyone seeing him carrying the thing and thought about leaving the bag in the car, but then he'd have nothing.

The door beside him jerked open and Office Wilkes stuck his head inside the car. "Comin?"

"Yeah." Declan stepped out of the car and threw the garbage bag over his shoulder.

His mom appeared beside him. Her eyes were all shiny and wet. Susan said, "Are you ready to start your new life?"

His new life. It had a nice ring to it. The bag dropped from his hand and Declan turned to his mom. A thousand words crossed his mind and he experienced an earnest desire to vocalise how awful he felt. But the long string of words wouldn't come out. Instead, all he could manage were two. "I'm sorry," he blurted, and then started to cry. His arms wrapped around his mom's shoulders. He hugged her hard and she shuddered in his embrace. He held her close to him and sobbed into her shoulder.

"Okay, okay," Officer Wilkes cleared his throat and tapped him on the shoulder. "Break it up."

His mom blinked back her tears and reached up to muss his hair. The smile on her face said it all.

Declan squared his shoulders and dried his eyes. Then he turned to the front door.

"I got this," he said over his shoulder.

His mom looked at him and frowned. "Honey, you don't have to convince me. Just do what they tell you and you'll be okay."

"I know..." Declan trailed off, realizing he didn't know. As a matter of fact, he didn't know jack shit!

Susan noticed his indecision and squeezed his arm. "You'll be fine."

"You think?"

"I think." She grinned at him.

"Okay." He nodded at the treatment center. "I'm ready."

"Good! Let's go," Susan said, hooking her arm in his.

Just like he had in first grade, Declan held tightly to his mother's arm as they walked through the front glass doors with Officer Wilkes trailing behind.

Chapter **56**

THE THREE OF THEM SAT FACING EACH OTHER. Lyndsey intertwined her fingers, fearful they might act on their own accord. What she really wanted to do was wrap Declan in a great big hug and take him home with her.

As she studied his face, any remaining doubts she had that he was her child disappeared. He had the same sprinkling of freckles across his nose that she did. The same dark hair and blue eyes. Although his nose, chin, lips, and forehead were an exact replica of HIM, there was still a lot of her features there.

Taking her eyes off Declan, Lyndsey turned to Susan and stopped. She caught the surprised look on Susan's white face as she stared at the picture on Lyndsey's wall.

Declan noticed his mother's surprise and turned to see what she was looking at. "Hey!" he pointed at the picture.

Susan's mouth hung open. She stared at Lyndsey as if she'd just seen a ghost. "Where did you get that?" she asked, her eyes glued firmly to the picture.

"I, ah," Lyndsey stumbled. "It's personal," she explained, not wanting to go into it.

Declan bounced up from his chair and strode over to the picture. Tracing the sun with his finger, he said, "Hey Ma, I remember drawing

353

this!" He turned, his brow wrinkling, and he stared at Lyndsey. "How did you get it?"

"Pardon me?" Lyndsey asked, playing dumb. What was she supposed to say? Things were going sideways, fast!

Susan stood beside her son and peered at the picture. "That's your artwork, alright. When you were little, smiling suns were all you ever drew." Her face clouded with confusion, as she glanced back at Lyndsey. "But why do you have it? He drew it for—" she broke off, and her eyes went wide as she whispered, "You?"

An image of herself in the back seat of an old car came rushing back to Lyndsey. She'd been in such pain. If that mother and her son hadn't been in the park that day…

Lyndsey shivered and goosebumps broke out all over her skin.

"Oh my god," Susan said, placing one hand over her heart. "Are you that poor woman we found in her car?"

Time regressed. Lyndsey was in the hospital strapped to a table, an IV snaking down her arm. She was in the doctor's office opening a brown envelope with a child's drawing inside. She was taking her first year cake. She was getting married. No matter where she was, Lyndsey had taken that drawing with her. Why? She'd asked herself that questions dozens of times and never had an answer, until now.

"I," she broke off, unable to talk due to the large lump in her throat.

Declan pulled the picture off the wall and walked over to her. He dropped down on the floor beside her and sat cross-legged. Susan pulled her chair up next to Lyndsey's and the three of them sat in silence for a minute, each lost in their own thoughts.

"Oh my god," Susan said, breaking the silence. "You're her, aren't you?"

Lyndsey nodded, still not able to speak.

Declan studied the picture and then raised his head. "Back then it was you who was messed up, and now it's me." He shook his head. "Funny how time changes everything."

Lyndsey sniffed and took a deep breath. Fighting the urge to reach down and stroke his hair, she admitted, "That was one of the worst days of my life." What she didn't tell him about was the worst day of her life. The day she'd had to give him away.

"How'd you do it?" Declan asked.

"Do what?"

"You know," Declan waved his hand around the office. "How'd you get from wanting to die to…" He trailed off looking for the right word.

Lyndsey bit her tongue to keep from finishing his sentence. Already she wanted to make things easier for him. She'd have to watch out for that.

"This?" Declan blurted.

"I started from where you are now." Lyndsey shrugged. "I walked through the front doors of this center years ago and they taught me how to live. Before that, I wasn't really living. I was existing. And I wasn't even doing that well, as you know."

Declan reached up and patted her knee. She swallowed, not sure how cool it was to be telling her story to a new patient, who also just happened to be her son. There was so much he needed to learn. But not all at once. *First things first, Linds*, she reminded herself. There would be plenty of time in the future to tell him he was her son. Right now, it would only overwhelm him, and his addiction would use the information as a reason to get high.

"Well, it looks like you're doing great now!" Declan exclaimed. "Hey, maybe I can be a drug and alcohol counselor one day."

Susan piped up. "Honey, you can be anything you want to be, once you get this figured out."

Declan got up and started to pace. The energy in the room changed. He stopped and stared at his mom. "Who am I kidding?" His shoulders sagged. "I can't do anything right!"

Susan blurted, "That's not true!"

"Yes it is!" Declan argued. "Tell me one thing I've done right in my life, Mom!"

The tables had turned; Declan was no longer in charge. The addict in him was seeking attention. Lyndsey broke in, wanting to spare them the entire nasty scene that was sure to unfold.

"I may not be your mom," she said. *Liar, liar*, a little voice whispered. She ignored it and continued. "But I know one thing you did right."

All the air left Declan. He'd been looking for a fight and didn't get one. He crossed his arms over his chest, looking more like a pouty little boy than a man, and said, "How would you know what I did right? You don't even know me!"

"I know one thing." Lyndsey stopped and bent down to pick up the picture sitting at her feet. She held it up in front of her and met his eyes. "I know you drew this. Not too many people can say their drawing inspired someone to live. I can't say that. But you can."

Lyndsey's eyes filled with tears and she let them fall. "If it wasn't for you and your drawing, I might not be sitting in this chair. I can't tell you how many times I wanted to give up. Recovery is hard. Being real is harder. I brought this drawing with me every step of the way, and sometimes when I didn't think I could do one more thing, I'd look at it, and I could move forward again. This picture represents love and life. I needed your smiling sun desperately. It reminded me that something cared for me, even when I didn't care for myself."

Susan handed her a tissue from her desk and Lyndsey stopped to blow her nose.

Declan stared at her with big round eyes. "Wow! My drawing did all that?"

Lyndsey grinned and nodded.

The door opened and Tammy stuck her head inside. She opened her mouth to speak but stopped when she saw the Kleenex in Lyndsey's hand. Tammy's eyes met hers with an unspoken question. *Is everything okay?*

Lyndsey nodded, and Tammy turned to Declan. "Are you ready to get started?"

The look of awe disappeared from Declan's face to be replaced with one of fear. He turned to Lyndsey and his mom. "What if I can't do this?" he whispered.

Susan said, "Don't worry, honey, you can." She forced a smile and stopped.

Declan's eyes met hers. No matter how tall he was, he was still a scared little kid. "It's my turn to help you now." Lyndsey grinned at him and winked. "I'll draw you a picture."

A big smile broke out on his face. Declan crossed the room to give her a hug. Susan joined in and the three of them hugged it out.

Tammy cleared her throat. "Time to go," she said.

None of us know what life has in store for us, but Lyndsey had a good feeling about this. Addiction tears families apart, but this family, her family, wasn't giving up. They were all striving to make better lives for themselves. Twenty years later, they had come full circle. Lyndsey may not have been there to watch her little man taking his first steps. But today, in this room, she watched her little boy taking his first steps to becoming a man.

Lyndsey and Susan wiped the tears from their eyes as Declan left with Tammy. He stopped in the doorway and turned to Lyndsey with a saucy grin on his face. He pointed a finger at the picture she held and said, "You've got a deal, and don't think I won't hold you to it!"

Then he blew a kiss to his mom, winked at Lyndsey, and disappeared out the door.

Two

WEEKS LATER...

THE PASTOR READ FROM 1 CORINTHIANS 13:4-13, New International Version. "Love is patient, love is kind. It does not envy, it does not boast, it is not proud. It does not dishonor others, it is not self-seeking, it is not easily angered, it keeps no record of wrongs. Love does not delight in evil but rejoices with the truth. It always protects, always trusts, always hopes, and always perseveres."

Lyndsey dragged her eyes from the pulpit and looked at the small urn on the side table. A colorful floral arrangement sat next to it. She shook her head, still trying to take it all in. The church where the service was being held was bare. Few people had come to sit in the pews or pay homage to Dee's life. Unbelievably, not even her mother was there. Then again, Lyndsey wasn't even sure if the woman was still alive. Sadly, the empty seats were just another tragic reminder of her friend's life.

A sob caught in her throat at the enormous finality of it all. Drake passed her a Kleenex and wrapped a warm arm around her shoulder. She'd known Dee was sick, but she had hoped and prayed that she would overcome it.

A hot kernel of anger ignited in her belly when she thought about Billy. He was the true victim in his mother's death. Lyndsey wasn't sure how she would explain it to him. It wasn't like Dee didn't love her son. She did. But something far more powerful than love had taken hold of her, and without treatment, Dee never stood a chance. It could have been so different! Lyndsey was living proof of that. If only Dee had stayed with Miriam and Charlie.

"If only," the two saddest words in the whole world.

A tear rolled down her cheek as she thought back. It wasn't hard to figure out what had happened. Like any addict, Dee had wanted to give it one last time. Go big or go home. Right? Unfortunately, the latter had occurred. Lyndsey just hoped the eternal home where her friend now rested was a place where she could find peace. Lord knew, Dee had experienced little of it here on earth.

The day after Lyndsey and Drake had gotten the news, Charlie and Miriam had stopped by for a visit. Between sobs, Miriam filled her in on the details. The chamber maid, who had found Dee in the hotel room, and the coroner's report had filled her in on the rest.

After Charlie and Miriam left, Lyndsey and Drake sat up most of the night talking. They realized Dee's death changed everything. After much thought and consideration, they decided to make Billy their own. They were meeting with the lawyer tomorrow morning to start the adoption proceedings. It was a huge undertaking, but they were going into it with their eyes wide open.

Only hours away from sunrise, they'd finally crawled into bed, but neither one of them had slept much that night. As her fingertips traced the muscles on Drake's back, Lyndsey told him everything. She rehashed how she'd first seen Declan and what had happened since then. Her fingers stilled as she spoke into his back. "I know he's mine. I'm absolutely certain of it."

At first Drake was skeptical, but as she poured it all out, he had come around. Lyndsey didn't know if it was the shock of hearing about Dee's death or something else entirely, but she could finally say out loud a name she'd been hiding for years.

Lenard. His name didn't sound nearly so scary with Drake curled up next to her.

Lenard was her first love. He was also an abusive son of a bitch who'd been nothing but a coward. He got her pregnant and then beat her up. Lyndsey repeated the word. Leon. Maybe she could find a way to forgive HIM, and calling HIM by his real name was a start. Even if she never saw Leon again, and she hoped she didn't, she was grateful for Declan.

Lyndsey still couldn't believe she'd found her son! It was so exciting to finally meet him. She looked forward to getting to know her grown son better, and hoped he would be a good big brother to Billy. With Drake's help, Lyndsey would provide Billy the life his mother never could.

And speaking of life… A small smile tugged at her lips as she touched her stomach. So much had happened, she hadn't even told Drake yet. Nor had it fully sunk in. She'd only just confirmed it that morning when the little stick she had peed on read 'pregnant.'

Miriam sobbed beside her. Lyndsey knew she was struggling. Miriam blamed herself for Dee's death, but Lyndsey had the feeling Charlie would help her see the truth of it. It wasn't Miriam's fault that Dee had stolen from her, or taken her medication. The tragic ending of her friend's life was a direct result of the poor choices Dee had made, not Miriam.

Beside Miriam, Charlie sat looking dapper in his charcoal gray suit. He whispered into her ear and placed his gnarled hand in hers. Miriam clutched a white linen hanky in her free hand and dabbed at her eyes. Charlie raised her brown spotted hand to his lips and kissed it.

The tender gesture brought a fresh wave of tears to Lyndsey's eyes. Love wasn't just a word, it was an action, and she had just witnessed it first-hand between these two.

Charlie was lovely, Lyndsey thought. He had kind eyes and behaved like a gentleman. She got the feeling there was a lot more to him than met the eye, and she hoped to hear his story one day. She felt a sense of relief knowing he had tried to help Dee. At least her friend had known that someone cared.

The pastor's deep, sing-song voice drew her attention back to the pulpit. "When I was a child, I talked like a child, I thought like a child, I reasoned like a child. When I became a man, I put the ways of childhood behind me."

Unfortunately, Dee never got past the damage she had experienced in her childhood. Without professional help, she had functioned as a child. Or more precisely, a hurt child. Instead of maturing, she'd become toxic and turned on herself.

Lyndsey stared at the pastor, feeling awed. His words rang out loud, echoing melodiously in the church as he wrapped up his sermon. "And now these three remain: faith, hope, and love. But the greatest of these is love."

When the church service concluded, they filed out a somber lot. After saying their goodbyes, Lyndsey climbed into the car and sat next to Drake. She couldn't stop thinking about what the pastor had said.

Faith, hope, and love.

In the end, wasn't that what it was all about? Faith had brought her great comfort in her darkest hours. Hope had kept her going when all she wanted to do was give up.

And love? Love was her higher power and the engine that drove all possibilities.

Possibilities like getting clean and sober, or raising a child who wasn't hers. Or even bonding with an adult child who was. Love had gifted her with the precious little babe now growing in her belly.

Love was home.

Drake snapped his fingers under her nose. "Earth to Lyndsey," he grinned over at her, and asked, "Where were you?"

"I was thinking about love," she said, and buckled her seat belt.

"Oh?" Drake put the key in the ignition and frowned. "How does love play into this?"

Lyndsey drew in a deep breath and wondered how she could explain it. Love was like the mother of all other emotions. Love was simplicity. Love was complicated. Love was… Life.

Maybe instead of telling him, she'd show him. Lyndsey reached over and placed Drake's hand on her stomach.

His brows drew together. "What are you doing?"

She grinned, hoping he might guess.

"Linds?" He tried to pull his hand away, but she held it firmly in place. Drake wasn't feeling playful. He shook his head. "Come on! I want to go home."

"Just a minute." She placed her other hand on top of his and pressed down gently on her stomach, hoping he'd get the hint.

"What the hell are you doing?" he snapped.

"Drake," she stopped, not able to get the words out.

The last trace of impatience disappeared from his face as he noticed her distress. Drake cocked his head at her and said, "Linds, you're worrying me."

God, she was such a mess today! This wasn't how she wanted it to go. She could barely see him through all her tears. Lyndsey let go of his hand and used her sleeve to clean her face. Then she reached into her purse and pulled out the stick.

Without a word, she held in front of him.

Drake stared at the stick and his eyes widened. "Pregnant?" He looked at her still not putting it together. "Who's pregnant?"

She held his gaze and smiled. Drake's eyebrows shot up and he sucked in a huge breath. His jaw dropped open as he stared at the word. "Us?" He shook his head and repeated, "Us?"

Lyndsey dropped the blue stick into her purse and turned to him. "Yes, us."

"What?" Drake scrubbed his face. His eyes met hers. "Really? How?"

"Um…" Now it was her turn to look surprised.

"Okay, okay," he backpedaled. "I know how, I just mean… how? I thought we couldn't have kids?"

"I didn't think so either. I mean, my doctor said we could, but it never happened, and after so long…" Lyndsey reached for his hand. "Do you remember a few weeks back when I was feeling nauseous?"

Drake nodded.

"Well, I thought the stress was making me feel sick. I figured that's why I missed my period too. With all that's been going on," Lyndsey waved her hand at the church outside, "I didn't put it together. It wasn't until my breasts became tender that I thought of it. So I picked up a pregnancy test and peed on the stick this morning." She waggled her eyebrows up and down. "I almost fell off the toilet when I read what it said."

"Wow!" Drake seemed at a loss for words.

"I know it's a lot," she said, squeezing his hand in hers. "We've gone from no kids to three!"

Drake stared at her, mute.

A cold finger of dread uncoiled in her stomach and the feeling of excitement faded away. "Aren't you happy?"

Drake pulled his hand from hers and placed it gently on her stomach. His eyes grew moist. "A baby?" he whispered.

"Yes," she nodded, noting the shock seemed to have rendered him dumb.

A huge grin broke out on his face. He let out a loud, "Whoopee!" Drake rubbed her belly, his eyes wide and said, "Linds, we're gonna have a baby!"

"I know, that's what I've been trying to tell you, silly." She grinned back.

Drake pulled his hand from her stomach and started the car. He looked over at her and winked. "We've got an important stop to make before we go home."

"Honey, I'm not up to going anywhere else. I'm beat."

"Sorry Linds." He shook a finger at her. "It's not up for debate."

A twinge of hurt poked at her but she let it go. "Where are we going?"

Drake pressed on the gas pedal and not taking his eyes off the road, replied, "For cigars, of course!"

Lyndsey chuckled and relaxed back against her seat. Her thoughts wandered to Dee and she said a silent prayer. Although Dee was gone, she lived on in her little boy, Billy. Lyndsey promised her friend she would keep her memory alive. Life was full of unpredictable twists and turns. It was crazy how fast everything could change.

Even in death, life marched on.

Years ago, Lyndsey had lost the will to live. Her life seemed hopeless. Her world was one of 'more': more drugs, more money, more drugs, more lies, more drugs, more heartbreak, more drugs, more pain, and to numb the pain, more drugs. It became a vicious cycle of more, more, more. At the end, she couldn't stand to be in her own skin.

Until then, she carried within herself a deep dark hole, exacerbated by the pain of a thousand jagged little edges, worsened by a lifetime of jagged little lies. But things could change. Where there was life, there was always hope.

Lyndsey sighed and reached for Drake's hand. She pressed her cheek into his work-worn palm and thought she must be the luckiest woman alive.

Drake, hearing her sigh, looked over at her. "You okay, love?"

Lyndsey nodded and smiled at him. "I couldn't be better," she said truthfully.

Thankfully, life came with second chances. It was never too late for a do-over. Although she hadn't had the best start, she was making up for it now. By the Grace of God, a supportive recovery network, and good old hard work, her life today was jagged no more.

About
THE AUTHOR

LORELIE ROZZANO HAS WORKED IN THE FIELD OF addiction for sixteen years, and is a recovering addict with eighteen years clean and sober. Her writing draws from a lifetime of experience, both professional and personal, and aims to break the stigma of addiction and give hope to addicts and their families.

She is the author of two previous novels in the Jagged series, *Jagged Little Edges* and *Jagged Little Lies*, and the children's book *Gracie's Secret*. She lives in Nanaimo, BC, with her husband, their teenager, and snuggly pug, Maddy.